The Love of a Family

REBECCA SHAW

ORION

First published in Great Britain in 2018 by Orion Books,
an imprint of The Orion Publishing Group Ltd
Carmelite House, 50 Victoria Embankment
London EC4Y 0DZ

An Hachette UK Company

1 3 5 7 9 10 8 6 4 2

A CIP catalogue record for this book
is available from the British Library.

ISBN 978 1 4091 7826 2

Typeset by Deltatype Ltd, Birkenhead, Merseyside

Printed in Great Britain by Clays Ltd, Elcograf S.p.A

The Love of a Family

Chapter 1

As usual Myra heard Graham enter the house, almost but not quite without making a sound; it was only the very soft click of the front door closing that alerted her to his presence. His foot-fall made no sound on the parquet flooring in the hall, either. She knew for certain his news would not be what she wanted to hear. She called out, 'In the kitchen, Graham.'

The door was ajar, he pushed it wider and walked in. In some ways he looked not a day older than when they married all of fifteen years ago, but today his familiar kindly face was a blank. He slumped down on a chair, rested his elbows on the table and covered his face with his hands. That lock of hair that fell over his fingers amounted to his trademark. Poor Graham, all his life overshadowed by his energetic successful brother, and by the looks of it, the news about John was the very worst it could be.

'Well?'

'He's fading fast. Another two or three days at best.'

'That's a real pity, I've always liked John.' But Myra's concern soon slipped back into her customary spitefulness. 'I preferred him to you when I met him, but he'd already met Mo so that was that. So I married you instead.'

Graham ignored her frankness because he was used to it, and today beyond caring about her cruel tongue. 'He's weaker than he was yesterday. They're very good at the hospice ... you can't fault them ... so kind ...'

'That's what they get paid to be ... kind.' Reluctantly Myra asked the million-dollar question, 'What about the boys?'

'The boys? Ah! Well.'

'Spit it out,' Myra barked, impatient to get to the nitty-gritty of the situation regarding John's two sons.

'It's been so long since they lost their mother, they're used to that of course, but now losing their dad … well, life's not too good. Piers doesn't want to believe his dad's not going to be here much longer but being two years older, Oliver knows where this is heading. Imagine being twelve and knowing you're going to lose your only parent. At least at the moment the two of them have stopped squabbling.' Graham shuffled awkwardly, trying to pull a handkerchief from his trouser pocket so he could blow his nose.

Looking at him, appraising him, Myra guessed he was going to mention the unmentionable. The forbidden topic. He'd hinted once or twice since John took ill, but she'd ignored him like she always did when something he said didn't suit her. She'd have to put a stop to this right now. Take in the boys? She simply wasn't having it. It was all too much to ask of her. She'd never been up to much since her big operation three years ago, so because of that − let alone all the other reasons − it wasn't up to her to step into the breach. 'It's my opinion your cousin Susan should take them in. We definitely can't, that's certain, not with my bad health.' She got up in an effort to change the subject. 'Tea?'

Graham nodded but wouldn't let it drop. 'Susan lives alone, how can she possibly bring up two young boys all by herself? She has to work to keep a roof over her head. That flat only has one proper bedroom, the other is no more than a cupboard. Anyway, she's not used to children.'

There was an awkward pause, and when Myra spoke again, her voice sounded as if it was caught in her throat. 'Neither are we, as you well know. So, you can forget the bright idea of them coming to live here, thanks very much. There'll be money once John's house is sold, Susan'll have to live on that.'

While Myra put the cups out Graham sat silently contemplating the pattern on the plastic tablecloth. They never normally disagreed on anything. Or at least, he never told her so. But this felt different. She could tell he had his heart set on those two boys coming to 12 Spring Gardens to live with them.

'What about them going to your mother's?' Myra asked.

'How on earth could my mother cope with two boys? She's in her seventies.' And she made my childhood a misery, he added to himself. She'd been open about preferring John to him, and even now, he felt he never measured up in her eyes. He wouldn't wish that on the boys.

'She has the bedrooms, and the garden and room for their bikes and things in her shed. No, that's the best, they can go live with her. She'll enjoy the money, you know what she's like about money.' Myra thumped the teapot on the table and looked at him as only she could, glaring meaningfully, daring him to challenge her decision.

Graham protested softly. 'We have the bedrooms, too. We have the garden and we have the space for their bikes and we are thirty years younger than she is. I've got a good job with the council – especially now I'm running the department. We're in a position to give those boys some security. In any case, it's what John wants and what I want.'

'What you want? Whenever has what you want had anything to do with anything? Never! Ever! And it's not going to matter now. Why should you get the last say? If it's not right for me then it's not right for both of us. In any case I have one bedroom, you have the other, I use the little bedroom for my textile business, and that only leaves one for when people come to stay. So all four bedrooms are spoken for.'

Graham gazed at the ceiling, pondering. 'When was the last time someone came to stay? Last week? No, last year? No, how many years is it? So long ago I can't remember, I really can't remember. Can you?'

3

So, thought Myra, Graham's strong will which so very rarely made itself felt had emerged, had it?

Myra poured them both a cup of tea. 'Like I said, I have my textile business to attend to, I haven't the time to take on waifs and strays. Think of the washing and the ironing and the cleaning up, and the rushing off to school and being *there* for them all the time. Think of the school holidays. No, it's just not possible. Sorry.'

'I've thought about that,' said Graham. 'We can well afford someone to clean. Very easily. They could iron, do anything you want.'

'I'm not having someone poking about amongst my belongings. Our home is my sanctuary, I'll brook no prying nosey parker. Not likely. And not just when my business is taking off. No. No. No.'

Graham leaned across the table and gently touched her fingers where they lay on the table, gripped tightly into a fist. Very softly, he said, 'Be honest for once in your life, Myra. The last craft fair you went to you sold what? Two tea cosies? That didn't even pay for the petrol, never mind the cost of the stall.'

'The business is still growing.'

'I suppose two instead of the one you sold at each of the last four fairs is better than nothing, but it isn't a full time occupation now, is it? People just aren't desperate to snap up a new tea cosy, even ones as carefully made as yours.'

'You've never approved of me having a career. You've always belittled it. You're so unfair. So jealous.'

'Who drives you back and forth?'

Myra ignored him.

'Who sorts it out when you're given a bad trading position? Who admires what you make? Who comforts you when you cry because it's not succeeding?'

'I don't cry. I never cry. Crying isn't my thing.'

Graham shrugged and changed tack. 'They're sharing a

bedroom at John's neighbour's while their father's in hospital so they can do the same here. It'll be better for them till they feel more settled. Oliver will need a room of his own soon really, being almost a teenager, but sharing for a bit longer won't be a problem.'

'How many times do I have to say NO? Do you not listen?' Myra leapt to her feet, accidentally swept her cup and saucer to the floor, stared briefly at the broken shards and the tea spilt everywhere and stormed out.

She daren't, she couldn't, she wouldn't. She mustn't allow it. In the quiet of her room, Myra sat on her bed and sobbed deep searing sobs that clutched at her throat and struck near deathly blows to her heart. Had he no memory of what she'd been through all those years ago? A late miscarriage the week Mo had given birth to Oliver. At the time she'd thought it was the worst feeling in the world. Then, hardly more than two years later, the week before Piers was born, just when she thought at last it was her turn to rejoice, her beautiful baby – the child that was meant to heal the pain of the miscarriage – was stillborn. She couldn't bear to think back to it. Had she not suffered enough? How could she have her memories stirred every hour of every day by Oliver's mass of blond curly hair, and Piers' laughing blue eyes so reminiscent of Graham and John's?

At the time, Mo had been so kind, so thoughtful, but it helped not one little bit. She, Mo Butler, was the favoured one, it was she who had the joy of the two little boys, the sound of their laughter, the glorious physical comfort of their tiny bodies in her arms, their smiles were for Mo, their plump little arms encircled Mo Butler's neck, not Myra Butler's. And what had she? Nothing. Nothing at all. A second-best husband. No cot. No pram. An empty house. A void.

All she had were the tea cosies she made that no one wanted to buy. And tea cosies didn't fill her heart, make her smile, make

5

her proud. Surely someone in Mo's family could take them in?

Then Myra recollected Mo's grief-stricken family when she was killed in that terrible car accident when Piers was only a few months old. Mo had been an only child and her elderly parents had been devastated. Mo's mother had never truly recovered from the loss. No good asking them to take the boys in. Myra wiped her tears away, realising as she did so that she was in a catch-22 situation.

The phone rang and she heard Graham answering it. She leaned over the banister and listened. 'For the worse?' she heard him say. 'I'll come. Yes. I know I have. But I'll come.'

Myra heard the receiver being replaced.

'Myra! That's the hospice. I've got to go.'

'Why?'

'He's not got much time left, they say.'

'Well, he's lasted this long, he could last a bit longer. Go first thing in the morning.'

Graham uncharacteristically came rushing up the stairs. 'I'll take an overnight bag just in case.'

'Do you have to? I mean ...' Myra hated hospitals and the thought of Graham going, even for John's last hours, made something inside her freeze.

'I'm not having him dying alone. Mind out of the way, I need that bag in my wardrobe. Can you get it for me ... please? I'll get my shaving stuff.'

Myra moved in a dream. She was unaccustomed to Graham having an opinion she hadn't already approved of. This was a Graham she didn't recognise.

Myra saw him to the door, kissed him automatically, as though he was just going to the office to do a day's work, and shut the front door before he'd even backed out of the garage. She was left thinking that the inevitable was about to happen. What could she do about it? She didn't know. A big blank ugly emptiness came over her. It was Saturday. She glanced at the clock. A quarter to five. She'd make another cup of tea. Read that library book she kept intending to finish. Perhaps she could pretend nothing was happening. Or maybe she should just imagine she was getting ready for some guests – temporary guests. What did she need to do – put towels in the guest bedroom? The beds were OK, they always had clean sheets on. It occurred to her those sheets had been on those beds since . . . like Graham she couldn't remember when. This four-bedroomed house, intended for their own family that never arrived, felt at that moment like a vast abandoned aircraft hangar where life had ceased and everything in it was meekly, patiently decaying, and her with it.

Myra heard the back door open – it startled her for a moment then she heard a voice calling.

'Myra, it's me.'

Of course, it was Viv, she'd bring life and normality with her.

'Just coming.'

Viv called up to her, 'I saw Graham leaving in a hurry, thought maybe it was an emergency, you know, his brother perhaps, decided I'd better come across. Thought you might need company. Are you all right, Myra? Shall we have a cup of tea? That's what you do at times like this, isn't it?'

Viv was Myra's only friend, she thought. She'd brought a cake across from number 11 the day she and Graham moved in and they'd been friends ever since. Well, Viv was effusively friendly and naturally caring, but Myra went only half way towards being friendly, though Viv never appeared to notice that.

'Get some cups out, Myra, while I put the kettle on. Is it an emergency?'

'Well, yes, it is. John's dying, that's why they've called him back again.'

'You didn't want to go with him, then?'

That idea had never occurred to her. It was always Graham and John, never Graham, John and Myra.

7

'No, I didn't fancy it. They're very close you see, they're better just the two of them. It was John I really wanted back then, you know. I'd already met Graham and then he introduced me to his brother and that was it. Just that bit more handsome, taller, straighter, lovely face, big personality, lots of get up and go. I didn't know then that he'd already met his future wife.'

Myra got up to get the sugar for Viv. 'So I married Graham instead.'

'But he's lovely, you've nothing to complain about with Graham. He's a good man – and you can tell he cares for you, just by looking. And he earns a splendid salary, you've said, plus he's always home on time, he tends the garden – and it is a picture, you have to admit; he takes you on lovely holidays and your home's beautiful. You shouldn't think of him as second best. It's not right.' Viv spooned sugar liberally into her tea and stirred it vigorously. 'Has he said anything about John's two boys?

Myra stared out of the kitchen window. Could she, should she confide in Viv? Viv with her bright outlook on life, still leading a busy life even now she had retired from being in charge of the secondary school kitchens. Viv always dashing somewhere, Viv with a house full of family and friends weekend after weekend. Viv with her springy wavy hair with not a white hair in sight, Viv with her bright complexion, with her understanding heart.

'He wants them to come here. He hasn't actually told them yet but that's what he wants, I know.'

'Oh Myra! At last the children you've never had! How wonderful. You must be thrilled. How old are they now?'

Myra knew the answer to that better than most. 'Oliver's the eldest and he was twelve last month and Piers is nine years and ten months old.'

'What lovely ages. At least they can get themselves ready for bed and all you've got to do is tuck them up. It's not as if they're two or three years old and you're toilet training them and heaving them out of the bath. Just the right age. They'll need mothering though, what with no mother and now no dad. The poor little things.'

'And what about me?' Myra burst out, almost without meaning to say it out loud.

'What about you?' Viv took a biscuit and snapped a corner off it. 'Heaven sent, I would have thought.'

Myra couldn't stop herself from letting the truth be known. 'I don't want them, all they'll do is remind me of what I lost, remind me of how empty our house is …'

'But it won't be, will it? Not with two boys dashing around. Graham will love it, too. Football matches and sports days and things. Wonderful! What a life-changing experience.' Viv glanced at Myra over the rim of her teacup and knew immediately she'd said the wrong thing. When would this woman *ever* pick up the strands of life and *enjoy* it? 'It won't be easy to begin with, they'll need an awful lot of understanding and forgiveness as they're bound to test the boundaries while they settle in and come to terms with everything, but Graham will help you with that. Always remember the way to a man's heart is through his stomach, even when they're only boys. Goes a long way does good food with boys, they're everlastingly hungry, believe me.'

'After that operation of mine …'

'But you're over it, it was three years ago. You're fit as a fiddle now.'

'I do have days when I need to rest … and… .'

'It was only a hysterectomy, Myra, for heaven's sake, and keyhole at that. It doesn't even have to be a consideration, not now.'

'We've been married fifteen years, we're not as young as we were, we need your kind of energy, I'm past it.'

Viv caught her cup just in time as she almost knocked it over in her amazement.

'Past it? My God, Myra you're twenty years younger than

9

me. Twenty years. Get away with you. No one's saying it'll be easy and anyone who does is plain daft, but worthwhile, so worthwhile. You should thank your lucky stars.'

The clock chimed the hour. 'Oh!' said Viv. 'My God, is that the time? Must fly. I've got the grandchildren coming for supper, I'd forgotten all about them, two of them overnight while our Sally and Bill go to a party. Now think on what I've said and if it's what Graham wants, take them on for his sake, he deserves having sons. I'll call in Monday, see how things have developed.'

Viv was gone in a second, tea spilled in her saucer, biscuit crumbs brushed to the floor, some still clinging to her cardigan sleeve, and her tissue screwed up on the table. Did anything ever change with Viv? But at least she remained faithful to her like all good friends should, Myra thought.

Myra studied the mess on the table and thought about two boys and how much more mess there'd be if they came to live in this precious monument to her barren useless life. Then her thoughts flitted to her 'design studio' upstairs. For a single moment she despised her idiocy in thinking she ran a business. Tea cosies a business?! 'Oh! Yes, I work in textile design,' she liked to say. It was all a fantasy, though. She could admit that to herself. She might be good at machine embroidery, none better, but as for ideas or *style* or *design* ... Viv's ginger cat Orlando would do better. Then it struck her: if the boys came then she could give it up; too busy she'd say and it would be a good excuse. But they weren't coming, were they? She just couldn't cope with all that energy, and noise and laughter. Laughter! She'd been short of that all her life. Graham had laughed a lot when she first knew him, but he hadn't for a long time now. Mainly because he was worried about her health, she had told herself.

The phone rang just after she'd finished supper. Before Myra picked up the receiver she guessed it would be Graham. Who else? His voice was thick and almost unintelligible.

'It's our John. It's all over. He was conscious right to the end, and knew the boys. Now he's out of his pain, no more chemotherapy, that's the only good thing about it. I won't be home, not tonight. I've got things to sort ... death certificate and that. Solicitors. Funeral arrangements. The boys are being brave, so very brave, it'll all come out sometime I expect, but right now they're being so strong. I'll ring again when I can.'

'Right.'

'In the morning, probably, when I know what's happening. I'm not very happy with the neighbour who's been helping John out with the boys. I'll fill you in tomorrow. Bye.'

Her own whispered 'Bye' he never heard because she was too late with it. She wondered about this neighbour Graham had declared he wasn't too happy about. Well, she'd meet her at the funeral and she'd see for herself. If she'd already been looking after the boys and was willing to continue, then why ever not? They could stay at their own schools, no disturbance there and ... just then little Piers' eyes came to mind. Bright blue, almost gentian blue they were, and he smiled so beautifully, his smiles captured your heart. But would they still capture it when you saw that enchanting smile of his every single day, Myra asked herself. When he was naughty and cross and broke things, would his smile still catch at her heart then?

Myra went upstairs and stood in the guest bedroom. It was twelve years since they had decorated it. Myra remembered how she'd insisted Graham spend every weekend on it – painting and papering until it looked nothing like the dream of a nursery Myra had treasured in her mind. It was modern and up to date then, but tonight it felt faded and disappointing. She caught a glimpse of herself in the wardrobe mirror and decided she looked the same ... faded and disappointing. Myra turned ninety degrees to study her side view and saw her figure didn't look too bad, her shoulders needed straightening a little, but her stomach didn't need pulling in. God! How long had she had this skirt? Black and white check, straight, neat, passable. Well, hard cheese, that was how she looked and there was no reason to change, she told herself. She was perfectly all right as she was.

Sleeping alone didn't upset her, she'd slept alone for years now. She wondered where Graham was sleeping tonight. In a hotel perhaps. Or John's house with the boys. Myra pulled the duvet closer, it felt cold tonight. How would the boys be feeling tonight? Deserted, she expected. Their remaining anchor gone. Well, life threw all sorts at people and the two of them would have to get over it and grow up and make the best of it.

Myra still felt cold. She got out of bed, put the light on and searched the cupboard for her extra quilt. It was only November; she usually made herself wait until December before she dug it out. She ran her fingers over the different fabrics – she remembered cutting and stitching each one meticulously, watching the geometric shapes grow and form a pattern all of their own. It had been her project the first winter after she'd married Graham. And as she'd spent the evenings sewing, she and Graham had talked of all their future plans. The places they'd go, the children they'd have. Somehow, after the lost babies, she couldn't bear to think of stitching another quilt. So this was the first and last she'd made. It was straight to tea cosies after that.

Myra slept fitfully the whole night; she'd thought she would be upset about John, but even those feelings, illicit and passionate though they had been in the early years, had dried up, as Myra had told herself they would never amount to anything. No, the worst was facing up to the thought that Graham might put his foot down about the boys.

She almost laughed to herself, of course he wouldn't. He never did. Even that time when he'd got the chance of a big promotion, which meant moving to the next county, and she'd said no, he'd given in without a fight. Move house, she'd said, just when we've got it how we want it? What about your garden, you can't leave that when you've put all that work into it, she'd said as her final gambit and he'd capitulated. No, in the end Graham would understand because if nothing else, he was understanding about her needs, and the last thing she needed now was two boys to look after. Some other arrangements would have to be made for them, she was determined.

Chapter 2

The funeral was at ten fifteen, so Graham and Myra set off first thing in the morning to make sure there was plenty of time to make an appearance at John's house and see how Piers and Oliver were coping.

The next-door neighbour, Delphine, popped out to greet them as soon as Graham pulled up in the drive. He'd always felt there was something curious about her, ever since John and Mo had come to live there. There was always the feeling at the back of his mind that if John had showed the slightest bit of romantic interest in her she would have stepped into Mo's shoes without a single protest, but unfortunately for her, John had mourned his loss with a deep and lasting passion, and thrown all his remaining energy into raising his sons.

Graham unlocked John's front door. 'Good morning, Delphine. Well, not so good, really, is it?'

'No, Graham, not so good.' Delphine was dressed from head to foot in black. 'The boys are almost ready. Good morning, Myra. Sad day, very sad day. Still, these things happen, don't they, life's never fair.'

Myra agreed with her, 'No, it never is.' She then added, 'Boys all right?'

Delphine came closer. 'Not too bad considering, they've been crying a lot, well, Piers has, but Oliver's bearing up. Cup of tea?'

Myra nodded and followed her into John's house. For one moment Myra got the distinct impression that Delphine was more at home in the kitchen than Myra had ever imagined. Graham went off in search of something while Delphine and Myra stood awkwardly for a moment, not knowing who should play host.

'The boys. Will they need something?' Myra asked, at last.

'They've had soya milk and biscuits over at mine. Would you or Graham like a biscuit?'

'I'll ask him.' Myra walked into the sitting room and got a shock.

There was Graham sitting on the sofa. Oliver on one side and Piers the other, an arm around each of them and the boys clinging to him as though ... well, a stranger could have been forgiven for thinking he was their dad. They looked so like him, especially Oliver. She hadn't heard them come in – they must have dashed out of Delphine's the moment they heard Graham arriving.

'Good morning, boys,' Myra said. 'You're looking very smart. Delphine wants to know, Graham, if you would like a cup of tea and a biscuit?'

Graham nodded. He'd been holding everything togther, but now he could barely speak. The two boys had clung to him the moment they walked in and he could feel their need. They had no one but him, their grandparents were too frail to cope, their mother gone, their father gone, who else was there? These boys needed him and Myra, but were either of them fit to become parents to two grieving boys? And were they willing? He'd had difficult moments with Myra many a time, when she needed his support, and he'd offered it, only to have it rebuffed. Now, this particular moment, he needed her support. He was certain he couldn't reject his own flesh and blood, his closest living relatives. They were so deeply in need. So afraid. So anxious. So desperate.

Delphine came in with his tea and biscuits. 'Now boys, I think you'd better be going to the lavatory, don't you? It's nearly time

15

for off. Come on, jump to it.' When they didn't move she said '*Now!*' very firmly. Graham didn't like her tone. Naturally, he thought, they were slow to react. Neither of them wanted to do anything today, least of all anything that brought them nearer the moment when they would leave for their father's funeral.

Graham released his arms and said softly, 'Good idea to go like Delphine says.'

Myra thought she sounded common. But she liked her being strict with them, boys needed someone strict. She glanced at Graham and saw he was angry, very angry. What was wrong with being a bit strict? But he was obviously very hurt.

Graham stood up as he heard the front door opening. 'I think it's Mo's mum and dad, I caught sight of them passing the front window. Yes, it is, that's her voice. Be nice, Myra, be nice,' Graham warned.

In came old Mrs Stewart. Graham took her arm and helped her to sit on the sofa. 'Mrs Stewart. How are you? A sad day for us all, especially for the boys. Good of you to come all this way.'

The reply came in a thin reedy voice, almost as if the effort to speak would bring about her immediate demise. 'It's brought it all back about our Mo, John dying. Nice man was John, proud to have him as a son-in-law. How are you, Myra? You look no different than the last time I saw you, at our Mo's funeral.'

'I can't believe it's been almost ten years. How are you keeping?' Myra knew without waiting for the answer that the Stewarts were not well enough to take on their grandchildren.

'Keeping body and soul together, Myra, but only just and my other half's not much better. His heart you know. Where are the boys?' Mrs Stewart delved into her handbag and brought out a handkerchief to dab her eyes. 'You'll be doing your duty then, Myra?'

'My duty?'

'Taking the boys.'

Graham intervened well before Myra had decided what to say. 'That's all in the melting pot, Mrs Stewart. Still to be decided.'

'That Delphine woman, she'd have married John at the first snap of his fingers. Fancied him for years, she did. Well, it's all too late, he didn't want nobody after our Mo died. Broke his heart when she got killed.' So wrapped in her misery was she, that Mrs Stewart had no idea Delphine had come back in and been standing behind the sofa listening to every word.

'Well really, Mrs Stewart, that's simply not true. I only helped because of the boys, he'd no one else, had he? Where were you at the end of the school day while the boys waited for John to get home?' Delphine's cheeks had gone a fiery red. 'I've done my bit, believe me, and it's more than can be said of you. I've slaved for John and the children, I have *slaved* and I mean that. Don't you think of mentioning a word of it in front of my boys.'

Mrs Stewart surprisingly found some energy to answer her back. Her lips curled, her mouth twisted and out it came. '*My boys* indeed! They are not *your* boys and never will be. You're not having 'em. Graham's having 'em, so you can forget that, lady.'

Myra reeled with shock. Just when she was forming a convenient plan of letting Delphine have the boys, old Mrs Stewart goes and says that. Her reply slipped out before she had engaged her brain. 'Oh no, Graham's not, because I won't allow it.'

At that exact moment the two boys walked back in, coats on, scarves wrapped about their necks, gloves on, looking like two very sad well-dressed angels.

Myra looked at Graham and thought he was going to boil over. She'd never seen him so angry.

Mr Stewart walked in just in time to hear Graham's emotional yet somehow positive reply. 'These boys have been left in my care by John in his will and that is how it will remain. Nothing, and I mean nothing, about this matter is to be discussed, ever again. The matter is settled as of this minute, it's what John wanted. Now let's assemble ourselves, the hearse is here, and remember it is these two boys who are suffering the most today and they've to have every consideration. From everyone.'

'But ...' protested Delphine.

Graham, in Myra's eyes, suddenly appeared to have grown.

'Come along, Myra, we'll go in the first car with Piers and Oliver. OK, boys?' He gently guided them to the front door, waited for the last of the mourners to leave and then locked it and preceded Myra, Oliver and Piers down the front path. He couldn't bear to even glance at the coffin. His dearly loved little brother was gone for ever. What his sons must be feeling, Graham couldn't even begin to imagine. For the last week or so he'd kept himself busy organising the funeral, notifying friends and colleagues, tackling a mountain of paperwork – but now he couldn't distract himself any longer. He would have to be strong while he said his last farewells, he would have to be the rock these boys could lean on now.

'Come along, boys, you get in first with your backs to the front of the car, these seats are just the right size for two boys, aren't they? That's it. Now you, Myra, facing the engine ...' dropping his voice, he added curtly, 'and like I said no more foolish talk, it's not appropriate right now.'

'But all I was going to say was ...'

'Drive on, please.' Graham, grim-lipped and stony-faced, stared hard at her and for once in her life she stayed silent, but it didn't stop her thinking. It had come to a pretty pass that Graham had silenced her. It had never happened before, he was always so patient, so gentlemanly, so courteous even when she knew she didn't deserve it. Somehow she'd have to read the will and find out the real truth of what John had decreed. After all, how would she know what was the truth if she didn't read the will? It was a bit surprising, John had always been so sympathetic about her poor health, surely he would never have intended for her to have the boys long-term. It must be a mis-understanding.

Here they were in the car park, the crematorium looming above them. Graham would have given anything to be able to get out and run, anywhere, anywhere but where he had to go this minute. The moment was finally here. His legs were stiff, his spine rigid, his heart bursting but the service had to be got through.

Myra watched Graham shepherd the boys to wait at the side so they could walk behind the coffin into the little chapel. There was a host of people waiting to follow them in. Who were they all? Smart, well-dressed, black ties, solemn faces, important-looking. Must be from John's office, she thought. They'd all be manoeuvring for his job now, Myra suspected. As she looked around at the sea of pained faces, she was determined not to let herself feel the pain of John's demise. She took pride in always being in control of herself, and she wouldn't be making an exhibition of herself, today or any other time soon.

Out of the corner of his eye Graham saw Viv in the crowd and it occurred to him that she would be an ally for him in the matter of the boys. Perhaps she'd convince Myra of what a chance they'd been given. But as for Myra … he glanced at her and saw her impassive pale face, emotionless, controlled. What on earth had happened over the years, was it his fault they never let their true feelings show? Had he been too considerate? Too willing to give in? Too eager to keep the peace? Before he could continue his train of thought, he saw his mother. He half rose but sat down again when he saw his cousin Susan had made a space for her. When he'd phoned her to let her know the funeral arrangements, she'd said she wouldn't come, that she couldn't face saying goodbye to her favourite son. That was how it had always been, she'd never made a secret of the fact that her youngest was the apple of her eye. John couldn't have hand-me-downs like other younger sons, her John had to have the best, even if it meant going without herself.

The service itself passed Graham by, his head too full of problems, his hands holding Oliver and Piers closely to him, sharing a service sheet, grieving for the brother he'd lost and for the father Oliver and Piers had had taken from them. It was all mixed up in his head and his tears didn't help. He hadn't a free hand to get at his handkerchief but he didn't care, so the tears fell unheeded. He glanced again at Myra. Impassive, carved in stone despite this being her last farewell to the man she'd once hoped to marry. Myra must have felt him looking at her and turned her head, her eyes challenging him briefly. But he said nothing.

Before he knew it the sliding organ music began and the coffin went on its final journey through the curtains. The service had ended. And now he had to take on life again.

Myra opened her mouth to speak, but Graham held his finger up to her and shook his head as he turned back to the children. 'Come along, boys, it's time to leave. We'll shake hands with everyone and thank them for coming. You've been very brave. I'm proud of you. Very proud, are we not, Auntie Myra?' His eyes told her to answer, but she didn't.

Graham was taken by surprise by the depth of sorrow John's work colleagues expressed as they filed out.

'Wonderful chap to work with.'

'So sorry he's gone.'

'He'll be greatly missed.'

They didn't any of them stay for a drink, but he could understand that. Even Graham half-wished he could skip the uncomfortable conversations he knew would abound at the small lunch reception he'd arranged in a nearby pub.

Arriving at the reception, Graham felt he should bite the bullet and talk to his mother.

'Boys, we'll go have a word with Granny Butler, she's over

there – look.' Piers was unwilling to let go of Graham, so trotted across with his uncle to say hello to a Granny he rarely saw. Despite doting on her youngest son, Mrs Butler was firmly of the generation that thought children should be seen and not heard. She visited as infrequently as she could, preferring instead to have John take her out for lunch (without Graham, ideally) while Delphine had the children. That way she could sweep in for a moment or two afterwards, ruffle their hair and leave without having to speak to the boys properly or, God forbid, play with them.

Oliver, old enough to be aware of his grandmother's disdain for him, point blank refused to talk to her. Myra was for making him go, but Graham said, 'Leave him be, please.'

Oliver spoke his first words of this dreadful day to his Auntie Myra. 'The miserable cow. Granny! Huh! If she's a typical granny then I'm glad I don't have anything to do with grannies. I mean, Granny Stewart is OK, but she always looks like she's about to cry when she sees us, and anyway, she lives so far away. Granny Butler lives so near but does everything she can to avoid seeing us, well, me in particular. She's an old bag.'

Greatly amused that Oliver shared her own feelings about his granny, Myra asked him what was wrong with her.

'Doesn't like me, never has, it's all Piers. Piers. Piers. Not his fault, it's hers.'

'She doesn't like me either, so that makes two of us.' They seemed to have established a conspiratorial relationship and Myra found herself surprisingly pleased by the idea. Then it occurred to her that that was how it had been for Graham, his younger brother the favourite when they should have been equal. It didn't soften her resolve, though, not to have them both to look after.

But Granny Butler staggered across to speak to them. 'Now then, Oliver, not speaking to your granny then? My little Piers has. Sulking, are you?'

Myra couldn't bear for her new-found conspirator to be spoken to like that.

'On a day like this I think that Oliver has permission to speak to whom he likes.'

'None of your business, Myra. None at all. If he can't be polite ...'

Oliver turned to walk away, but not without making sure he trod heavily on his granny's toes.

Secretly delighted he'd done what she wished she would have dared to do, Myra said, 'Oh! Oliver!'

Granny Butler shouted in pain, and someone Myra didn't know came across to help.

'Come along, Mrs Butler, you've been standing far too long. Let me help.'

She hobbled off, complaining loudly about ungrateful grandchildren.

Graham, witnessing the whole episode, said nothing. What he'd overheard was history repeating itself and he couldn't blame Oliver. Piers had been given a five pound note by his Granny, was there any wonder Oliver was filled with rage towards her with that kind of favouritism? Graham remembered the anger he'd felt as a boy at the same treatment and he couldn't in his heart ask Oliver to apologise.

The buffet lunch was excellent. The atmosphere, as at most funerals, was one of people wanting to chat, having met up with relatives they didn't see from one funeral to the next, but at the same time aware it wasn't really a time for laughter or excessive noise. Graham was glad when it was all over and people were shaking his hand saying their goodbyes. The whole thing was awkward and regrettable and he needed to pay attention to the boys and explain what was going to happen. He'd said nothing to them until he'd seen the will and there it was plain as plain: the house, the money in the bank and most importantly, the boys were in Graham's and Myra's care now. John had hoped everyone else would understand that Graham would need the money to help feed and clothe and educate his boys, so there was nothing at all for anyone else.

His mother would have something to say when she found out. Her favourite son not leaving her anything! Not that she wanted for anything. Graham's father had left her comfortably off when he died, but the value of money was one of her favourite topics of conversation.

Delphine came to have a word before she left to go home. Graham knew she would, there was no avoiding it, but he wished he might walk away today and deal with it when he felt better able to cope.

Delphine had assumed John would have decreed the boys should stay with her, it seemed to her to be the only common-sense solution. Convenient, no massive upheaval at a time of such distress to the boys, and yes, of course they'd be left to her along with plenty of money to care for them. She knew exactly the amount that would be available because she'd peeped at his bank statement a week or so ago when she guessed the end was almost there. She was glad to have the chance to catch Graham right now. After all, that embittered cold-as-ice wife of his had made it clear earlier that she didn't want the boys. She'd be relieved to be rid of them.

'The boys can come straight home with me, Graham, I'll sort their clothes out from John's house tomorrow, move everything across ...'

'Delphine! Delphine, I'm sorry to have to tell you that John has decided I should have the boys. It's in his will. He asked me to give you a big thank you for everything you've done for them and ...'

Delphine went a ghastly shade of white. Her mouth opened, closed, and then opened again. Then she said in a loud raucous voice, 'You! You and that cold fish you call your wife? What does she know about caring for children? Nothing! I've cherished them, I have. They need me!' Instead of calming down, Delphine was getting ever more shrill and wild-eyed. 'I'll fight you in the courts for them. They belong to me! I'm like their real mother after all these years. They're mine. Mine! You're stealing them from me.'

Graham had anticipated resistance but not on this scale. 'I'm sorry, I know you've done heaps for them and John always appreciated that, all those evenings before he got back from work, those long school holidays, but this is for a lifetime, you see, and he wants them to be with family.'

'I can't believe John's done this to me after all I've done, day in day out, I thought he'd want me to look after them. I'm devastated. It's been a privilege to me to look after them.'

Graham couldn't stop himself from saying, 'You did it all out of the kindness of your heart then, did you?' He knew John had paid over the odds for the hours she had the boys. He'd been so grateful after Mo's loss that Delphine had been on hand to give the boys some stability – someone to make sure they didn't get into trouble hanging around after school or falling in with a bad crowd – that he hadn't minded it cost more than any childminder or nanny Graham had ever heard of.

Delphine hesitated. 'Well … not exactly. John insisted on giving me a little something for the time I spent with the boys. And he always paid me any expenses I had, from time to time, if they needed new trainers or anything …' Her voice trailed off for fear of incriminating herself. What had happened to this blasted mouse of a man standing so defiantly in front of her? Money! That was it, the lure of it, the power it gave him. Damn him. All the money should have come to her, as she'd always expected.

Graham knew different. 'I know for a fact he paid you for every hour you cared for the boys. He told me in the last few days. I'm glad they had you for support though, you did a good job but now I am doing what John wanted according to his will. So, we'll come and collect their belongings right away. In the circumstances, the sooner the better I think. I have my own key,' he dangled a brand new key in front of her, 'so there's no need for you to worry. I got the locks changed first thing this morning.'

That was a shock. She'd purposely waited until Graham had let her into John's house that morning, not wanting people to realise she had free access to it. She'd intended taking various pieces out of John's house and saying not a word to anyone. Just a few mementoes, she told herself. In her mind she saw Mo's jewellery – that beautiful gold chain, so delicate, so costly, which she knew John had kept, because she discovered it one day when she was having a poke about in his bedroom. Plus there were some pictures she'd always fancied and those sovereigns in that leather box right at the back of the cupboard under the stairs, she'd have got a tidy sum for those. With the boys out of her house at school all day, she could have been in and out, with no one the wiser, taking what she wanted, over the back fence of course so the neighbours wouldn't notice.

First thing this morning, Graham had said. Delphine struggled to absorb this information. She'd heard a van pull up while she was still in her dressing gown – that must have been when it happened. Graham hadn't mentioned a thing about it when they all met at the house for tea before the service.

Graham continued with his devastating news with Delphine listening but barely able to absorb it. 'I didn't know who John had given keys to, so just to be on the safe side I thought I'd get them changed. After all, the house and its contents are the boys' inheritance, isn't that right, Delphine?'

Myra, a surprised witness to this exchange, was even more amazed when Graham took hold of Delphine's forearms, leaned forward and kissed her on both cheeks for all the world as though they were kissing cousins.

Graham produced a beaming smile, saying, 'That's a thank

you for all you've done for the boys and for John's sake. If there's anything owing while John's been in the hospice, let me have a list and when the money is released by the solicitors I'll see you get remunerated. I know you have my address, John told me.'

Delphine nodded, dumbstruck by the unexpected turn of events.

No one had noticed that Piers had snuck up until a small voice piped up, 'Don't let's forget Little Pete.'

'Little Pete?' Myra asked.

'Oliver's rabbit.'

'Oliver's rabbit? I didn't know he had a rabbit.'

'He got it for his birthday, it's only a baby, it doesn't eat much, Myra.'

Myra, on the verge of suggesting they took it back to the pet shop, was silenced by Graham, who after fifteen years of being married to Myra knew exactly what she was intending to say.

'We mustn't leave him behind, must we, Oliver?' Piers looked for support from his brother who'd come across to see why all the grown-ups were speaking in raised voices.

'No. You'll like him, Myra.'

Not entirely convinced that Oliver was right about that, Myra shook her head at Graham to indicate she really wasn't keen. But he ignored her.

'Mightn't you boys prefer to stay with Delphine a little longer while we get organised? Find the best place to put Pete? Get your beds ready. That would be a good idea, wouldn't it?'

Her apparently helpful, considerate remark was met by two pairs of bleak blue eyes, and a blank refusal from them both. Oliver said, 'No way, we're not going back to Delphine's.'

Piers uttered the single but very firm word, 'No.'

Delphine's eyes widened but before she had a chance to chastise them, Graham ushered Myra and the boys away. He knew if he didn't take them now while Myra was still in shock at the thought of taking on the boys, she would come up with a thousand reasons why they couldn't take the boys home. How he and Myra would cope with bringing up two boys he had no idea, but cope they would, it was most definitely a better solution for them than foster homes or a childrens' home or Delphine's for that matter.

Graham swept Myra along with a tide of suggestions as to how best she could help the move. 'If you could supervise their clothes, Myra, get them into cases or bundled up as best you can, don't forget the coat hangers because we haven't enough at home, I'll do the toys and books with the boys' help and sort out the transport of Little Pete. Before we know where we are we shall be home. I think we'll have a meal out tonight just to round the day off, how about it, Auntie Myra?'

Numb with shock, Myra agreed. 'Of course. Yes.' In the circumstances what was there else to say?

Graham gave her a chaste kiss on her cheek for agreeing and Myra almost blanched at the unexpectedness of it.

Back at John's house, Graham unlocked the front door and forced himself to go in. He hated this bit, he might look brave and positive but he was anything but. It had only been a few hours since they'd sat in the living room this morning, but the finality of the funeral service had changed the atmosphere. The house felt chilled and unwelcoming. Myra followed him in but the two boys hesitated.

Graham forced himself to sound cheerful. 'It won't take us long, boys, let's get on with it.' He opened the door wider and beckoned them in. Piers ran upstairs, Oliver opened the back door and went into the garden to find comfort with Little Pete.

In no time at all with Piers' help the books and the toys were packed in large plastic boxes Graham had found in the garage, obviously new and purposely bought by John with removal in mind when he was told he had terminal cancer. Graham was amazed at how John had had the bravery and presence of mind

27

to prepare so many thoughtful details when he must have been reeling from his diagnosis.

The clothes packing was much slower. Myra was inspecting every single item to see if they were suitable and if they would fit in the empty drawers in their guest bedroom. Graham, discovering her slow progress, said, 'It's no good Myra, for goodness' sake. Sort them out at home. Just put them in any old how. Look, I've found another case in Oliver's bedroom, that'll help, won't it.'

Finally the Butler family car was loaded to its roof, with Oliver and Piers packed in the back seat surrounded by belongings. Graham had finally realised that they had no hope of getting everything in, so had declared that before they went out for a meal he'd come back and pick up Little Pete and the hutch and run and his boxes of food, along with the boys' computers which also wouldn't fit in this first car-load.

Myra panicked. In a low voice she protested that she couldn't manage the boys by herself, what was he thinking of?

'There's no alternative, is there? It won't take me long.'

'Leave the blessed rabbit behind with the door open by mistake. I told you I didn't want it as soon as I heard about it. Do you understand, just leave the hutch door open, *please.*'

'Haven't they lost enough already? It could do untold damage to them both if that happened.'

'What about the damage to *me?*' protested Myra.

'Pull yourself together, Myra, life's quite difficult enough without you inventing things to worry about.'

Myra protested vigorously. 'It's not fair, you're not fair. I'm not putting up with it. What's happened to you?' She heard the petulant strain in her voice, knew she was meant to be an adult in this situation, but couldn't stop herself.

★

They drove home across town in total silence. The two boys weren't into speaking much that day anyway. Graham was struggling to come to terms with this new situation which had suddenly hit him with a force he hadn't bargained for and as for Myra ... she was in a complete spin. This was the first day and already she couldn't cope. How did you speak to boys? What did you talk about? Weather? Formula One? Football? School?

Myra made her first stab at speaking to them at their level. 'It's school tomorrow, isn't it?'

The disgruntled mutterings which came from the back seat should have warned Myra she was on difficult ground.

'We're not going.' This was Oliver.

'I'd rather they didn't, not the rest of this week,' said Graham. 'We'll talk about it later.'

She ignored Graham, it was as if he'd never spoken. 'Piers, your school is too far away for you to go to. You'll have to change schools.'

This remark got no reply from the back seat and she realised she might have broached the subject more gently. Tough, she thought. She wasn't going to be walking on eggshells around the boys.

'Oliver, your school will have a bus going across town, so we'll inquire about that tomorrow.'

Still no reply. So what did you do when they wouldn't answer? How did you know what they were thinking? She glanced at the pair of them via the vanity mirror on her sun visor. They looked miserable. Briefly a moment of sympathy flooded Myra's heart, quickly dispelled when Piers poked his tongue out at her. Had he seen her looking at him? He did it again! Did he *want* her to see him doing it? She was baffled. A flicker of a smile crossed Oliver's face and she knew he liked the idea of Piers doing that to her and then he stuck out his own tongue and grimaced. She'd thought they were friends because of what he'd said about Granny Butler. She folded her sun visor up, rooted in her bag for the house keys and, hand on safety belt, waited while Graham swung the car into their drive.

With everything unloaded, Graham said, 'I'll be off then for Little Pete. Do you boys want to stay here with your Auntie Myra? I won't be long.'

'Why not wait until tomorrow? It's five already, and almost dark?' remarked Myra.

Oliver turned to Graham. 'We can't leave Pete there all on his own all night, he needs locking up 'cos of foxes. We'll come with you, Uncle Graham.'

'That's fine by me. Come along then, we'll put all this away when we get back.'

So they went, her wishes apparently counting for nothing.

Myra knew she was losing her grip on Graham and she'd no idea how she'd get it back. Life had suddenly turned completely upside down. Graham seemed to forget it wasn't just for a few days; *one* night with guests was bad enough, they were talking here about a *lifetime*! And a blasted rabbit too! She'd had no experience of animals, not even a hamster, because her mother wouldn't let her have one. Come to think of it her mother wouldn't let her have anything or do anything she wanted at all, like wearing hairbands when they were the fashion, or skirts the same length as a pelmet when they were in, or holes in her jeans when everyone else her age had artfully ripped denim. Graham had been her bid for freedom and now look what was happening. Surrounded by the mountains of the boys' belongings Myra plunged down on to the nearest chair and wept; outfaced and inconsolable.

Chapter 3

They'd got the boys into bed in their pyjamas decorated with mysterious emblems from some children's TV programme that Myra didn't recognise, and Myra, glad for a touch of normality, had switched on the television. They'd just about managed to eat a meal out, pretending they were a normal family, and get back in time for a stab at a bedtime routine and now the quiet in the house felt like a blessed relief. But before she could savour it, Oliver appeared in the sitting room like some ghostly apparition, holding out a thin stick. He stood in front of Myra saying, 'I'd forgotten this. Here you are.'

Myra was puzzled, what on earth was the stick for? Was this a game boys played? 'What is this for, Oliver?'

'To make me good tomorrow.'

'To make you good for tomorrow? Why does giving me a stick make you good tomorrow? I don't understand.'

Oliver sighed at her lack of understanding. 'It's from Delphine's. I had to hold out my hand and she hit it with this stick to make me good tomorrow.'

Both Graham and Myra struggled to get a hold on what the boy was talking about. Graham, swallowing hard, asked the stupidist of questions. 'How many times?'

'Five.'

'Oh God!' Hit with a stick for nothing at all. To make him good. Graham was appalled – he didn't know whether to shout or cry. His instincts about Delphine had been right then. No, he thought. In truth it had been worse than he'd ever imagined.

He tried to stay calm. 'Well, Oliver, I'm glad to say we don't use things like that in our house.' He was going to be sick, his heart was pounding, his knees trembling, covered in a cold sweat, he fled the room.

Myra and Oliver solemnly stared at each other, neither knowing what to do next. 'Sit down, Oliver, here beside me. Did this happen every night you stayed in Delphine's house? Even when you'd been good?'

Oliver stared at his bare feet sticking out at the ends of his legs as though they didn't belong to him. He nodded.

'And Piers, what happened to him? Did she hit him with it?'

'No, she said he didn't need it.'

Myra cringed. She'd no understanding of boys but even Myra could see what a terrible thing this boy had suffered. How could anyone do this to a child? 'I'll go get Uncle Graham a glass of water. You'll have to excuse him, he's so upset.' She added to her own surprise, 'And so am I.'

Oliver sat looking at his feet, they still didn't belong to him, nothing did. Not a single thing was right, here in this house. All he wanted was his dad there right beside him, laughing and talking like he did before he got so ill. He couldn't remember his mother at all, not her face, nor the smell of her, nor her voice, so she didn't count in a way. He didn't miss someone he didn't remember. And now he was trapped in this strange house with two people who didn't know about children. What was his alternative though? There wasn't one, so he was stuck with it till he was old enough to look after himself. He remembered a boy at school, Iain was his name, whose mum was on her own and she'd died. He'd been sent to a children's home and once he'd seen him weeks afterwards out in town and he'd looked so sad that Oliver hadn't been able to allow himself to recognise him and he'd walked past stricken dumb by the change in him. He looked so ... wounded.

Uncle Graham came back in saying, 'Sorry about that, couldn't help myself. I had no idea. Did your dad know?'

'I never told him.'

'Why ever not? He'd have wanted to know, of course he would.'

'We didn't sleep at her house till Dad went into hospital and somehow ...'

'You couldn't tell him, of course not. But I think you were brave to put up with it. Too brave in fact. I'm horrified. I want you to know that all the time you live in this house this stick will never be used.' Graham picked it up, and flexed it a little. 'You can break it into little pieces right now. Go on.'

Oliver shook his head.

'She'll never know because we shan't tell her. I want you to break it, then you know for certain it can't be used any more.'

Oliver shook his head.

'Then I'll do it.' And Graham did. He snapped it in half and amazed himself by his strength, it was so flexible, so bendy he never thought he'd manage to break it. It was the anger that did it, he was so furious. Then he snapped it again and again until the stick lay in pieces on the rug. 'There, that's the end of it. No more stick. Show me your hand. Go on.'

Oliver opened his right hand and Graham could see the faint weals made by Delphine on his twelve-year-old hand.

Graham shook with temper. 'I'm so sorry, if your dad had known ...'

'I couldn't tell him, could I, he was so ill ...'

Myra came back into the sitting room carrying three mugs on a tray, and the smell of hot chocolate floated ahead of her and warmed Oliver's heart. 'Here, Oliver, before you go back to bed, hot chocolate, specially for you. I've put a bit of sugar in it, makes it tasty.'

They sat watching the TV, mugs cradled in hands, silent, each lost in their own thoughts. Graham sick with the pain of it all. Should he be calling the police, he wondered – perhaps he should have kept the stick as evidence. He'd talk to Myra about it later. But right now, all he cared about was making sure Oliver was OK.

Myra was silently swearing vengeance on that dreadful woman. Thinking how if she'd got her own way they'd have stayed in Delphine's house and he'd have been hit every night of his life. She couldn't bear it. Myra had had a devil of a mother but even she didn't descend to hitting her with a stick on the pretext of making her good.

Oliver, pressing the marks on his hand against the heat of the mug, thought perhaps, just perhaps, things might not be too bad in Spring Gardens. 'I'd like to go back to school – not this week, but on Monday ... when we've sorted the school bus out. That'll be soon enough for Piers. He's crying upstairs; well he was, he might be asleep by now.'

Graham leapt to his feet. 'I'll go see.'

Piers was curled up under the duvet, a rather unsuitable one for a child, Graham thought, covered as it was in sprigs of roses. The whole room looked like it would better suit an old lady rather than two boisterous young lads. Not that Piers looked boisterous now. In the soft moonlight that crept through the curtains Graham could see his sad sleeping face, his eyelids fluttering a little. Piers was still baby-faced, and Graham's heart ached a little at the sight of him. He didn't properly know how to make contact with a child, he'd have to stumble along making mistakes, sometimes getting it right first time, sometimes not. All he could do was his best, and at least he'd stopped Oliver from being beaten every night. At the thought, his hot chocolate almost came back up. Just the thought! He swallowed hard, leaned over the bed and placed a kiss on Piers' forehead. He thought he caught sight of a sleepy half-smile. Ah! That was all that was needed, love in capital letters. But did he have, in fact did either of them have, love to give these two boys? That was the question.

He stood there in the moonlight staring down at Piers, thinking about Myra and wondering when and where love had slunk away from the two of them. Life had been so bitter for so long he'd forgotten the sweetness of love, of how it coloured the day, warmed the night, flavoured every mortal thing.

He heard Oliver coming up the stairs in his bare feet because they couldn't find his slippers, and thought about that blinking stick, whippy and bendy and full of hurt. He was glad John had died not knowing the truth about Delphine and her evil ways.

'Hop into bed, Oliver, and try to sleep. Myra and I will try our very best to make things right for you and Piers, you know.' With that, he kissed his forehead, but this time there was no sleepy half-smile as his reward.

Somehow Myra had survived the first night, including the catastrophe when Piers couldn't find the 'cuddly' he went to bed with, Oliver's refusal to clean his teeth with Myra's toothpaste because his own still lay on the washbasin at home, and the utter exhaustion of the day, and now here she was, the next morning, awake far too early, planning how she would survive her first full day. There wasn't a sound from the boys' bedroom when she crept downstairs so she closed the kitchen door so as not to wake them when she set the table for breakfast.

But Graham was already in the kitchen.

He'd laid the table for four, boiled the kettle, got the toaster out, the cereals, the butter, the jam she liked and the marmalade, and brought the milk in so all she had to do was sit down and eat. Breakfast was her favourite meal of the day. This was more like it. Graham being considerate towards her, thought Myra, that was the Graham she knew.

'Sit down and eat while they're still asleep. You were too tired last night for sorting things out so we'll do it now while we're on our own.'

'I've been thinking ...'

Graham nodded. 'So have I. You tell me first.'

This was how it had always been. Her feelings at the top of the agenda. 'What on earth are we going to do with them all day? No school. No nothing. What do boys do all day? I've got my housework, and my tea cosies to work on, I can't be finding time for entertaining them.'

'Well, first of all we're taking them to the local school, let's hope they have a place for Piers. We'll tell them what's happened and get the paperwork in our names. Then we're going to Oliver's school to get him sorted, a place on a new school bus and letting them know he'll be back in next week. After that I thought we'd take them out to lunch by the river, that place we like and if I can find a shop that sells kites I'm going to buy them each a kite.'

'A kite? Whatever for?'

'For fun. I never had a kite as a boy and I thought I might quite like one. I'll buy three, or if you'd like one we'll buy four.'

'I haven't the time. No, you go with them and fly the kites. That's better, just the three of you.'

'Myra, they're not going to be *my* boys, they are *yours* too – you've got to belong.'

'Well, not today. I'll get the food side sorted. Make a nice supper. Viv says boys like good food. It all helps, she says.' She pushed away that panicky feeling she kept getting. 'Graham ...?'

'Yes?'

'I'm frightened to death. Absolutely frightened to death. However am I going to manage?' Myra trembled, but just as she was about to burst into tears – something she would never normally do because she kept such a tight control of herself – the kitchen door burst open and in walked the two biggest problems of her life. They were both looking clean, Oliver had found his slippers, and Piers was wearing quite the oddest selection of clothes, standing there, looking lost and withdrawn.

Graham sprang into action, the fastest Myra had seen him move in years. 'Now, boys, sit yourselves down. Myra's going out shopping today to get just what you both like for breakfast and so on, but for now you'll have to make do with what we eat. Sit down, it's laid for four so it must include you. Piers, you sit next to Myra, that's it, and Oliver, you sit next to me here. That's the way. Now. Choose your cereal.'

That first breakfast time was the most agonising it could possibly have been. Two silent children, playing endlessly with their food and basically eating very little, two grown-ups trying desperately to be jolly and understanding, but not succeeding.

Finally Myra stood up, the tension having built up in her more than she would have thought possible without her actually exploding, and she said straight from her heart, 'We are trying, you know, it's hard for us just as it's hard for you, just make an effort. Please. We are trying to give you a *home*.' With that, she stormed out.

The silence in the kitchen grew deeper. The three males left behind silently working out what to do next, even more withdrawn than before she spoke. Graham finally broke out of his bonds by saying, 'We'll have to forgive her, she's not used to a houseful and doesn't know how to go about it. She feels just as bad as you do. Completely at sea.'

Piers slapped his spoon down in his bowl and said, 'We didn't want to come here. We want to be at home with our dad, but we're not and we wish we were and we don't know what to do in your house. We can't try, honest, we can't *try*. All our trying's used up. And we're only boys not men, not yet, and I want my dad.' Two large tears traced a steady path down his cheeks.

Graham, torn apart by Piers' plea, stared at his toast awaiting him on his plate and choked at the thought of eating it. Now what did he do to make things right, was it ever going to be possible to do so? Perhaps if he tried hard enough it might.

37

'Today, when it gets to nine o'clock we're going to sort out your schools, the new nearest one for you, Piers, and arrange transport for Oliver to his old one. We'll let them know you're living with us now and that you'll be back on Monday. Then I'm going to a shop I know that sells kites and I'm buying one and if you like the idea you can have one each too. I always wanted one as a boy and my dad couldn't afford it, but I can afford it now and that's what I'm going to do. I know exactly where to go to fly it, and I shall watch it soaring up into the sky and think about it being me flying all that way in the freedom of the skies.'

Oliver looked rather sceptically at him.

Graham smiled. 'Just you wait and see! When you've finished your breakfast would you go and feed Pete and let him into his run? Clean your teeth and then we'll be off.'

Somehow Graham's positivity did all of them good, they scurried through their cereals, ate a piece of toast each, cleared their dishes into the dishwasher and disappeared into the garden. All the way to the school Piers talked about kites and he'd decided he'd like one too if that was all right?

After they'd left Myra stood in the kitchen and wondered what on earth to do next. She happened to be facing the garden while she pondered and caught a glimpse of that blasted rabbit. Something else to make a mess and look after. She paused for a moment: it was a very pretty rabbit, long-eared and kind of milky-coffee-coloured, hopping about the run. She stopped herself. It would crucify Graham's immaculate lawn, there'd be no grass left inside a week. The whole patch where the run stood would be bare.

Should she let it out? Accidentally of course. She wouldn't be to blame. She practised an innocent look with her face, but somehow she knew it would look grotesque. So she stopped trying to smile.

There was a sharp tap on the kitchen door and then Viv's voice calling, 'It's me, Viv.'

'Hello Viv! How are you?'

'Never mind about how I am, I saw Graham going out with the boys so I thought I'd come across and give you some moral support. How are they?'

'They've gone out to see Piers' new school and to re-organise the school bus for Oliver. Then they're supposed to be going to buy a kite for Graham. Can you imagine Graham with a kite, he won't know where to begin.'

Viv plonked herself down on the nearest chair saying, 'You should have gone with them.'

Myra shuddered. 'Well, no, thank you very much, I've enough to do here in the house.'

'You looked as though you were very busy when I walked in, staring out of the window.'

'Have you seen what I was staring at?'

Viv leapt up from her chair and peered out of the window. 'What a little darling, isn't it sweet, is it a boy or a girl?'

'Must be a boy, it's called Pete. I didn't want it and I still don't want it, and I've a good mind to let it out by "mistake".' She glared at Viv, daring her to object.

Myra joined her at the window. Viv said very softly, 'They've already lost their father and their home, to lose their rabbit would be the last straw. Don't do it, Myra. Please don't do it, they'll be devastated.'

'I didn't ask for a rabbit, nor did I ask for two boys, but I've got them, Viv. Don't I have a say at all?'

'You've had your say for far too long, Myra. Now it's Graham's turn and Piers and Oliver's turn, they all need you, believe it or not. The boys are not going to say, "Auntie Myra, we need you." But they *do*. Bear up, stiff upper lip and before you know it you'll feel like a mother and that's what you will be, and that's what you've yearned for for years.' Viv dared to pat Myra's arm, even though she knew any kind of contact was alien to Myra. 'Well?'

Myra hurriedly snatched her arm from Viv's grasp. 'I've had my way far too long? What does that mean for heaven's sake?'

'Can I be frank? Blunt even?'

Viv sat at the kitchen table, resting her forearms on it and looked straight into Myra's face. 'Round here we all realise that you and Graham don't share a bedroom any more and haven't done for some years. That's no way to go on. Now is it?'

Myra's face flushed dark red. 'And what makes you think that?'

'Bedroom lights. You never have visitors staying so they must be yours and Graham's lights on. Nobody would think twice about my house having bedroom lights on, some nights I swear my house looks more like Blackpool Illuminations 'cos every bedroom's lit up, but every night it's always just two rooms lit at yours.'

'It's no one's business but ours where we sleep. You're all a load of gossips, cruel, evil gossips. Go on get out, leave this house and don't come back.' Myra was so angry she forgot about her renowned self control and shouted.

Viv didn't move an inch. In fact she settled herself more comfortably and it infuriated Myra. 'You're nothing but a nosey parker, that's what. Wait till I tell Graham.'

'Judging by your reaction, I guess that was your decision, not Graham's. I'm right, aren't I? And furthermore I guess you won't mention it to him because it will bring the whole matter into the open and then where will you be? Decisions to make? Truth to be spoken? Oh! No Myra, that's the last thing you want.'

Myra expected Viv to march off, but instead she got up calmly. 'I'll make us a coffee.'

So she did while Myra sat silent in the chair she'd slumped down on when Viv had started her speech.

'I've put plenty of sugar in, do you good, there's not a peck of flesh on you, you could do with fattening up. I'm going to the supermarket after – shall we both go and you can shop for these boys of yours and that gorgeous husband? Get plenty of stuff in, fill the freezer and the cupboards, then feeding them won't feel such a task. I don't need a lot today, so there'll be plenty of space for a big shop for you. How about it?'

Cleaving her way through the terrible anger she felt, Myra realised the sense of going shopping in Viv's car and nodded her head. The hot sweet coffee felt good. The neighbours noticing! The neighbours talking about her! But did she care? No! It was her house and she'd do exactly what she wanted in it, and sleeping in the same bed as Graham was not a thing she wanted. Not after losing the babies, and certainly not after her operation. No, certainly not, that side of things was over with for ever. She forced her thoughts back to practicalities. She'd need more butter, and extra milk and ...

'Finished your coffee? I'm glad to see you drinking it all. You skimp on food, don't you, Myra? Why? Are you punishing yourself for something?'

'Now you're being ridiculous. Of course I'm not. What have I got to punish myself about? I've never done anything wrong.'

'Denying yourself any joy? Shutting yourself off from your husband when you could be holding each other close? A shared bed makes the wheels of a marriage go round better than anything I know.'

Myra stood up. 'You may have been a friend since the day we moved in here, but speaking to me like this is just not right, it's all too ... intimate.' Using that word made her blush. God, what was she thinking of? Blast Viv. 'Are we going shopping this morning or next week?'

'Right away. I'll get my purse and lock up and we'll be off.'

★

The traffic was heavy and slow-moving, the car park was full to bursting, the supermarket packed, and in the end Myra and Viv decided to eat a quick lunch in the cafe and do the shopping afterwards. By the time they got home it was after three o'clock and just as they turned in to the drive to unload Myra's shopping Graham and the boys came home.

More used to the tiny quantities of shopping for two, the mass of bags and mountains of food overwhelmed Myra and she had to rely on Viv to help her sort all they'd bought. What angered her was that both Oliver and Piers took to Viv immediately and spent lots of time describing their kite-flying expedition. Finally the shopping was all put away, her bags for life in the cupboard where they belonged and Graham was carrying the tea tray into the sitting room with a generous plate of biscuits included.

Viv made her farewells. 'You enjoy that tea together just the four of you, I'll have a cup with you all another day. Bye boys. Glad you've had such a good time with the kites ... and I like little Pete, by the way.'

With Viv gone, Myra sat down, unable to recall what it was she'd planned for supper, despite all the food she'd bought, and by the time she'd finally remembered, she found herself involved in a decision about bringing Pete into the house. 'Do you want to know what I think?' she said. 'I think it's all new for him at the moment, new garden, new noises, maybe we'd do better to leave him to get settled and then try him in the house in a few weeks, we don't want to confuse him, do we?'

Graham gave her a grateful smile and Oliver agreed they'd better wait until he settled.

Piers meanwhile had been wolfing biscuits down as though he hadn't had any for weeks. Was it good for him to eat so many? It certainly wasn't good for the housekeeping. Myra decided to say something. 'You like those biscuits, Piers?'

He blushed and nodded his head, replaced the one he had in his hand but hadn't bitten into and sat back looking mortified.

Oliver explained on his behalf. 'Delphine always gave us cream crackers with no butter on and they tasted funny, kind of old, that's why. Old and musty.'

'Help yourself,' Myra said, determined to score a victory over that dratted Delphine. 'I don't mind.' Though in truth she did mind when to her amazement, the entire plate was emptied by the two boys. Was this how it was then, eating a plateful of biscuits and then not wanting their supper? She'd not get it ready until a bit later, give the biscuits time to go down.

Suddenly there she was making allowances for the pair of them when she'd sworn she wouldn't. They must abide by a few basic rules she'd thought up last night, and now before she'd even had a chance to explain them, they'd unwittingly broken them. She sat silently thinking about the cross she'd given herself to bear.

Graham cut through the strained atmosphere by suggesting the boys went to the car and brought in their kites to show Myra.

'Look Myra, there's a picture of mine on the box.'

'Oh! So there is.'

'Uncle Graham got it going really high,' Piers said. 'Up and up. It was lovely wasn't it, Oliver?'

'If you say so.'

'It was fun then?' asked Myra.

Piers' sparkling blue eyes twinkled at the thought of how much he'd enjoyed himself, but seeing Oliver's face he remembered he wasn't supposed to be happy and his eyes shut down and he lay back against the sofa cushions, his painful memories right there in his cherubic face. Graham took hold of his hand saying, 'It was fun and I'm sure your dad would have loved to see you flying it.'

'He would, wouldn't he, Oliver?'

Oliver gave Piers a long stare then stood up and walked out. They could hear his feet tramping solidly up the stairs, then the thud of the bedroom door being slammed and a sound like someone throwing themselves on a bed.

Piers, with tears beginning to brim in his eyes, set off to follow him, but Graham caught his hand, saying, 'Piers! Let's leave him for a while, maybe he wants to be alone.'

Chapter 4

In fact Oliver did want to be alone. He lay on his bed fighting back the tears which he'd promised himself, from the moment his dad died, he would not allow. But God, it was hard. At twelve he thought tears were for wusses, not for a boy who would be in his teens very shortly. He stared at the old-fashioned wallpaper with the roses as big as cabbages dotted all over. What kind of wallpaper was that for a bedroom? It was rubbish, just like Myra. Never ever as long as he lived would he ever call her Mum. He didn't know his mum, hadn't the faintest memory of her. Dad had shown him pictures of her holding him when he was a baby, some faded snapshots of her holding his hand as he learned to toddle, and a clutch of photos taken from the only holiday they'd had together – a windswept beach under a grey sky. He tried to turn the pictures into memories, to bring them to life but he was only two when Piers was born and his mum was killed when Piers was three months old. For a moment he grieved not for her, but for himself never having known his mother.

So here he was, laid on this bed in this bedroom, alone, and what was worse, afraid. Afraid of going back to school and everyone knowing he was an orphan, and them all, even his close friends, feeling sorry for him. Afraid of Myra and her un-predictability and that icy calm that sent shivers down his spine. Afraid that Uncle Graham would favour Piers and not like him just as his granny did. She truly was a nasty old bag. Piers had very kindly given him £2.50 from his money box to make up for the five pound note granny Butler had given Piers. Piers always shared the money she gave him, and he was tempted to refuse it out of pique but then he would have upset Piers. It wasn't Piers' fault his granny thought the sun shone out of his bottom. Brothers, especially ones with no Mum or Dad, had to stick together.

Oliver rolled over onto his back and, putting his hands behind his head, thought about his dad. He had the same name as his dad, John Oliver Butler, did that mean he'd be the same kind of person? Loving and laughing and kind. No matter how hard Uncle Graham tried, he didn't sound as sincere as his own dad. He tried, oh how hard he tried, and he meant to be kind and jolly but it didn't quite work. Perhaps with a bit more practice, a bit more experience of being a pretend father he might, just might learn how to do it right.

But those blessed kites he was so proud of! The sight of Uncle Graham prancing and dancing after his kite was enough to make a cat laugh. He was so clumsy, so awkward, Oliver was glad there was no one else in the field to see. He imagined having to go to Parent Teacher evenings with Uncle Graham and Auntie Myra in tow. What an image – her in her old-fashioned dowdy clothes and Uncle Graham trying so hard to be fatherly.

On the other hand he was glad his dad hadn't chosen Delphine to take in the two of them. He'd have run away from her, he most definitely would; a backpack full of clothes, food from that cupboard she called her larder that had more spaces on the shelves than it had tins and jars. He'd have bought two pints of real milk instead of that horrible soya stuff she thought would do them good (even though she always kept proper stuff for her own tea, he'd noticed), and he and Piers would have sat in the bus shelter down the road and drunk their pints of proper milk right to the bottom, while they waited for a bus that would take them anywhere at all because nowhere could be worse than

Delphine's. The dried-up old stick that she was. Bitter, mean, and very peculiar.

He thought back to the biscuits he and Piers had just scoffed. He felt embarrassed about eating them all, but they couldn't help themselves, and he was surprised how Myra didn't appear to mind them being greedy. However, just as a precaution in case things went pear-shaped he'd have a stash of money and keep adding to it in case of an emergency. He'd ask Uncle Graham about pocket money and he wouldn't spend his except for a very little bit then it would soon mount up. He studied the bedroom and decided the top shelf of the wardrobe would be best, inside a pair of socks. He had to stand on a chair to reach the very back of the top shelf of the wardrobe, and just as he almost overreached himself, the bedroom door burst open and he narrowly averted being knocked to the floor by clinging to the top shelf. It was Piers.

'What are you doing?'

'Ssshh! Close the door!'

Piers whispered, 'Well, what are you doing?'

'Don't say a word downstairs,' he pointed to the bedroom floor, 'I'm storing money in case we decide we have to run away.'

Still whispering, Piers asked why should they want to run away?

'Sometimes you are an idiot. It's early days yet, but Myra might decide she doesn't want us after all, or start acting like Delphine. We need a Plan B.'

'Where would we run to?'

'I haven't thought about that, yet, but I will.'

'Not Granny Butler's, not Delphine's, not Granny Stewart's. And Auntie Susan's flat smells terrible with all those cats. Last time I counted it was six and they make me wheeze. We've got nowhere to go. But I've got lots of money saved, shall we put mine with yours in the wardrobe?'

47

'How much have you got?'

'About fifteen pounds.'

'Right. Give it to me and we'll put it together and save it up. That'll make twenty-one pounds fifty pence.'

'That's not enough.'

'No, I know that, Piers, but it will start to add up because I'm going to ask Uncle Graham for some pocket money and we'll save it all.'

'But I like spending my pocket money. Like Dad always said, money burns a hole in my pocket.'

Oliver got down from the chair and grabbed Piers by the throat, saying, 'Don't mention his name again, I don't want to hear it. Right?!'

'That hurt!'

'It'll hurt even more if you say his name again. So shut up.'

Shaken by the strange bullying tone of Oliver's, Piers relayed his message to him, with a funny tremble in his voice.

'I've come up to tell you supper's almost ready and we have to go and shut Pete up for the night and check his water.'

'Right. Remember, don't breathe a word of our plans.'

'We're not really going to run away, are we? The money's just in case, isn't it?'

'Shut up, Piers. Or else.' Oliver shoved his fist under Piers' chin and frightened him out of his wits with the threat in his voice. This wasn't Oliver, not the real Oliver, what had happened to *him*? Where had he gone?

Together they went downstairs and out through the back door and with the torch Uncle Graham handed them, they went to shut up Pete for the night.

Crouching close together talking to Pete healed the breach a little, they were both good at one-sided conversations with Pete and they could keep going for ages when all they got for an answer was a glance from Pete's warm brown eyes.

'Do you think he's settled yet, Oliver? I want to bring him inside.'

'No, not yet. We'll give him a week.'

They heard Myra calling, 'Supper!'

Piers grabbed Pete, kissed the end of his twitchy little nose, popped him in the hutch and Oliver slammed the door shut before Pete could race back out. Piers watched Pete trying to scrabble his way back into the run. 'I'm glad I'm not a rabbit, shut up all the time. Do you think we could let him out to run in the garden one day?'

'If you want to lose him, fine. He'll burrow his way out and that will be that.'

'Supper! Come along, boys.'

'That's Myra again, better hurry up. "Wash your hands boys after touching the rabbit, not hygienic you see."' Oliver copied Myra's voice exactly and Piers began to laugh and was still laughing when they reached the kitchen door.

'Wash your hands, boys, after touching the rabbit, not hygienic you see,' Myra reminded them.

Neither of them could help it, they immediately broke into even bigger peals of laughter and Myra was annoyed. 'I don't know what you find funny in that, you should always wash your hands before eating, plus heaven alone knows what you might have picked up from Pete.' She turned to look at them and scalded herself with the hot water from the greens she was straining.

'Run your hand under the cold tap, quick!' Piers shouted and turned the cold tap on himself. Oliver busied himself straining the abandoned greens and began serving the food. Myra stood there with her scalded hand under the cold tap, her wrist gripped by Piers who'd no intention of letting go until he was satisfied he'd done all he could.

Uncle Graham came into the kitchen as Piers was allowing Myra to dab her wrist dry. 'Dab not rub, remember. Fresh air is the best for scalds if there's no broken skin, just a very red patch.

Try not to catch it in case it blisters because then you might break the blister and that really will hurt. Sit down. That's for shock, is sitting down.'

Myra, gratified by his obvious concern, asked where on earth he'd learned all this first aid.

'We had a a nurse come to our class to teach us first aid. Scalds and burns were my speciality,' Piers said proudly. 'She said I was a natural. I remembered everything she told me. Dab not rub,' he repeated.

'All right, Myra?' Graham inquired, cautiously. Normally Myra would have deemed herself in need of serious medical aid in similar circumstances, but for some reason she'd accepted Piers' treatment without a murmur. 'How did you do that?' he asked.

Oliver spoke up. 'Straining these greens. Is that enough veg for you, Uncle Graham?'

'Yes, thanks. I must say the two of you are coping very well, I shall be redundant soon.' He smiled that odd lopsided smile that made Oliver wonder if Uncle Graham ever did anything natural without having to think hard about it first.

Oliver placed Myra's plate in front of her. The food wasn't arranged on the plate as meticulously as she would have served it, and she couldn't stop herself from saying so.

'You've not served the food very tidily at all.'

Piers held his breath, waiting for the inevitable outbreak of temper from Oliver.

'I did my best. I saved you from having to do it when your hand hurts.'

'It needs to be neater altogether, just remember that. Not potatoes covered by the greens and one sausage this side of the plate and the other sausage half hidden under the sage and onion stuffing.'

Oliver looked down at the floor for a moment, then without warning he swept Myra's supper plate and all the food on it off the table and onto the floor. In a voice full of scorn he shouted,

'Is that neat enough?' and left the kitchen. For the second time that day they heard him climbing the stairs, slamming the door and flinging himself on his bed.

Piers had half a mind to run after him to avoid Myra's reaction but somehow he was pinned to his chair by panic.

Uncle Graham; stunned by the situation, sat motionless too. It was the most dramatic thing that had happened in that kitchen since the day the two of them, full of happiness, moved in.

Myra couldn't understand why Oliver had done what he'd done, all she'd spoken was the truth. What was wrong with the truth? He'd have to come and clean it up, and eat it and she'd eat his. As she headed for the stairs a dull flush crept over her cheeks, an outward sign of the temper boiling within. Without knocking on the bedroom door – why should she, it was her house, she reasoned – she flung it open and said in her icy tight-lipped tone, 'Come downstairs and get your supper. Now, this minute, and *you* can eat the food you flung on the floor.'

Oliver's answer was to turn over and let his back say it all.

'Do you hear me?'

She got no reply. Then she made the biggest mistake yet. She took hold of his arm and tried to drag him off the bed, but Oliver – well versed in fights with his brother – had both hands wedged under the edge of the mattress with his weight laid on them and he held on, and so long as he kicked out hard with his feet, he knew she wouldn't be able to move him. Myra, not having done anything really physical in years, let alone faced the stubborn rage of a twelve-year-old boy, couldn't get him off the bed.

'I said, go downstairs and eat your supper.'

Silence.

More angry than she could ever remember being, his silence aggravated her into saying the unforgivable. 'I never wanted the two of you in the first place, and if you think you can behave badly and get away with it with me, you're very much mistaken. I'll send you back to Delphine and you can see how you like that. She'll be glad. I'll keep Piers but not you. You wicked boy. *Now* do as I say.'

But Oliver, devastated by her threat, didn't move a single inch. He didn't beg, didn't argue, didn't do anything except weep inside, which she could neither hear nor see.

There came the sound of Graham's footsteps pounding rapidly up the stairs. He sized up the situation immediately, and for the first time in years he told Myra exactly where to go.

Myra resolutely folded her arms and said, 'No. I'm dealing with this.'

'No, Myra, I am. I've heard every word you've said to this boy and if you think I'm going to tolerate it you are very wrong. He is not going anywhere, most certainly not to Delphine's. Now I'm not saying anything goes – Oliver is going to apologise when I've talked to him. But I will not have threats and cruel words you don't mean. Now you go downstairs and see to Piers. The child is terrified of what is going to happen to them both and you are to go down there and reassure him.'

Graham had done it again, growing in stature until he brooked no opposition, and Myra, her temper waning through exhaustion, decided to do as he said. Only because she wanted to reassure Piers, she thought, not because Graham had told her to. So down the stairs she went, to find Piers scooping her dinner off the floor and onto a plate arranging it neatly as best he could.

He looked up and said, 'This is my supper, I've given Oliver mine, and you've got Oliver's. We've got to stay together, I'm no good without Oliver.' The tender dependence on his brother stirred a slight softening in Myra's heart. Not much, but she could at least empathise a little with his predicament. As for Graham Butler, just wait till she got him on his own.

'If Oliver goes to Delphine's I'll go too.'

Myra couldn't understand what made her answer as she did.

'You're a good boy Piers. At least let me give you two new sausages, I was going to save them for Uncle Graham's packed lunch on Monday but you have them and we'll throw away your two that rolled under the table; the floor is clean, but I wouldn't fancy them.'

Piers couldn't help but notice that the two sausages from the floor were wiped and put in a piece of foil in the fridge. Piers felt very sorry for his Uncle Graham having sausages off the floor for his packed lunch.

Not long after, Oliver came downstairs with Graham and sat at the table, picked up his knife and fork and said in hushed tones, 'I'm sorry, Myra, I was trying to do my best and you were critical and it hurt. But this is my apology for being so badly behaved. I am sorry.'

Piers smiled with relief, Oliver began eating Piers' supper, Piers ate Myra's and Myra tucked into Oliver's and silence fell until Graham decided it was time to break it.

'The next chance we get, I thought we'd take the kites down to the coast and fly them up on the cliffs, how about it, Myra? Then we could have lunch in one of the fish restaurants and walk along the cliff top to see the lighthouse and go up it if it's open, which I believe it is at weekends.'

Graham might have thought that the matter was concluded, but as soon as the two boys were settled in bed that night and Myra was convinced they were sleeping, she launched into what she considered to be her very righteous battle royal.

'You may have won the battle but you certainly haven't won the war.' Where on earth had she got that from? 'I will not stand for Oliver losing his temper like that, if it happens again, he'll have to go.'

Graham gave a long steady look while he found the right words. 'Myra, he was not to blame. When I came in Piers was attending to your hand and Oliver was trying to help by serving the supper. If that isn't being kind I don't know what is. I was most impressed and then you – yes *you* – had to go and spoil it all.' He looked gravely at her and she felt his accusation come creeping up her back, up her neck and up her cheeks. She damn well wasn't going to be made to feel guilty about this. Definitely not.

'Excuse me, it was Oliver who flung my supper on the floor, not me.'

'But it was you who didn't, wouldn't, recognise how helpful they were being. Two boys torn to shreds with grief, we need to make allowances and you should have carried on eating with tremendous graciousness and not a single word of criticism, and you should have *seen* the effort he had made to please you.'

'He still shouldn't have done what he did. I mean, he's twelve, not two.'

'Myra, he's watched his father slowly dying with not even his mother to help him, and all the while feeling responsible for his younger brother. Think about it.' Deciding there was no use continuing the argument, Graham picked up the book he was reading at the moment and opened it up.

Myra repressed the guilt which kept creeping up her spine. 'Listen to me. All I said was— '

Graham interrupted her. 'The matter is closed, Myra. We're the adults here and it's up to us to bend the rules, to understand, to feel pity for them, up to us. You and me.'

How dare he? She hadn't finished. 'I might have guessed. I take third place in your mind now, those two boys I didn't want and I told you I didn't, are now ahead of me in your affections. I did not think for one moment that this would ever happen. Up till now I've always come first with you.'

She waited for him to tell her she was wrong, that she would always come first. But instead, Graham neatly placed his bookmark at the right page, got to his feet, said 'Goodnight' softly, and went upstairs to his bedroom.

Chapter 5

Monday morning brought a whole slew of new problems for Myra. On edge after a weekend of trying to get used to the presence of the boys, messing up her house, making noise where she was used to quiet, leaving lights on in empty rooms and strange silences in full ones, she'd got up in really good time to make sure that everything was organised for the week ahead. Something told her the boys should not leave the house without a good breakfast. But her greatest anxiety was having to take Piers to his new school. Seeing Oliver to the bus stop was no trouble but Piers was far too young to be crossing the main road by himself, so she had to go part of the way with him at least and then she knew, though she did wonder about ducking out, that she should take him right into school, seeing as it was his first morning.

Piers didn't have to worry about Myra holding his hand and showing him up as they walked along, because he knew she wasn't a holding hands kind of person, but he did worry about a new school and making new friends and what his teacher would be like.

Mothers and children flooded the pavement the nearer they got to the school, and Myra was surprised how everyone knew everyone else and was amazed how they chatted: arranging others' children going to their house for tea after school; re-minding each other about the new time for their exercise class; had they remembered the New to You Sale in aid of school funds; offering lifts; their reasons for communicating appeared endless.

But she still had to face going into school. They found the headmistress's room immediately so there was no choice but to knock and introduce themselves.

'Good morning, Mrs Butler. I'm afraid the headmistress is not here this morning, I'm her deputy. This must be Piers. I've been told to expect you.' She shook hands not only with Myra but with Piers too. From her desk she took a file with Piers James Butler written on the front in bold letters. 'I have all your details in here, Piers, the ones your dad gave my colleague when he brought you last week. Now come along with me and I shall take you to see your teacher, her name is Mrs Fletcher. You remember her, don't you, Piers, I think you met her when you came to school with your dad.' She turned to Myra. 'By the way, have you decided, is Piers having packed lunch or school dinners?'

'Ah! Didn't my husband arrange it?' Myra was so thrown by hearing the teacher refer to Graham as Piers' dad that she couldn't think to answer clearly. Did she think that she was Piers' mother, then? She thought anyone could see a mile off that she couldn't possibly be mother to this lively young boy. Maybe it wasn't as clear as she thought. What on earth had Graham told them?

Still flummoxed she turned to Piers. 'What do you want to do for lunch?'

Thinking about Uncle Graham's packed lunch sausage sandwiches he chose, 'School dinners, please.'

'Wise choice,' said the deputy headmistress, 'our school dinners are excellent. Come along then, young man, say bye-bye to your mum. See you at three fifteen.'

Piers opened his mouth to say 'She isn't my mum', but changed his mind because he couldn't remember having a mum and he quite liked the idea, so he decided not to enlighten her.

Myra said, 'I'll be here when school finishes, Piers, wait for me, won't you?'

Piers nodded and left her standing in the corridor, feeling like a spare part. As she squeezed her way through the crowd of mothers still cluttering the pavement and exchanging news it dawned on Myra that the teacher wasn't the only one who would get the wrong idea while they were out and about. The whole wide world would think of her as the boys' mother. She set off on her journey back, trying to ignore the small glow of pride that lurked deep beneath her horror at the teacher's misapprehension. Her, a mother? Ridiculous.

By the time she got home, her whole morning thrown out of kilter by having to turn out so early, Myra felt exhausted. She'd have this to do every morning, so her leisurely time pulling herself together after Graham left for work was over and done with for ever. Coffee! She'd have a coffee with sugar in and sit down to read the paper.

As though Viv had a private line to Myra's kitchen, she was there as soon as Myra got a mug out for herself. 'It's me!'

Myra got out another mug.

'Everything all right?'

'Yes. I think so. You having sugar this morning, Viv?'

'I need it. I think I'll have to begin going away for weekends.'

'Why?'

'The last four weekends I've had one lot after another staying. They never think I might like a break myself.'

Myra placed Viv's mug in front of her, the coffee still swirling around after vigorous stirring. 'I've been to the school with Piers. Seems nice.'

'It is, all my lot went there and I think the new head is the best one of all. Was Piers OK?'

Myra nodded. 'Can I tell you something?'

'Be my guest.'

'She assumed I was Piers' mother.'

'That's a laugh!'

'Perhaps Graham never told them ... '

Viv thought it odd he hadn't but said instead, 'Maybe they've just got confused – did you see the same teacher he spoke to? Still, perhaps it's for the best, Piers won't get extra sympathy that might make him feel very different from everyone else.'

'I'll ask him tonight what he said.'

Viv nudged Myra's arm. 'Nice though, isn't it?' and grinned.

'Nice?'

'Yes, them thinking you're his mum. Nice for you, you must agree.'

'Not the truth though, is it?'

'Sometimes the truth is best left unsaid.'

'When can it ever be better not to tell the truth?'

Viv's expressive eyebrows shot up her forehead. 'So as not to hurt someone's feelings?'

'Perhaps.'

Myra stared out of the window and remembered that in the rush that morning Little Pete hadn't been let out. 'They forgot the rabbit, before they went.'

'Well, you can let him out. Come on, we'll do it together.'

Myra unlocked the back door thinking it was one thing after another. Not even half past nine yet.

'His food's in a plastic thingummy in the shed. I'll get it out.'

Viv opened the door of the hutch and out came Little Pete. In the morning sunshine he looked very appealing and Viv cooed over him. 'Does he bite?'

'I don't know, I've had nothing to do with him, the boys look after him.' Myra poured a meagre amount of food out of the plastic container and put it down in the run. 'I'll get him some fresh water from the outside tap.'

When she came back with Pete's water bowl, Viv was cuddling him in her arms.

'He really is the sweetest little thing. Lovely eyes. He enjoys cuddling, here, you hold him.' Viv knew she wouldn't want to, Myra didn't like touching anyone, and certainly not an animal.

'No, thanks, shall we let him get his breakfast?'

'You know, Myra, when you've got children you've got to learn to touch them. Comfort them. Hug them. Maybe even let them hug you back once in a while.'

'Pete's a rabbit not a child.'

'Same thing except he's got fur. Reach out your hand and touch him while I'm holding him. Go on, just a little touch.'

Myra darted a finger out to touch Pete's fur for a brief moment. 'There, I've done it. I'm going back in for my coffee, it'll be going cold else.'

She wouldn't have admitted it for the world but in fact she found she hadn't minded touching Pete at all. Not one little bit. When no one was there she might even pick him up, she thought, or perhaps stroke him first and get used to him.

'So how're yer doing?' Viv asked once they'd settled back indoors. She cocked her head to one side and looked quizzically at her, looking rather like a robin with her red sweater and her bright inquiring eyes.

'I don't know. I'm not getting this discipline business right, I do know that. I seem to expect all the wrong things.'

'You've got to walk on ice in the circumstances you find yourself in, emotionally they're in a very delicate state. They don't really know you from Adam, do they? What's more, you've no experience of kids either, it all takes time. You'll have to let them grieve, you see, and be thoughtful of them.'

'Graham seems to know better than me how to go about it.'

'He's spent a lot more time with them, you never used to go on their expeditions with John and Graham, did you? Left it all to him.'

'Someone had to take care of things and I had my fairs to go to.'

Viv looked a mite sceptical. 'How many? Four a year? Come on!'

'It all has to be done.'

'Ye-e-ess. They're very nice tea cosies, but ...'

Myra sat up straighter than usual. 'But ...?'

'I've never said this before and I shouldn't, but I'm going to ...'

She went silent so Myra, preparing herself for a fight, said fretfully, 'Well?'

'I mean, for example, I have that one you gave me two Christmasses ago and it's beautifully worked, you're very clever with the sewing machine and the embroidery, but ...'

'Yes?'

'Well, Myra, it doesn't grab you.'

'It isn't supposed to grab you, it's a tea cosy. They don't.'

'You know what I mean, it's not exciting. I'd like a tea cosy that's bright and cheerful and makes me want to get it out of the drawer on a morning, makes me smile when I look at it, you know.'

'Does it keep your teapot hot?'

'Oh! Yes, nothing better.'

'Well, then, what more do you want?'

'Like I said.' Viv knew that she was about to be turned out, so she got up to go before Myra got her chance to say it. 'I'd better be off, anyway. Let you get on with your morning. Be seeing you!'

Myra was bereft. Even her textile design business was a waste of time according to Viv. She'd known it for a long time inside herself, she even acknowledged Graham felt the same as Viv, but Graham had never said it so forthrightly as Viv had just now. Myra drank her coffee almost to the last dregs and put the mug back on the table, but was so distraught that it slipped from her hand before she'd placed it down properly. It fell over; the remains of the coffee slowly flooded out onto the table and began to drip down the tight join between the leaves. Had she felt anything like normal she would have leapt up and wiped it up, because she couldn't bear mess. Instead she sat perfectly still staring at the coffee leaking onto the floor. Myra had always loved the table, how thrilled she'd been when it first got delivered, at the time it had seemed smart and up-to-the-minute, like she felt – well, almost felt. Now she wouldn't care if it spontaneously combusted. She pictured it now: she'd ignore the bright red fire extinguisher provided and fixed by Graham, and go happily into the garden to watch from a distance as the once prized possession would slowly disintegrate. She wouldn't even mind if the chairs went too and the padded cushions she'd so eagerly made to match the curtains. Whatever had possessed her to think they were splendid? As she gazed round her precious kitchen Myra decided that the whole of the kitchen required a refit. Every cupboard, every door, every centimetre of skirting board was boring, boring, boring. Safe, that was it, a safe choice. It had been like that all her life: always safe choices.

She glanced down at the apron she wore, the one she'd made with such care. That was appalling too, so neat, so dreary. She yanked it off and unfortunately for the apron her kitchen scissors were on the table where she'd left them after she'd cut the greaseproof paper for Graham's sausage sandwiches. Snatching them up, Myra cut the apron to shreds. Snipping, snipping, snipping, relentlessly. She didn't clear away the pieces, didn't care that bits of apron were soaking up the cold coffee from her mug, didn't care the clock was ticking the morning away.

Then with the decision made – and making decisions was not her forte – she marched with deadly intent up the stairs, scissors in hand and went directly to the smallest bedroom.

Myra paused in the doorway and knew without doubt that her cutting frenzy was not due entirely to Viv's criticism. The worst of it was knowing that Viv had only put into words what she herself had been feeling for months and months, feelings she had doggedly refused to acknowledge.

The tea cosies were lined up neatly in their plastic jackets along the shelves, lying in wait for their buyers. Methodically, without passion, she began their complete destruction. Tearing off their wrappers one by one, each tea cosy was cut into pieces, the padding spilling out on the floor, the very pale green gingham covering fluttering down to the carpet piece by piece. In total thirty-one tea cosies met their Waterloo in the space of an hour. The pieces left were so small they looked almost like fallen leaves. She was ankle-deep in the ruins of her so-called career, in the room which for so long had been her refuge, but somehow she didn't care.

Down in the kitchen she got out two dustbin bags, shook one of them open and put the bits of her apron in, then marched upstairs and stuffed the remains of the tea cosies in until the bags were full. Out came the upstairs vacuum and she cleaned the floor. All that remained of her former business was the state-of-the-art sewing machine and two linen baskets of wadding and material, plus a leaflet advertising a Christmas Arts and Crafts Fair.

She'd cancel the stall she'd reserved this very minute. Her reason?

She couldn't very well say my stuff didn't sell because it was dreadful.

I've given up trying.

I'm wasting my time.

The fair will be better without my tea cosies, believe me.

Then the excuse hit her. She'd say she and her husband had been lucky enough to take in two boys and she was too busy to sew. That was it. The very, very best of reasons. No need to say she'd cut everything up in a mad frenzy. Just that at the moment she couldn't find time for sewing, being busy helping the boys to settle in. A perfect cover story.

The sitting room clock chimed the hour. Myra counted and found to her amazement it was already eleven o'clock. Where had the time gone? She marched downstairs, picked up the phone and told the organiser what Myra knew to be a lie. The organiser was delighted for her. Thank you for being so understanding, said Myra. No, she couldn't see her way back to sewing just yet, she was too absorbed in making a good life for the boys. No, no, it's Graham and I who are privileged, they're such lovely boys. And a Merry Christmas to you too. Having listened to her own lies Myra couldn't believe how easily they had slipped out, and how readily they'd been believed.

She replaced the receiver and wondered what to do next. The ironing, of course. One moment of madness couldn't be allowed to let everything go to hell in a handcart, she thought.

Three o'clock came round all too soon and the challenge of managing not to get spoken to as she fought her way through the crowd of mothers would have to be faced again. They all gathered at the school gates: a horde of them, chattering while hanging on to their pushchairs or their toddlers. One of them was giving out leaflets and she handed one to Myra. 'You're new, aren't you? You won't have heard of the New to You Sale. The details are on here. Stunning stuff, believe me. Some wonderful bargains. You'll be most welcome. Which class is yours in?'

Myra saved herself from looking a complete chump by re-membering the teacher's name was Mrs Fletcher.

'Ah! She's very good, my eldest was in her class last year and he did brilliantly. He'll like her. See you then!'

The doors opened and the children poured out. Just as Myra was beginning to think Piers would never come out, he did, shivering slightly in his shirtsleeves.

'I can't find my coat.' He was holding back the tears as best he could.

'I see.' Myra did not know what to do. Did you go in and ask? Did you go in and look for yourself? Did you go in and speak to Mrs Fletcher? Or did you just go home without it? She was terribly keen to go home without it rather than draw attention to herself. But it was so cold.

She took hold of Piers' hand to give her some confidence, and though she suspected it made him feel a baby, he let her. They found the cloakroom because it had a smart notice on the door. There, under a bench, was Piers' coat.

'I can see it!' he yelled and rushed to get it. He struggled into it, fastened the buttons and the zip and tried to get out of school without holding her hand but she was determined and gripped it tightly. As an excuse he suggested he should put his gloves on as his hands were cold, so she let him, delighted to have navigated this small hurdle without having been seen or needing to speak to anyone else. She wished she'd listened to the other mothers greeting their children so she might have a better idea of what to say to him.

'Did you have a good time?' was the best she came up with,

'Yes, thank you. They're nice in Mrs Fletcher's class. Two of the boys let me play with them.'

'Did you find out their names?'

'Yes. Aidan and Carl.'

Spontaneously Myra declared she liked his name best. 'Well they sound like nice names, but Piers is much nicer.'

'Do you think so? I used to get teased about my name at my other school.'

'What did they say?'

'It was posh but it isn't, is it? My dad said it was my mum's choice.'

'It was. I remember.'

'Did you know my mum?'

'Of course. She was lovely.' After that Myra was silent, thinking about Mo and how envious she had always been of her. Mo

64

with two babies and herself with none. How grossly unfair it had all seemed. Now they were both supposed to be hers, yet they weren't, and things had come round full circle.

'Tell me something about her. Dad never said much.'

What was there to tell? How pretty she was with her blonde curly hair, her huge blue eyes that Piers had inherited, how kind she was, how she loved life and how John wept for her when she was killed? And how she, Myra Butler, didn't.

'You've got her eyes and Oliver has her fair hair and her curls.'

'Did she smile a lot?'

Myra nodded.

'Was she happy?'

'Oh yes. And you boys are what made her happiest of all.' Alarmed by the direction the conversation was taking, Myra steered things back on to safe ground. 'When we get in will you feed Pete, I'm not sure I gave him enough this morning.'

'Oh no! We forgot about him.'

'Never mind, I fed him, well, Viv and I did.'

'Thank you. I'll do it as soon as I get in. Oliver's never home before half past five on Mondays because he has football. He catches the late coach.'

'I'm glad you told me. There we are, in we go in the warm. See to Pete before you take your coat off, it's so cold. I'll start on the supper.' There, she'd managed the coming home quite nicely, no awkwardness at all. She put her keys down and looked at the leaflet for the New to You Sale. She wasn't going, not likely. All the crowds and the prattle. How did you chatter like they did? What was there to endlesssly chat about? A lot apparently. She spotted a scrap of fabric on the floor she must have missed earlier. She wouldn't tell Graham about what she'd done to the tea cosies. So long as she kept the bedroom door closed he'd never know. She'd tell him when she'd sorted it all out in her mind.

But Graham came home that night with a present for the boys. A bumper car game with two cars, two remote controls and loads of batteries to make them go. 'Flashing lights,' he said, 'loads of noise, just what kids like. I'll surprise the boys with it in the living room. But I'd better get the big scissors from your room to cut the box open.'

Before Myra could offer him her second-class pair of scissors he had raced upstairs with this new enthusiasm he'd garnered and it was all too late. He walked down more slowly, came into the kitchen and stood in front of her. He gave her a long slow stare and when she didn't provide an explanation, he asked, 'Myra? What's happened? What have you done with every-thing? All your work? All the tea cosies?'

She put down the vegetable knife and with downcast eyes muttered, 'Got rid of them.'

'Where?'

'By the bin.'

Piers had sneaked in to see what all the fuss was about, and now he rushed back out to look and saw the two bags lined up against the wall. He prodded them with his fingers, poked a small hole in one and by the light of the outside lamp he took a peep inside to prove she was speaking the truth. Dashing back in, he said with his big blue eyes wide with amazement, 'She has, Uncle Graham, she really has. They're all cut up. In very little bits.'

Graham's attention was focussed on Myra in a way it hadn't been for years.

'*You cut them up? All of them?*'

Myra nodded. 'All of them.'

'But why? They're your pride and joy. You love your cosies. What made you do it?'

Her voice trembled. 'I-I-you've known for ages, but never said.'

'Known what?'

'They were dull. They were plain. They were ... safe.'

'I've never said so.'

'No, but you knew. I knew you knew, but I wouldn't have listened, even if you'd said.'

'What about your stall at the Christmas ...'

'Cancelled.'

'Did you tell them why?'

Myra turned away so he couldn't see her face, she couldn't say what she'd said. She couldn't have him thinking she'd suddenly accepted the boys willingly as a blessing, because she hadn't, had she? 'I said I was too busy and hadn't been well.' What had happened to the truth, she thought to herself, lying twice in one day. What were these boys doing to her?

'But you're not ill ... are you?'

Was she? Was that why she'd had that cutting frenzy, maybe she was going mad.

'No, not really.'

'Well, I'm sorry. Sorry for your sake, Myra. But maybe it was time to move on – try something new. There's so much you could do.' He said this so sympathetically it didn't feel like criticism at all.

A few days ago she would have lambasted him. Today, she hadn't the energy to do it and just suggested he took the bumper car game into the hall, it would run better on the parquet floor and she could get the supper ready. He and Piers took her at her word. Within minutes everything was out of the box, the batteries fitted, the aerials in place, and the two of them were playing the game as though nothing else in the world existed. And that was just how it felt to Myra. She was on the outside of this male-dominated world she'd so abruptly found herself in. Now she not only had no work to take refuge in, but no Graham either.

The bleeping and the flashing of the car lights and the whoops of excitement drilled holes in Myra's brain. How could she concentrate on the plaice and chips and the parsley sauce with all that going on? She glanced into the hall readying herself to silence them, and caught a glimpse of the delight in Piers' face. And it was not only Piers' face which was full of pleasure, but Graham's too. She couldn't remember when she'd last seen him so delighted.

By the time Oliver got home off the late bus, Graham and Piers were completely absorbed in the bumper car game and couldn't wait for Oliver to have a go.

'Oliver! Look what Uncle Graham's bought! Isn't it great? Come and have a turn.'

Oliver flung down his school bags and took over Graham's car. Within moments he had mastered the concept of the game and he and Piers were playing as furiously as Graham and Piers had been. The shouting, the cheering, the applause felt deafening to Myra, unaccustomed to such goings on in the normally silent house. Graham was sitting on the bottom step watching the boys and the look on his face baffled Myra. It was a mixture of . . . well, what exactly? Pride, boyish enthusiasm, childish glee, mirth, happiness? Yes, happiness definitely and then something else she couldn't quite evaluate.

'Supper's ready.' She may as well have said nothing because she got no response.

'I said supper's ready. Go wash your hands.'

But they didn't. Neither Graham nor the two boys moved a muscle.

After all the slaving she'd done to get it ready and that lovely pudding too, all home made.

'I *said*, supper's ready. Go wash your hands.'

'Sorry.' Graham stood up. 'I'm counting to ten and then we stop and have our supper.' This worked, but even then when they eventually came to the table, they could talk of nothing else but the bumper cars, not a word about the lovely fish, not a word about the fruit crumble and cream, they just wolfed it down as fast as they could, said 'Thanks' and asked to leave the table to play with the game.

Myra intended to give them a lecture on manners but Graham beat her to it. 'I'll clear your dishes for you tonight, you go play the game.'

She was furious. She closed the kitchen door so the noise level was reduced and she could think what she was saying and burst out with, 'I won't have bad manners. Not one word about how nice their meal was, all they can think about is that blasted game.'

'Myra, have you noticed anything about that game?'

'It's noisy and silly and stupid and I wish you'd never bought it for them. How much did it cost?'

'Too much, Myra, but worth every penny judging by the enjoyment they're getting out of it.'

'It's ridiculous, what a waste of money.'

'You haven't answered my question.'

Myra stood up and began shuffling plates. 'I haven't time. There's all this to do.'

'I'll answer it for you then. It's the first time they've really enjoyed doing anything at all since they've been in these four walls. These bumper cars have really engaged them and being taken out of themselves is what they need. Forgetting their grief, just for a while.'

'So that's it, is it? That's why I'm having to tolerate all the din? What about me?'

'What about you?'

'I've given up my business because I've too much to do with four of us in the house, what with all the washing and ironing and cleaning and tidying. They were my pride and joy.'

'I thought you said—'

'I got rid of them all so they aren't reminding me of what I've lost.'

'Actually, Myra, you've lost nothing. You were quite clear earlier: you cut them up because you realised all by yourself that they were not interesting enough to make people want to buy them. And if you want to know what I really feel, I think a part of you knows that you can do better. You've got so much talent if you'd just take a chance or two. That's the truth and you know it. I'll advertise for some domestic help for you, there'll be plenty of people who'd like to clean and iron and put clean sheets on in a tidy house like ours. You don't have to stop your work. But right now, why don't you go and sit down and switch the TV on. I'll clear up in here. You're doing a brilliant job with the food, Myra. The boys might not say anything, but they do eat it all up, and if that isn't a recommendation I don't know what is.'

Myra flopped down on the sofa after tiptoeing across the hall in an attempt to avoid treading on the bumper cars. So he did still care about her, right when she thought she'd lost him to the boys. Thinking about getting help in, clearing up the kitchen for her, he must still care. He was right about the food, too, the boys didn't need persuading to eat it. So she must be good at something. The memory of Graham's face when he was playing with Piers flashed across her mind. Why had it been so long since she'd seen him so happy?

Chapter 6

Graham and Myra never came across each other once they'd gone upstairs for bed. Myra's bedroom had its own shower room and Graham used the main bathroom. So it came as a shock to Myra that night when he tapped briefly on her bedroom door and walked in wearing his pyjamas.

Her heart leapt and she could feel it pounding in her chest. Oh no! He didn't, did he, not after all these years. 'Yes?'

'I've come to say goodnight and a great big thank you.'

Was she about to get the one reward she couldn't stomach?

'Thank you? What for?'

'For trying so hard with the boys. How did you go on at Piers' school this morning by the way?'

'I'd have got on a lot better if you'd told the truth. They thought I was his mum! I didn't know where to look.'

'I didn't pretend anything. I told the head teacher everything – she'll be an important voice when Social Services approve us becoming guardians – or I certainly hope so. But I know plenty of people assume we're their parents when we're out and about. And even if we have to fill out forms or give our names, people are bound to think we're a normal family because our surname is the same as the boys'. You must have met with a different teacher today who just glanced at the forms and made a logical guess. Did she call you his mum?' He had a kind of tentative grin on his face.

Myra pulled the duvet up a little higher, just in case. 'Yes, and Piers didn't contradict her.'

'Did you?'

'No.'

He patted her leg where he could make out the shape of it under the duvet. 'I know we'll never replace John and Mo – we wouldn't want to, and it's important the boys always know how much their parents loved them and didn't want to leave them. But if we can't be Mum and Dad to Piers and Oliver, we'll be as close as we possibly can. We're family already, and now we're just even closer family. And if other people call us their mum or dad from time to time, that's fine by me, as long as it doesn't upset the children. You know John's lawyer talked me through the next steps – as well as Social Services giving us the thumbs up, we need approval from the Family Court. They need to see we're serious about our responsibilities, and that the boys are happy. But I'm not going to hide anything from you, Myra. I'd like to do more. I'd like to make it permanent and adopt them. And there's no hurry on that, we don't want to overwhelm the boys. For now, getting the legal guardian status is my priority. What do you think?' He stood there smiling down at her, with that lock of hair flopping down his forehead as always, waiting for her reply.

Myra turned over to face away from him. 'It's permanent then?'

'It is for me.'

'I'll think about it, it's not a decision to be taken lightly.'

'It certainly isn't and we'd have to ask them first, of course. We mustn't rush things. Here, I'll turn out your light for you.' He reached down to her bedside lamp and she smelt the mingled toothpaste and soap. Normally even just the thought of anyone being close, invading her space, made her tense up. But just for a moment, there felt something comforting about his presence. Before she could even fully register this strange emotion, he'd gone, leaving her to the quiet and the dark.

★

Graham had got his bedroom organised just as he wanted now. It had taken a while to adapt to being the equivalent of a single man in this regard, but he rather felt he had achieved it. The wallpaper sprayed with bunches of appleblossom had been painted over, the curtains swapped for a more masculine pair, the carpet and the bed linen changed to match, and together with the computer on a sleek desk down one side and some smart shelves for his files above it, it felt like a space he could call his own.

He'd loved playing with the bumper cars, it took him right back to going to the fair with his father and sharing a bumper car with him. The thick oily smell, the excitement, the roughness of it all really appealed, even when he was as young as four. He'd dreamed of being the man who swung from car to car when they were going round, unravelling the cars locked together, setting them free again. What more could he ask of life but travelling from town to town setting up the stand, unstacking the cars from the huge transporters, bringing them to life again, and giving children like him all the pleasure in the world. The bumper cars had been the only ride he wanted to go on. Playing with that toy today had brought back all the thrill of the fair, brought back something of the boy he used to be.

Then he remembered the annual bonfire fair would be coming to Moor Top Fields the next week. He'd forgotten all about it. He hadn't had a reason to go for years. Myra hated the noise and the crowds, and going by himself would have made him look ridiculous, but this year he had a cast iron reason for going. He and the boys could go on the real bumper cars. Oliver would be old enough to drive one himself and he and Piers could share. He almost jumped out of bed to tell the two of them about the fair. But of course they'd be fast asleep. Tomorrow would have to do.

Graham was on the verge of falling asleep when he was disturbed by a tap on his door. 'Myra?'

'No. It's me, Uncle Graham. I can't sleep.' Framed in the doorway was Oliver, looking lost and forlorn.

'Come in, Oliver, sit on the bed. What's up?'

'Thinking about Dad.'

'Exactly what about him?'

'I don't know. Just thinking about him. I miss him, you know. I try not to, but I do.'

'Of course you'll miss him. You're bound to. I'm no substitute for him, I'd be the first to admit that, all I can do is try to help you through it.'

'I know. And I'd rather be here than Delphine's.'

Oliver was silent after that so Graham filled the silence by asking, 'Do you think some hot chocolate might be a good idea?'

'Yes, please. Piers won't want any, he's fast asleep. Nothing ever stops him from sleeping, not even the night Dad died.'

'Put your slippers on, the kitchen is cold this time of night.'

They sat together at the kitchen table, each with their hands wrapped round their mugs of hot chocolate. Thinking. Right out of the blue Oliver asked, 'Myra doesn't want us, does she?'

'Myra finds it very difficult to share things.'

'Not even her bed.'

Unable to touch on such a delicate subject with anyone at all, least of all a boy of twelve, Graham closed the subject off immediately.'Well, that's a matter for me and her. I meant she can't share her emotions easily. I do believe she's on the verge of coming round to you two boys though. We've never had children, you see, so ...'

'Why?'

His frankness wrongfooted Graham briefly, but he decided honesty was the best policy. 'Well, we wanted them – very badly. We even had two – almost – but each time they didn't make it ... and it broke Myra's heart ... and mine.'

Oliver sighed. 'That's why she's always sad then.'

74

'It's kind of closed her away from people. It will take a while for her to come round to the two of you, but there's one thing for certain, this is your home now and this is where you are staying.' He almost added, 'Whether Myra stays here or she doesn't,' but bit back the words and said instead, 'I've got lots of plans for us all and bit by bit, it will work out. Have patience.' Graham smiled his forced lopsided smile that so amused Oliver, but tonight he recognised it was a genuine smile even if it was a bit stiff.

'You're very perceptive, Oliver, you'll turn into a lovely grown-up. And if you get the right moment, tell Piers what I said about you both being here forever. I know he's worried about getting sent somewhere else and he'll believe you more than me or Myra.'

The two of them sat in companionable silence sipping their drinks for a few minutes.

'Bed now, Oliver.'

'How old are you, Uncle Graham?'

'Forty-three.'

Oliver's face registered complete amazement. 'So you're not an old man then! You seem like one. Sorry, that was rude.'

'Is that what I seem? Old?'

'Er … yes. Sorry. I'd better be off.' He scuttled off upstairs before anything further might be said about his rudeness.

It was three o'clock before Graham went to bed, mainly because he was in a state of shock. It took an intelligent perceptive boy of twelve to come out with the truth then. Maybe it was his work that had aged him, he thought: as the youngest head of the county waste department there'd ever been, Graham hadn't wanted anyone to think he was too junior for the top spot. But who was he kidding – it wasn't just his job that made him act this way, look this way. He went to the mirror Myra had for checking she looked presentable before she answered the door to the few callers who actually came to the house. Granted it was

the middle of the night but even he had to admit he looked ...
well, yes ... old. His haircut needed to be sharper, his eyebrows
could do with taming, his skin was weary, he needed a new
razor that was obvious. Even his pyjamas were old fashioned.
His dad must have worn ones identical to these.

Tomorrow he'd do something about his appearance.
Definitely.

But fate had other ideas, it seemed. Not long after Graham
had finally gone to bed, full of ideas for reinventing himself, his
work phone rang. No call at that time of the day could be good
news, and true enough, a harassed voice at the end of the line
told him there had been a massive shutdown of the emulsifiers
at the waste treatment plant. He knew even before he put the
phone down that it would mean working around the clock to
get the plant back up and running. There would be precious
little time for seeing the boys or spending time with Myra until
the crisis was solved – and certainly no spare time for worrying
about what he looked like.

It took nearly a week of feverish endeavour on his part to put
right. He left home at the crack of dawn, arrived back long after
the boys were in bed. Finally he got the necessary new parts
from the manufacturers in Germany fitted and life returned to
normal, by which time he was so tired he didn't care about
looking older than his years because he knew without looking
in a mirror again that he definitely did.

On Thursday night when there was just him and Myra still
up, drinking their tea and eating their biscuits before going to
bed, he asked her, weary though he was, how she'd managed
this week with his long absences.

Unfortunately she had dropped a piece of biscuit in her tea at
the exact moment that he'd spoken so he had to wait until the
fussing was done with. 'Oliver has moved his homework desk
and his computer into the small bedroom. I said yes when he

asked me, he says Piers talks all the time he's working and it was driving him mad.'

'And you said it was OK?'

Myra nodded.

'But that's your textile ...'

'Not any more. I can make the sewing machine do whatever I like, I know that, but I've no bright ideas. No inspiration, you know. Nothing new to say.'

Graham was surprised by this remark – it was so un-Myra-like. She'd clung to her 'textile design business' for years and here she was discarding it, apparently without any regret.

'I'm sorry about that. Very sorry.'

Myra looked at him, more directly than she'd done in years, saying as she did so, 'Time I realised my limitations, Graham.'

'I don't know what to say.'

'Don't say anything then.'

'But it's like I said last week. Maybe this is the clean slate you needed. You've been so set on making those blasted tea cosies for years. Now you're rid of them you can start again – do something new. Have you something else in mind? '

'Not especially.' Myra's tone made it clear the topic was closed.

'How about the boys, then, how are they doing? I've barely seen them all week.'

'You haven't, but they've managed. They've played that infernal dodgem game every spare minute. Oh, and Oliver showed me some of his art work the other night. He has talent.'

'He has?'

'Says he has a picture in an exhibition at school on Parents' Night.'

'When's that?'

'Two weeks' time. He brought an invite home tonight.'

Silence fell while they both contemplated the implications. There would be so many moments like this ahead for the boys – little occasions like a parents' evening, or big landmarks like graduations or weddings – where it was just assumed you had parents to attend, to listen, to watch you, congratulate you.

Myra broke the silence. 'I shan't go.'

'We'll have to go.'

'You can, but I'm not.'

'Myra, we must.'

'Graham! I'm not.'

'Very well then, one of us has to go and it'll have to be me, then.'

'He gets As, you know,' said Myra.

'What for?'

'Nearly everything. If not As he gets B+. He's terribly bright. John would have been pleased.'

'Well, now we must be pleased for him instead. Show him how we appreciate his efforts.'

'I don't approve of making children believe they're better than others.'

'But you've just said ... '

'I know I have, but that's between you and me.'

'I'd like to see this picture, though.'

'Well, you will when you go to Parents' Night. I shan't because I'm not going. And don't try to persuade me.'

'I really wish you would, couldn't you make an exception?'

The whole prospect of attending Oliver's school and being *in loco parentis* in public was more than Myra could possibly contemplate. She began to shake inside and the more she thought about it the more she shook. It was bad enough having to take Piers backwards and forwards to school without a new tribe of parents and teachers judging and gosssiping. No. Absolutely not.

Myra got up feeling harrassed in the extreme, collected the tea cups, caught her toe on the curved leg of the coffee table and tripped full length. As she fell, she caught her forehead on the corner of the table and blood spattered as she made contact. Myra and the tea cups lay splayed across the carpet.

Graham leapt up too late to help her as she was standing upright again in a trice.

'The mess!' Myra muttered weakly.

'Sit down, you might be dizzy. Your head, here, I'll catch the blood.'

With Graham's pristine handkerchief pressed to her head, Myra sat down again, clutching her head. 'Graham, the carpet! Clean it up.'

'Never mind the carpet, it's you I'm thinking about. Have you a headache?'

'Of course I have.'

'I'll get you a drink of water, it'll help.'

Briefly Myra felt quite faint and it silenced her. The drink of water helped, but the blood did keep coming.

'Let me look!'

'No! You know what you're like about seeing blood, Graham.'

'I insist.'

'No!'

Graham finally snapped. 'For God's sake I want to look.'

He tenderly lifted the handkerchief away from her forehead and saw a clean but deep cut still bleeding profusely. He gently replaced the handkerchief while he thought what to do. She hated hospitals after ... well, anyway, she never set foot in one unless it was completely unavoidable. But she was even whiter than normal and he feared she would lose consciousness.

'It needs stitching, Myra, believe me.'

'It's half past ten, we can't leave the boys, what if something happened and we weren't here?'

Graham knew she was right. But she had to have medical attention. The handkerchief was soaking with her blood, and she looked paler than ever.

They needed help and for the first time since they moved in

Graham decided to call a neighbour for help, something Myra had always refused to do no matter the circumstances.

Viv! Of course. Myra had gone very quiet so Graham crept into the hall, searched the phone book for Viv's number and rang her. He filled her in quickly.

'You want me to come across to look after the boys, Graham, is that it?'

'Yes, that's it. Please, if you can.'

'Of course I will. I'll get my coat. Won't be a tick.'

True to her word, Viv was knocking almost before he'd had time to open the front door for her.

When Viv saw the blood and the colour of Myra's skin she said, 'Off you go. I know you won't want to, Myra, but you absolutely must. Just *go*. Don't worry about how long it takes, I'll have a nod on the sofa while I wait. The boys will be OK with me. No ifs and no buts, Graham's right. You must.'

Myra felt so ill she meekly allowed Graham to put her coat on for her and let Viv pin a scarf around her head to hold another of Graham's handkerchiefs in place. She even let the two of them to help her into the car.

It was after four in the morning before Viv heard the car in the drive. She shook herself awake, and went to the door to open it up for them, but there was only Graham there.

'They're keeping her in for observation because she's been sick, and they're worried about concussion. They've X-rayed and she hasn't fractured her skull, it's severe bruising and a flesh wound. That's been stitched now so she didn't want to stay in, but they insisted.'

'Quite right too. I thought she looked awful. Look, have a cup of tea before you go to bed. Do you good. Put some sugar in for shock. In the morning I'll come across and take Piers to school so you can go back to the hospital a.s.a.p. OK?'

'Thank you, Viv. Thank you.'

'No probs, only being neighbourly. See you about half past eight. 'Night now.'

Graham made a cup of tea and took it upstairs to drink in bed. After he got into his pyjamas he decided to check on Piers and Oliver. Helped by the landing light he saw Oliver was tucked up in a tight ball, with the duvet right up to his chin and no hands to be seen, while Piers had his arms flung wide and the duvet halfway down his chest. Graham felt his hands and decided they were cold, so he pulled his pyjama sleeves down to his wrists, tucked his arms under the duvet and pulled it up to his chin, and then impulsively kissed his forehead. A strangely alien sensation filled his heart and his mind and he realised he was overcome with a love that had welled up inside him completely unbidden.

In bed he picked up his cup and drank his tea slowly, thinking about that eruption of love when he looked at the boys, and how long it had been since he'd felt emotion like that. The ability to love perhaps hadn't withered away completely in spite of Myra's withdrawal from him and the rest of the human race then? It seemed not. He'd definitely done the right thing, taking the boys on, doing as John asked him, shouldering his responsibilities as a brother should. Winning Myra over would be a mountain to climb, but for her own sake, climb it she must. He thought about her in her lonely hospital bed and hoped she didn't feel too frightened by her predicament.

These two boys could be the start of a whole new life for him and Myra, and as he slid down under his duvet he rejoiced at the prospect.

Chapter 7

At school the next day Piers found time to make a get-well card for Myra. He decorated it with sparkly stuff held on by glue from the craft box and wrote, 'Please get better soon, Piers', after all, he thought, she belonged to Uncle Graham who was the nearest he could get to his dad, and ... he didn't love her, but you never know, he might in time if she just cheered up a little. He remembered he'd gone to tea with a boy from his old school one day and he'd really wished he belonged to that boy's mum because she was so cheerful and jolly. He could feel the boy loved her and she loved him and he longed that day for a mother who could be like that. For every day his dad had been enough but just sometimes ... a mum would have been nice. So underneath he wrote 'with love' and drew a scroll around it to make it important.

Oliver had art that day too and he was finishing a collage made with quilted fabric. He'd made a sailing ship on a beautiful blue sea and he'd crafted the sails so they looked as though the wind was making them billow out by padding them slightly and covering them with pristine white fabric, and for a moment you would swear the ship was sailing along, it was so realistic. In the marine blue of the sea he had placed a small pinky octopus he'd made with minute shiny glass beads for eyes and a mermaid with shining pearl sequins to represent fish scales on her body.

His teacher had given him an option. 'Do you want to take that home, Oliver, or shall I keep it for the exhibition?'

Oliver thought about this and about Myra in hospital and he

said, 'Could I take it home for my Auntie Myra, and bring it back to hang for the exhibition? She's in hospital, you see.'

'Of course you can. She'll love it.'

Oliver's teacher was right, she did love it, but Myra froze, completely unable to express any emotion about it, and therefore giving the impression to Oliver that she'd rather not have been given it. It had taken Graham some effort to persuade the boys to come with him to evening visiting hours, and now they were all here it felt awkward. He'd realised on the way over that the last time they'd been to a hospital would have been to visit their father. But mercifully, Oliver had seemed distracted by looking forward to seeing what Myra would make of his collage.

'Don't you like it?' he asked. 'I've to take it back to school to hang in the Parents' Evening Art Exhibition and then I can bring it home again.' He waited for Myra to give her opinion, then as she could muster nothing more than a strained smile, he quietly put it back in the carrier bag he'd brought it in and leant it against the bed leg.

Piers, proud to bits of the card he'd done for her, hesitated about giving her it. He couldn't understand what was happening, didn't she like getting presents? Anyway he'd give it a try. So he handed it to her, saying, 'I've made this for you to get you better.'

Myra thanked him politely and managed a few stilted words to Oliver, too, but her gratitude was clearly lacking in enthusiasm.

'How thoughtful of you two boys to make these for Myra,' Graham said instead. 'When yours comes back from the Exhibition, Oliver, we'll find a place at home and we'll put it up, won't we, Myra?'

Myra nodded, her face bleak and miserable. 'I'm sorry, the three of you, I've got such a headache, you shouldn't have come.'

'Shall I fetch the nurse?' Graham hovered over her, making her feel worse.

'No, thanks. I'll have a little sleep. Thank you for coming, all of you.'

'Right then, Myra. Ring me tomorrow – let me know when you can come home. OK?' When he got no reply, he patted her shoulder saying 'Bye-bye!' The boys said nothing. What was there for two young boys to say in the face of such disappointment?

Myra held herself together as best she could, but eventually, as the ward doors swung shut behind Graham, she had to give in and the tears began pouring down her cheeks. At first they fell silently, and then more noisily and before long she was sobbing and thrashing about in her bed so alarmingly, the other patients became concerned.

One of them in the bed directly opposite her rang for help. The sister, the bossy one who appeared to believe that patients were there to annoy her and not because they needed to be nursed, hustled in. 'Now, Myra, now, now, dear, are you in pain? Tell me where the pain is.' Sister propped her up on an extra pillow, felt her pulse, stroked her forehead with her ice-cold hand, and rang the bell for more help when she didn't appear to be having any effect.

'Have her visitors upset her? Does anyone know?'

The patient who'd rung the bell shook her head. 'Didn't look like it, they were lovely, it was her husband and two boys.'

A nurse rushed in responding to the demanding bell.

By now Myra was even more hysterical and out of control, and the other patients were becoming increasingly anxious.

'Cup of tea, nurse please.'

'Yes, Sister. Straight away.'

'Calm down, ladies, we'll soon have her right. Now, Myra, I'm going to have to give you some pills to calm you down if you don't stop, we can't go on like this. If you don't want one then stop this, you're tearing yourself apart.' She drew the cubicle curtains round the bed and Myra took in a huge halting breath. 'That's better, that's much better. Now try to lie still and we'll have a talk. There, there. I'll straighten your sheets, and we'll get that clean nightie out of your locker and we'll put it on, this is soaked with sweat. Better now? Here comes the nurse with a cup of tea for you. Get her face cloth out of her toilet bag, nurse, and we'll wipe her face and then we'll put the clean nightie on.'

'Sorry. Sorry. So sorry,' Myra stuttered as she still tried to catch her breath and speak without a sob catching in her chest.

'No need to apologise, Mrs Butler. But I do need to know what brought this on. Has someone said something to upset you. A nurse? A patient?'

Myra shook her head. 'No. No. He gave me a picture he'd made at school.'

'Who did? One of the boys that was just here? That sounds wonderful. Look, it's right here. Can I have a look?'

Myra nodded.

'Why, it's beautiful, very artistic, he's a very clever boy, isn't he?'

Myra nodded. 'I couldn't say thank you. I can't, not to him.'

'You've just said the words. "Thank you", you said, right this minute.'

'I didn't want him, you see, and I still don't. Neither him nor his brother.'

The sister passed her the cup of tea. 'Drink this, now you're all tidy. I'll sit on the chair here and wait for you to explain.' Sister found Piers' card on the floor and admired it. What more could a woman ask for but two sons so thoughtful? She watched Myra gulping down her tea and felt nothing but pity for her. There were thousands of women who would love to have two such caring boys.

'Sister?'

'Yes?'

'They've no business bringing me presents. I don't deserve such kindness. I know it's mad but I rather hoped they'd go away, that they'd have somehow gone when I get back home after this.' She pointed to the dressing on her forehead. 'I don't know where, but I wish they would just go. I want my old life back.'

'But you've brought them up so far, what's gone wrong?'

'They're not mine, not ours,' Myra whispered. 'They're my brother-in-law's children. He died recently and their mother died nearly ten years ago, so they've had to come to us. It's all too much.'

'I think it's the fall you've had, you're not feeling A1 at Lloyds, that's the trouble, it's all been such a shock. We'll keep you in another day, don't go home tomorrow, stay with us, give you time to think, eh? How about that? We'll talk again tomorrow, shall we?'

Myra nodded her agreement, still half in shock at her own outburst.

'Now, supper's coming soon. What did you order?'

'The salad.'

'It's fresh salmon salad, you'll enjoy that. See you later.' The ward sister turned smartly on her heel, leaving Myra alone behind the cubicle's flimsy paper curtains.

Myra slithered down under the sheets and felt ashamed. No, embarrassed more than ashamed. She couldn't understand why she'd screamed and cried like that. It was like the outburst of a teenage girl. But making such an exhibition of herself! How could she? She who'd been so self-contained for so long. What had happened to that woman who'd married Graham? She'd been reasonable then, able to chat to people, a bit shy, but able to overcome it. But being back in a hospital meant she couldn't hide from the truth. It had been having a miscarriage and then

86

the stillborn boy ... well, that had almost killed her. Outside she still functioned, inside she had died.

Clear as crystal in her mind was that moment when Graham had gone to the office for the first time since they'd lost the second baby. She'd stood in the hall at home, her arms shaped as though rocking a newborn baby, and the searing pain had been unbearable, the emptiness so appalling. Who was that howling with the agony of it all? It must be her, it must be her because there was no one else in the house. Oh God! Where was this baby she should have been holding? Why wasn't he in her arms right now? When her tears had finally dried that day she'd sworn she'd have to keep a tighter hold on her emotions if she was going to hold it together.

Six months after their second loss Graham had timidly brought up the subject of adoption but she wouldn't even discuss it. Hadn't he realised that she couldn't take a chance again, hope that something might work out? It was too much to expect of her.

She'd only survived all that because Graham had been so understanding, so kind, so patient. And what had she done in the face of his love? When he too had been distraught by their loss, she'd rejected him, left him comfortless, abandoned him. Myra cringed at her thoughtlessness, her lack of compassion.

All that dreadful time, John and Mo were so lucky by comparison. It had been hard enough when Oliver was born, but when Piers arrived Myra fell apart completely. What had she done for life to treat her like this? Why should Mo have such joy while she was rotting away? Nothing in the world touched her heart any more after that. Whatever tragedy she heard about in the world, she shrugged her shoulders and said to herself, 'So ...?'

Myra caught sight of Piers' card standing on her locker. How kind he was. Then she looked at Oliver's collage, really looked at it for the first time and saw all the detail. She loved the mermaid, the realistic way the sails appeared to billow out in the wind. Sister was right, he was a clever boy. She wasn't even one thumbnail's worth as creative as Oliver. One look at those stupid, boring tea cosies would have told you that. But, for once, she didn't feel jealous of someone else's good fortune.

The salad arrived. Every mouthful choked her. One half wanted desperately to eat it but the other half, the half that dealt with her emotions, the half she'd crushed all this time, rebelled. She left it barely started and never touched the pudding. Her head pounded, she ached inside, her legs felt numb, she didn't know if she was hot or cold, happy or sad, alive or dead. She felt both trapped in her body, lying there on the hospital bed, and also very far away from it all. She stared ahead of her letting the noises of the ward wash over her, barely registering the passing hours, and the nurses who came and went, checking various readings. The upshot of it all was the sister asked the consultant to take a look at Mrs Butler before he left for the day.

He was the handsomest of men, Myra thought when he approached her bedside; elegant, white-haired, beautifully mannered, with a peace and a contentment about him that made her feel he'd met with every possible sort of human condition and nothing could faze him. He was the kind of man who made you feel, no matter what kind of a mess you found yourself in, that right then, you were the most important person in all the world.

He didn't let go of her hand after he shook it, but held it clasped to his chest as though he didn't want to let go. 'Mrs Butler, may I call you Myra?' He spoke so considerately it seemed he had all the time in the world to spare for her.

'Of course.' At that moment, if he'd asked her to fly with him to the moon she would have done.

'Now what is the problem? Sister tells me she is worried about you and if Sister Goodchild is worried then so am I.' He let go of her hand and pulled up a chair. 'Now tell me,

I want to know what *exactly* is troubling you?' The emphasis he put on the word 'exactly' persuaded Myra that perhaps she could tell him, really truly tell him because she knew he would understand without laying blame on her.

Myra explained about the fall and then somehow or other began talking about the situation she found herself in. 'So you see I'm landed with these two boys I don't want, and I just want them to go away. I want to get back to my own life like it should be.'

'Describe to me what your own life consists of.'

'I look after my husband, I look after the house, I've plenty of time for myself ...'

'And what do you do with that time?'

Frankly Myra couldn't think of a damn thing she did with her time. What did she do? Watch TV? Listen to the radio. Make the tea cosies ... no, not now. So she didn't answer.

'You've no children of your own? Do you mind me asking why not? Don't feel you have to answer if you'd rather not.'

She couldn't believe it of herself, she who'd kept the whole story from everyone she ever met, bottled up all these years, and now out it all poured to this lovely sympathetic man she'd never met before.

'I see. So after the stillbirth you never tried again?'

Myra shook her head. 'And now I've had a hysterectomy, so it's all too late. Too late anyway at forty-five.'

'Have you ever thought that sometimes life takes a turn for which we are totally unprepared? We rebel, we say this isn't for me, but if we stand still and *listen* to our inner selves we realise that in fact it's the best thing in the world? The best for us. That life has worked out just as it should be? That what has happened is our just reward for all our pain and struggles?'

Myra listened, but didn't answer him.

'You see, believe it or not, you have your answer in your own home. What you would have had if things had gone right was two children of your own. Now you have just that, in a funny roundabout kind of way. How old are the boys?'

'Oliver's just twelve and Piers is nearly ten.' She turned to show him Oliver's picture. He studied it, saying, 'My word but he's very talented. What a privilege to have the bringing-up of a boy with this kind of life in him. Look what wicked eyes that octopus has, and the mermaid you can see is a lively lass. And the card?'

'That's from Piers, he did it at school today for me.'

'Myra! Myra! Stand still and listen. Someone somewhere is telling you something. I'll be back tomorrow before you leave.'

In fact she didn'tsee the consultant the next day, he had an emergency operation, she was told, and couldn't spare the time. But he hadn't forgotten her and there was a note left with Sister Goodchild ready for when she was discharged. Just one line. 'Remember what we talked about, Myra.'

She remembered what he'd said but decided she would not be taking his advice. Him in his smart suit, with all his money, who did he think he was telling her to look inside herself? She did and what did she see? A failure. A total failure. She couldn't even make a career for herself. She'd failed at having children. Her marriage had failed in all but outward appearance. What was there left? Absolutely nothing.

When Graham and the boys came to collect her, Sister Goodchild admired the boys as though they were Myra's own, and winked at her behind their backs. She could. After all she didn't have them to look after.

Arriving home, she found Graham had made a lovely casserole and laid the table in the dining room before they came to collect her just to make it feel special, and Viv had baked a pudding for her homecoming. But all she really saw was a small square patch on the wall. Graham must have taken down that framed picture of Paris they'd bought on their honeymoon (he'd not liked it for years, she knew). As soon as they'd walked through the door, and the boys had vanished to their bedroom, he'd sat her on the sofa, reached into her hospital bag and hung Oliver's collage proudly on the wall. Piers' card he stood nearby on the mantelpiece. She tried to look away but the picture on the wall ... somehow it almost kept making her look at it, demanding she look at it. That mermaid was a lively lass just as the consultant suggested and as for the octopus, well, he did have wicked eyes, he was right about that too. Then she saw Piers' get-well card and she felt her eyes begin to brim with tears. One thing was for certain, she wasn't going to cry over a get-well card, most certainly not. That was until she read *with love* in its scrolled border, and that did it. It was ridiculous to be watching the TV news with tears rolling down her cheeks. The more she tried to stop the more the tears ran down.

Graham turned to ask her if she'd like a cup of hot chocolate. 'Myra, what is it? Is your head bad again?'

He went to sit beside her on the sofa and took her hand. 'Can I get you one of those tablets the Sister gave you? Is the pain bad?'

Myra answered softly, 'It's Piers' card, "with love", he's put. What love have I given him since he came here? None.' The tears kept coming.

Graham got a clean hanky out and dabbed her cheeks, but to no avail. 'This'll have to stop, otherwise we'll have to put the washing machine on just to keep me in handkerchiefs. You have tried, you know.'

'Tried what?'

'Not to love him exactly but you have made an effort. All those meals, the school run and they've had clean clothes whenever. It all takes time.'

'I wish I was a natural mother like Viv. She seems to know instinctively what to do and when to do it. I don't.'

'Myra! She's been a mother for over thirty years, you've been a mother for not even thirty days. Like I said it all takes time.'

'I quite like the rabbit, Pete's a sweet little thing. I've stroked him, you know.' Saying that, she realised that Graham was still holding her hand and she hadn't snatched it away like usual.

'Viv's been very good while you've been in hospital, she's taken Piers to school and met him and brought him home, and both boys went there to tea each day so I could either finish up at work or come and see you. She's a very nice person, Myra, I'm so glad you've got someone like her to rely on as a friend.'

'Viv?'

'Yes. Viv. And you know the woman next door on the other side? She came round and brought you those flowers there in the vase. Her name's Betty, and her husband's Roland.'

'It's taken them fifteen years to speak to us.'

'And us fifteen years too, don't forget.'

Myra studied the flowers and decided they were in good taste for someone who hadn't spoken to them ever before. They weren't a bunch snatched up in the supermarket, they were from a proper flower shop. If she felt like it tomorrow she might dig out one of her tasteful notelets and write her a thank you. On the other hand she could always call round and say thank you in person, get a chance to meet this Betty properly. But of course she might not be well enough, she quickly reminded herself.

Rather to her surprise, Myra found herself feeling much better the next day, the pain relief tablets were obviously doing her good.

She determined that when Viv came across to take Piers to school, she'd go with her. Graham didn't want her to, but because he said no she decided she definitely would.

She wore sunglasses to help disguise the bruising and the swelling but nothing could disguise the cut and the stitches. She thought of covering it with a dressing but Sister had said it would be better left to get the air.

'I'm coming with you, Viv.'

'Are you sure? I go right up to school, he seems to like that. Will you manage all that way?'

'Of course. I go right up to school, too, when I take him.'

'You know that New to You Sale they keep talking about, it's tomorrow night.'

'Oh, right. Are you going?'

'The clothes'll all be too young for me. All right for you, though.'

'I couldn't wear their stuff, they're all young women.'

'You're hardly an old lady, Myra – wait till you get to my age and you'll think you were still a spring chicken in your forties!'

Piers joined them in the hall ready for off and unwittingly Viv demonstrated how to be a mum without even trying. 'Now, Piers, have you cleaned your teeth? Good. Got your homework? Yes? It's football day your Uncle Graham said, where's your bag? I knew there'd be something. Go get it. Handkerchief? Yes. Let's be off then.'

The sharp air caught the wound on Myra's forehead, making it hurt badly. The cold seemed to worm its way right inside the cut and into her brain, but she wouldn't give in and turn back. They saw Piers in, and headed back swiftly, harried by the cold.

'Thanks for looking after everyone while I've been in hospital, Viv.'

'Not at all, it's been a pleasure. Any time, they're thoroughly decent boys, Myra, you're very lucky.'

Myra was glad to get back home, but not fancying being on her own right now, she invited Viv in for coffee on the pretence of her perhaps liking to see Oliver's picture and Piers' card. The most ridiculous, most unaccustomed, feeling of pride came over her when Viv showed her delight at Oliver's collage, but all she said was, 'It is good, isn't it? The art teacher wants it back for Parents' Evening so she can hang it in the school art exhibition.'

'Not one of my children were good at art. Absolutely hopeless they were. The best was Sally in pottery. I've got some
clumsy bowls and vases in a cupboard somewhere, and that was
the nearest any of them got. Here, sit down. I'll put the kettle
on, you look tired.'

So they sat in the kitchen enjoying their coffee until Viv
said, 'Oh God! I'd forgotten I've got the the dentist. I should
have left already. Blast. Never mind though, he always runs
late. Must go. Remember, I'll collect Piers this afternoon, I'll be
leaving at three. Come with me if you feel up to it.'

Myra slept for most of the morning and woke feeling better
able to cope with life. She inspected the cut and decided it was
looking a little better than when she'd got up that morning. She
put on her coat and went outside to see Little Pete. The sun was
out so the cold didn't strike her so badly as it had earlier.

Pete was hunched up in a corner of his run looking, she
thought, rather glum. She hitched her scarf round her throat
and bent down to poke a finger through the mesh and touch
poor Pete. It must be rather lonely for him on his own, and she
wondered about having two rabbits. She didn't want an army
of them though, and surely two buck rabbits would fight. Or
maybe they could have separate hutches. One could be Oliver's
and the other could be Piers'.

Her knees ached bent down all the time, but as she straightened
up she decided she quite liked the idea of company, so, pushing
aside her revulsion at touching another being she reached in and
picked up Pete. Anxious not to drop him, she rushed inside with
him. He was such a dear little thing, rather like a Siamese cat in
his colouring, sort of coffee and cream. She took a fresh piece
of lettuce from the fridge and gave it to him. Was lettuce, cold,
straight out of the fridge good for a young rabbit, maybe there
were rules about it? She'd ring Graham, he might know. She
never rang him at the office, but just this once she would. Pete

94

was eating it with relish, should she take it from him? She hadn't the heart to. Myra dialled Graham's office number and asked to speak to him.

'Graham! It's me—'

'Myra! Are you all right?'

'I'm fine, I'm ringing about Pete, the rabbit. You kept a rabbit when you were a boy, didn't you? Is it all right to give him lettuce straight out of the fridge?'

'Won't do him any harm.'

'Good. He's in the kitchen eating away.'

'How on earth did he get in there?'

'I carried him in.'

'Oh! Right. I see. He'll be fine, Myra, don't worry about him. Anything else?'

'No. See you tonight.'

Graham put down the receiver and sat staring into space. She obviously wasn't right, had he better go home? He'd loads of work on hand and couldn't really afford the time. But Myra carrying a rabbit into the house? She hated anyone touching her at the best of times, and she always said pets were riddled with germs. The rabbit in the kitchen? What was she thinking of? Then he began to laugh, a rip-roaring, powerful, joyous laugh. His PA came in with some figures he'd asked for and stood stock still, astonished. In the whole of the seven years that she'd worked for him she had never seen him laugh like this. Not once. Not even at the office Christmas Party. It was such abandoned laughter and he showed no sign of stopping. She quickly shut the door so no one else would hear.

'Mr Butler?'

He paused briefly, said, 'In the kitchen of all places . . .' and laughed even louder.

'Are you well? Mr Butler. I said, are you all right?'

Graham tried to quell the laughter that kept spilling out. He knew what his PA would be thinking – had he finally tipped over the edge, this hard-working man of few words, devoted to the business of waste as he was? He'd better get himself under control before someone thought to ring Myra. Not that anyone at work knew her – she'd never shown her face at the office, never came to any events as his plus-one, the excuse being she didn't 'do' parties.

'I'm fine, thank you, never been better. Got those figures? The meeting's in fifteen minutes and I need to make myself *au fait* with them before I go in.'

It was all right then, he was back in his usual mode, though he did wonder if she heard him burst into laughter again just as she closed his door.

The rabbit incident was the last thing on his mind by the time he was driving home. The meeting hadn't gone well despite the encouraging figures, there'd been another minor breakdown of the new equipment, and a promising chap coming for interview tomorrow had rung to say his wife had gone into premature labour and he couldn't possibly come for a few days.

But the nearer he got to home the more his boys filled his mind. Had they had a good day at school? He'd been enormously impressed by the collage Oliver had done, and by the thoughtfulness of Piers' get-well card. They truly were decent young boys and well worth getting to know. Thoughts about the challenging day he'd just survived fell away the closer he got to the house and it occurred to him that it was a long time since he'd so looked forward to getting home.

He thought of Myra, too. She'd frightened him to death with the way she looked after her fall. They might not be close like they'd been in the first five years of their marriage but his passionate love for her had never entirely faded away. Put on the shelf perhaps, neglected probably, allowed to wither definitely, but not entirely gone. That was how he felt, but how did she feel about love? It seemed on the surface that for her, all of it had gone. Disappeared in the dreadful double blow of losing their prospective children. Six months after their second loss he'd timidly brought up the subject of adoption but Myra wouldn't even discuss it. She had withdrawn so thoroughly from life. It was as if taking a chance or hoping that something else might work out for them wasn't possible any more.

His own profound grief had for a while masked the fact that she appeared to want nothing more to do with him. It was already too late by the time he'd realised that was exactly what had happened. He'd assured himself at the start that the separate bedrooms was a temporary state of affairs. After all, it had taken them a while to try again after the miscarriage, so the mourning after their stillborn son felt completely understandable, but the days turned into weeks and the months into years. Perhaps he should have done something, pushed for more – but instead he'd retreated into the state of limbo they existed in, afraid that rocking the boat would wreck the fragile shell of the relationship that remained.

As he switched off the engine he heard shouting coming from the house. It was Myra and Oliver. Both of them, by the sound of it, were past caring what they said. Graham leapt out of the car and shot into the house to find the two of them screaming at each other, saying unforgiveable things and Piers hiding behind the sofa begging them to stop.

'Say you're sorry, Oliver. Say you're sorry.'

Graham shouted above the din, 'That will do! Oliver, be silent as of this minute! Do as I say!' It had no effect, so he took hold of Oliver's arm and clapped his hand over his mouth. 'I mean it!'

Oliver wriggled free just long enough for him to say, 'I'll never apologise, it wasn't my fault, I didn't do it.'

Myra burst out with her complaint. 'He's come home from school wrong side out and there's no reasoning with him. I sent him to tidy their bedroom and he refuses to do it. He's just not grateful, and he should be, he should be grateful to you and to me for taking him in.'

Graham winced at her use of words. 'But what is it he is saying he didn't do?'

Myra drew in a great breath. 'He smashed a vase just to annoy me, because he didn't want to do as I said.'

'I didn't do it. Honest, I didn't break it. I've not even been in the sitting room since I came home.'

Myra stamped her foot. 'You must have. Who else could have done it? It certainly wasn't me.'

The three of them stood looking at one another and finally their eyes rested on Piers. If it was possible, he appeared to have shrunk, and his bright red guilty face told the whole story.

Graham took charge of the situation. 'Piers, you and I will stay in here while Myra and Oliver go in the kitchen. We need to talk. Before you go, Oliver, can you bring a dustpan and brush in here, your brother will need to use it.'

Piers, on the point of collapse with the fear that anyone could see welling up inside him, came out from behind the sofa now Myra had left the room. He sat scrunched up on the sofa. Graham could tell he was waiting for his wrath to descend on him. He imagined all the thoughts that would be running through the child's head – he'd probably already imagined he'd be sent packing for this.

'Now Piers, what's this all about?' He said this in the gentlest voice he could muster. 'Tell me what happened, there's a good boy.'

'I thought she'd get that stick out.'

'What stick? Myra hasn't got a stick.'

'I mean Delphine's stick.'

'I should have told you. We broke it in pieces the first night you and your brother were here. As soon as Oliver showed it us, we made sure it could never be used to hurt anyone again.

We don't use sticks on anyone in this house. Believe me.'

Piers looked relieved. 'I'm sorry. I didn't do it on purpose.'

'How did it happen?'

'I was looking out of the window for Oliver coming home, I just wanted him to be here, I couldn't wait, I felt so lonely and he was late and I knocked the vase with my elbow by mistake. It fell onto the carpet and hardly made any noise, so I knew she wouldn't have heard it breaking, and I ... I ...'

'Yes?'

'I thought she'd send me away.'

'She won't.'

'She will.' He stamped his foot.

'I'm telling you *she won't*. You belong here, this is your house, your home and you won't be sent away. Now, why did you let Oliver get the blame? That wasn't fair, was it? He's your brother and brothers look after each other.'

Piers flung himself down on the sofa face first. 'I don't know. I was scared.'

'So first you apologise to Myra properly, and then, really meaning it, you apologise to Oliver. I prize honesty above everything, Piers, and I want you to grow up honest just like your dad would want you to do ... if he were here. You understand? If you're in trouble then you have to face it and be upfront with the truth. People prefer that to great big fibs.'

'I'll do it. She doesn't like me anyway, does Myra. You do, but she doesn't. She'll convince you to send me away. I want to stay here, and not go back to Delphine's or a home.'

Oliver came in with the dustpan.

'I'm sorry, Oliver, Uncle Graham says he won't send me away. I shouldn't have told fibs.'

Oliver gave him a smile and a thumbs-up.

For the first time since the whole horrible incident had started Piers' face lit up with a smile.

Oliver said, 'Go apologise to Myra then, she's waiting.'

99

Piers looked across at his uncle wondering if he might just get away with not having to confront her, but he saw from the look on his face that he would have to, so he took a deep breath and marched in to the kitchen, determined to speak up.

Myra was turning down the gas under a pan and didn't even look up at him, that in a way made it easier to apologise.

'I'm sorry, Myra, I told a fib and I shouldn't have. Sorry about the vase, I didn't do it on purpose.'

Myra stared him straight in the eye and was about to be cruel and then into her mind came the *with love* on his get well card and the scroll drawn round it and she reminded herself he was the only person who'd said that to her in years.

'Thank you. No more fibs, Piers? I don't like fibs.'

'No more fibs. And I'll clear it all up.'

'Thank you.'

Later, they sat down to supper, the flowers from the broken vase now on the kitchen window sill in a pale mauve vase the same colour as the flowers, their bedroom tidied and the water and shards of glass cleaned up in the sitting room, and the two boys reconciled.

Oliver laid his knife and fork together and said, 'Uncle Graham . . .'

'Yes.'

'I've got maths to do tonight and I'm not sure about it, could you look at it with me?'

'Of course. If I can remember my maths, that is. Straight after we've eaten. What about you, Piers?'

'I haven't got any homework tonight.'

'In that case then you and I have something to discuss,' Myra said.

Piers' heart sank right the way down to his trainers. Wasn't one apology enough? He'd better say it again or else you never knew what might happen. He glanced at his Uncle Graham and wondered if he really was able to say no to Myra, if he could change her mind about letting them stay. 'I'm very sorry about the vase, Myra.'

'I know you are. You've said it already and I've thanked you.'

'Yes, but I thought …'

'Wait and see.'

Piers saw a mysterious smile on her face and somehow the grilled tomatoes, which he didn't normally like, tasted better than he'd expected.

With Uncle Graham and Oliver sitting hunched over books spread out over the kitchen table and the dishwasher pumping away, Myra gave him a brisk nod of her head in the direction of the sitting room, and Piers followed her.

'It's only three weeks to your birthday, so I wondered if you had any ideas about what you would like as a present.'

Piers was so stunned by her question not a single idea came into his head. It was unusual for him because in other years he had always thought a lot about his birthday and would in normal circumstances have had a long list of requests, from little often-craved treats to some totally, impossibly expensive wishes. But since his dad had died, it was as if time had stopped still. 'I haven't thought about it.'

'You haven't thought about it? Well, you'll have to, won't you?'

'Yes, I suppose I will.'

'Now you and I have agreed to always tell the truth to each other, it can always be like that for the two of us, can't it? So when you come up with an idea, tell me straight away. I have a good idea, but we'll wait until you come up with yours first.'

But Piers being Piers couldn't wait to hear her idea. 'What is your idea, Myra?'

'Well, I was thinking this morning that Little Pete seems

very lonely in that hutch all on his own night and day and I wondered if you'd like to have a rabbit as a friend for him. It would be yours absolutely, no one else's. We'd have to make the run bigger but Uncle Graham could do that.'

'Right.' His birthday hadn't seemed important, in fact he hadn't known if anyone even knew it was coming up soon. Piers thought he hadn't minded. But something about Myra's suggestion, and the fact that she'd been thinking about what he might like opened up something inside him. Before he knew it was going to happen, he was sobbing with grief: heartbreaking sobbing over which he had no control whatsoever. Between his gasping sobs he said repeatedly, 'I want my dad.'

Myra felt a wave of tension and panic at this open weeping. Her head throbbed, there was that piercing pain back again in her brain and she realised she longed to sob herself but couldn't. Instead, very tentatively, she patted his hand, then his shoulder, gave him a tissue and tried to console him with muttered words. Finally in desperation, she put her arm round his shoulders and he leaned against her and sobbed louder than ever. She couldn't leave him alone while she went to get Graham, so she had to sit there in silence, hanging on to him with both arms now, hugging him because she didn't know what else to do.

Had she but known, it was the best thing for Piers, he hadn't had a woman hug him since he could remember. Neither of his grandmas had been the hugging kind and definitely not Delphine. For Piers, Myra's hug spelt bliss. She was bony and all sharp angles and not very comfortable to lean against but she comforted him in the way he needed most right then. When the sobbing ran its course, he'd cheered up no end and feeling lighter than he'd done for a long time, he went to speak to Uncle Graham. He and Oliver had sorted out the maths.

'Sorry again, Uncle Graham, about telling fibs, I was so frightened I'd get sent away and I don't want to be, I want to stay here.'

'That's right, Piers, you'll stay here because this is your home now.'

'You were right, Myra will take time to get used to us. But she doesn't sound like she wants to send me away. She says she thinks I might like a rabbit for myself.'

Graham's bushy eyebrows rose up his forehead in surprise. 'Does she?'

Piers nodded. 'Yes. I'm thinking about it. They'd need a bigger run though.'

'Of course, well, that's easy. You have a good think then and let us know what you decide.'

That evening Graham told Myra what Piers had said and she nodded her agreement.

'You know I never like touching fur or going near any animals normally, but I've taken to Little Pete. Two rabbits will hardly be any more trouble than one and if that's what Piers would like . . .'

Graham went to sit beside her on the sofa, taking her hand in his as soon as he sat down. 'I'm so glad you're beginning to feel better about the boys. Just think, by Piers' birthday this time next year, it'll feel like they've been here forever.' He added softly, 'They even look like me, don't they?'

'They do, yes. Anyone who sees you out with the boys just assumes you're their father. But I'm still waiting for the big row and the great big upset, because there's bound to be one, I mean we nearly had it tonight.'

'If there is and, like you said, I expect there will be, we shall weather the storm together. You know, Piers is terrified of having to leave this house, that was why he lied. We'll have to be so careful with him – we mustn't forget he's still frightened inside, even when him and his brother put on a brave face. I'm surprised they haven't grieved more than they have.'

Myra absentmindedly stroked Graham's hand. 'Piers cried a lot tonight when we were talking.'

'You didn't say.'

'No, well, we resolved it, he just needed … well … I suppose he needed … mothering.'

Graham disguised his surprise as best he could. Mothering? From Myra? He supposed she just meant someone to hold him. In a different way, it was what he needed too. Just a sign that love still lingered somewhere. He held Myra's hand to his mouth to kiss. She snatched it away from him but he knew if he didn't say something now, the moment would be lost. 'I've never stopped loving you even if you've stopped loving me. All these years, turning away from each other, such a waste. Why did it happen, Myra? Why?'

Myra knew that since the boys had arrived she'd found herself in deep water. The kind of deep emotional turmoil she hadn't felt since she left hospital twelve years ago. But something had been stirred by Piers this evening, and even though she couldn't answer Graham's question, for once she wasn't scared at the very thought of it. She didn't even know the answer herself, all she knew was that shutting everyone out had enabled her to batten down her emotions and in time, ignore them completely.

'Perhaps if we'd had the courage to try again after … our little boy … we'd have been successful.'

Myra glared at him. 'You don't know that.' The prospect of trying for another baby and perhaps losing them was one emotional hurdle she most definitely couldn't have faced.

'No, but perhaps we should have tried. Cutting ourselves off from one another was no answer.'

'It was my answer and that should be enough, after all *I* would have had it all to go through, not you.'

'You don't imagine, do you, that the father of a baby experiences nothing at all? I know we don't do the hard graft but we're involved. I grieved too, but you couldn't comfort me, you didn't even realise I needed comforting, and you certainly wouldn't let me comfort you. It was as if I didn't exist. That was when you went dead inside.'

Myra turned to look him straight in the face the first time since they'd sat down. 'I died inside? Is there any wonder, when the baby died *inside* me. *Inside me, do you hear!* You never thought about that, did you?'

Graham went still and then said so softly she strained to hear, 'Of course I did, what do you think of me, that I'm inhuman? Unfeeling? I couldn't bear the distress, the despair you were suffering, it crucified me, but you wouldn't let me even talk to you about it.'

'I shut down, that's why. If I didn't talk about it, it was because I couldn't. I just couldn't. Every time I passed a woman in the street pushing a pram, I died all over again. I couldn't even look inside it to see the baby in case the baby was awake and looked at me.'

'I'm sorry, so sorry, Myra, we could have made things so much better for each other, if we'd both tried. We each had our own private grief – of course, we still do – but there was a shared loss, too; we could have helped each other through it somehow.'

The only sound in the room was the crackle of the log fire, the only light the flames flickering in the grate, the only movement Graham's hand taking hold of Myra's again.

'Graham?'

'Yes?'

'I've never asked before.'

'What?'

'I don't know if I can.'

'For heaven's sake say it, there's been too much "not saying" between you and me. Just ask.'

He heard the great breath she took in, felt the tremor of her hand, so he begged her again to say what was in her mind. 'Say it, whatever it is, just say it, please.'

Her reply came out in a rush. 'What did you do with all the baby things?'

It was Graham's hand that trembled now. Eventually he answered her devastating, heart-wrenching question. 'I think you guessed I put it all in the loft before you came home from hospital. I didn't know what else to do at the time. But a few months later, that day your mother had that last operation and you went to spend the weekend visiting her, I went up in the loft after dark and brought everything down, put it in bags and carried them out to the car when the neighbours had all gone to bed. The next morning, a Saturday it was, I took them to the vicarage because the vicar's wife knew someone due to have a baby who was short of money and badly in need of help. I thought that was best, thinking we could always buy new if . . . if we had another.'

Myra gripped his hand and thought about what he'd said. The wound inside herself, so long concealed, felt like it was now gaping horribly, and didn't allow her to speak. Vicar's wife? They didn't know any vicars, nor a vicar's wife. 'When did you meet a vicar?'

'It was the hospital chaplain – the one who did the burial service for the baby.'

'I didn't go to a service. No one told me,' Myra replied indignantly, shocked into speech again.

'No, I did though. I went, while you were still in hospital.'

'Oh Graham. I'd no idea.'

'You were too ill, you'd lost all that blood, remember? They were worried about you. And you weren't yourself, you barely knew what was happening, between the drugs and the trauma of it all. I thought even if you were well enough, you wouldn't want to be there, because that would make it real and I knew you couldn't face that after everything you'd been through.'

They sat silently holding hands, the fire burning lower, the night getting colder, each with their own thoughts. They'd both lived through it, but the paths they'd taken were very different, and Myra knew it was her inability to speak about their loss that meant they hadn't shared their feelings before. Perhaps it could all have been so much easier if they had.

Eventually Myra said quietly, 'Did ... you give the baby a name?'

'I called him George, after my dad, and Brian after yours. They were the only ones that sprang to mind, at the time.'

Myra stood up. She dared to say his name. 'George Brian Butler. I see.'

She drew back the curtains and looked out at the night sky for a few minutes.

She sighed several times. 'We've been such fools, you and I. Me more than you.' She closed the curtains again. 'Cup of tea?' It was the closest Myra could come to a peace offering.

Graham nodded. She went into the kitchen and he got up to throw another log on the fire.

As they drank their tea, Graham said out of the blue, 'I kept one thing.'

'What do you mean?'

'Three vests. I kept three little baby vests. Still in the packet. Untouched. I thought I should, I don't know why, I just did. I look at them sometimes. Thinking.'

Silence from Myra, then feeling that wound inside once again, she asked, 'Where are they?'

'On a shelf in my wardrobe.'

'I won't want to see them.' But lurking at the back of her mind was a need to see and a greater need to face up to her memories. She promised herself when she was in the house alone and no one would see her, nor hear her if she cried, she'd take a peep. Just for a moment. Not long. Just long enough.

Chapter 8

Immediately after taking Piers to school on Monday morning, Myra went up to Graham's bedroom and opened his wardrobe doors. She was struck by how neatly his clothes were stacked on the shelves, how his hanging items were all perfectly organised. Normally she just left his laundered clothes in a basket on his bed, never seeing inside any of these closed doors. It was his domain. Now she looked up to the very top shelf that ran the full length of the wardrobe. She was going to need the steps.

She went downstairs to get the folding steps she used to reach high-up things in the kitchen. Back in Graham's room, she patiently made her way along the wardrobe shelf, carefully turning things, trying not to disturb anything, but desperate not to miss her goal. She peered underneath every item and eventually, there it was ... an old Marks and Spencer's carrier bag, in the furthest most inaccessible corner. Myra climbed down and stood on the carpet, her hands shaking, her heart thumping. She could barely see, her eyes were so full of brimming tears. She blinked them away resolutely then slipped her hand inside, fearing it might not be the right bag, but out came three baby vests. They were just as they were the day they were bought, still in their packet, folded perfectly. Her heart raced at the memory of how excited she'd been, buying those vests. The very first purchase for their longed-for new baby. Pristine, tiny, beautiful, so full of promise, so filled with hope.

Myra sat down on Graham's bed and fingered the packet. It rustled as she stroked it, the end of her finger rubbed up a corner of the self-adhesive flap and before she knew it the vests were out of the packet and laid on her knee. One fell to the floor so she bent to pick it up; she laid it against her cheek and it comforted her. Where she'd expected tears she felt relief, a closeness to their lost baby she'd never permitted herself before. It hurt, but a kind of soft glow came over her, the injustice of it all melted, the anguish gone. Tenderly she refolded them, replaced them in the packet, sealed the flap, returned it to the carrier bag and put it away right where Graham had laid the vests all that time ago. She thought of him silently looking at them for all these years and never saying . . .

The phone rang.

Myra ran downstairs to answer it, quickly clearing her throat in case she sounded choked with emotion. It was the head teacher from Piers' school.

'I'm afraid Piers is not at all well, Mrs Butler. Is it possible you could come to collect him?'

'Not well?'

'He's deathly white and being sick, three times already, and it's only a quarter to ten.'

'Oh! I see.' Myra didn't know what else to say.

'Will you be able to come?'

'Yes, yes, of course. I'll have to walk, it'll take me ten minutes.'

'That's fine. He's in the sick room with our nursery helper keeping an eye. I'll tell him you're coming.'

'I'll set off straight away.'

'Thank you – see you soon!'

This unaccustomed state of affairs threw Myra into a panic. Any change to her routine, any shift in plans or pressure to be spontaneous was enough to send her anxiety levels skyrocketing. But she knew she couldn't dither about leaving the house, so she pulled her coat on and headed out.

Viv was heading towards her as she shut the front door behind her.

'I was just coming across for coffee, is something the matter?'

'It's Piers, he's been taken ill at school and I've to fetch him home.'

'Oh! the poor little chap.'

'Will you come and have a look at him when I get him back? I'm not used to sick children.'

'Of course. I'll look out for you, it won't be anything serious you know, not appendicitis or anything. Don't worry too much.'

She waved Myra off as though it was quite normal, but it wasn't normal to Myra. She was horrified that she could have been so careless as to send a sick child to school. She'd need to apologise, she really would.

The walk home after collecting Piers was horrendous. He kept retching over the gutter but nothing came up, for which she was thankful. But it was the ghastly pallor of his face she didn't like. She held his hand for which he appeared grateful. What on earth had she done to cause this? Was it something she'd cooked? Should she call the doctor? Viv would know what to do.

As she put the key in the latch Viv came dashing across.

'I feel awful,' said Piers, his face twisted into a grimace.

'Get your coat off and let's have a look at you.' Viv felt his forehead, asked him where it hurt, did he feel sick right now? Had he got tummy ache? If she pressed his tummy did it hurt? Piers shook his head.

Myra asked if she should give him something, but she hadn't anything to give him. Her medicine cabinet was rarely used and full of ancient pills and bottles that would be no use for a young child.

'What shall I do?' She wrung her hands with helplessness.

'If I were you I'd let him sit in a warm room reading or better still watching telly, to take his mind off it.'

'Is that all?'

'Give him a warm drink, not hot, just warm so's not to aggravate anything. What's your favourite, Piers?'

'Hot chocolate.'

'Good idea, perhaps with just a bit of sugar, Myra. And Piers, you must sip it gently, just see if you can keep it down.'

'Right.'

'Give him a bucket just in case it comes over him again. I'll come across in an hour or two to see how he is. Lots of TLC.' She winked at Myra and left for home.

Myra couldn't think what on earth her wink meant but then forgot about it as she busied herself with her tasks. She switched the TV on, put a rug over Piers' knees as he seemed to be shivering, made him a hot chocolate and one for herself and sat down in the other armchair to keep watch. She'd strategically placed a bucket with Dettol in the bottom, a glass of water and a box of tissues ... just in case.

The two hours Viv was away passed without further incident, which made Myra wonder what on earth was going on. Was he sick? Well, he had been at school, they said so. But it was all over, it seemed, and Piers was looking, quite frankly, rather sparkling.

Viv knocked and walked in at the back door calling out, 'Come to see the invalid. Oh! You look better. Thank goodness.'

'He's not been sick again.'

'Well, that's an excellent sign. Any coffee going?' Out of Piers' eyeline she nodded her head towards the kitchen. Mystified, Myra went with her to put the kettle on.

Viv quietly closed the kitchen door. 'If he's not sick again it might not be a bug, you know. I reckon he might just be homesick.'

'Homesick? For his real home, you mean?'

'No. For here.' She pointed at the kitchen floor.

'I don't understand.'

'I don't think *he* does either. I bet he just wants to be sure it's still here while he's at school.'

'But of course it is, where else would it be?'

'When you think about it, he's never had a mother that he's known, his dad's been dying while he's been looked after by that horrible Delphine and now he's living somewhere where, quite honestly, he sensed you didn't want him. So he's panicked and all he needs is some comfort to reassure him all's OK. You're not the only one who lives on their nerves!'

'That is ridiculous. I'll take him straight back to school, we can't have this.'

She handed Viv her coffee. She would, she'd take him back and apologise for his foolishness. He'd have to brave it out. She wasn't putting up with this kind of nonsense.

'A few hours off school won't set his career back, believe me. He won't learn anything if you do take him back, he'll be too upset. It's what he needs. He needs to sit with you playing Ludo or something, anything to give him the feeling that *you* care.'

Myra decided she wanted her own way about this. This was what being a mother was about, she felt. Making sure they toed the line, did as they were told. There'd be no end to this caper if she didn't, he'd end up being off school every other day. Viv could see this in her face and said, 'Please, Myra, one day off won't hurt.'

'He's in my care and I say he's going back to school straight after lunch.'

Viv got up abruptly and left, a look of thunder on her face, still holding one of Myra's coffee cups. Myra called after her, but Viv didn't, or wouldn't, hear her.

★

Myra prepared lunch and the two of them sat in the kitchen, Piers chattering away and Myra answering him as best she could while wondering how to phrase what she had to say. He appeared perfectly fit, judging by the eagerness with which he was eating his lunch. If he got upset, well, then he got upset. Not that she cared if he was upset because he was being naughty fancying a day off school, otherwise he'd have been sick at home as well as school.

His reaction to the news was more like an explosion than anything, but she didn't care. He was going back to school even if she had to carry him there, someone had to discipline him and it was going to be her. He screamed and cried, flung his chair to the floor, overturned her chair and the two others, his mug joined them and smashed as it landed on the tiles.

She put her coat and gloves on, forced him into his outdoor clothes including his hat, which he pulled off three times before he gave in, and they struggled out of the front door with Myra gripping him hard.

Crossing the main road was the hardest, as soon as the lights went red he redoubled his efforts to escape homewards. While hanging on to him on the pedestrian refuge in the middle of the road waiting for the lights to change, Myra ran out of energy and in the split second she took to regroup herself he slipped from her grasp and was scooped up onto the bonnet of a passing car. The screech of its brakes and the screaming of the driver were to stay in Myra's head for years.

Chapter 9

The police rang Graham at his office because Myra was inco-
herent, so he was at the hospital almost as soon as the ambulance
taking Myra and Piers. She saw him arrive and tell the A&E
desk that he had a message telling him a family member had
been brought in after a traffic accident. The receptionist pointed
at Myra and he turned to look at her. Words could not describe
the anguish in his face. Myra felt the same, she was horrified by
what she'd done.

'Myra! What was he doing out of school, had he run away?'

'No.' Myra sobbed out the whole story alternately crying and
sniffing, standing aloof, untouchable in her guilt. 'It's all my
fault. Whatever shall we do? I knew I wasn't up to the task.'

'Is he OK? Where is he hurt?'

'They're examining him now. He's hurt all over. Somehow
he got thrown on the bonnet of the car and then he fell on the
road. The driver must have had good brakes because she didn't
run over him. Oh Graham, the screams! It was terrible.'

Graham's Adam's apple bobbed furiously up and down as he
tried to swallow. 'You don't mean ... Piers' ... screams? Do
you?'

'No, the driver's. He was completely silent.'

'He's not unconscious ... is he?'

'No, he's been talking to me and ...'

A nurse came. 'Mrs Butler?'

'Yes?'

'We've examined Piers and the doctor would like a word.'

To Myra the doctor appeared fresh out of primary school, never mind medical school.

'Your son is very lucky. He's broken his right arm, it appears to have taken most of the shock when he fell back on to the road. It's a tricky break, we think it will need an operation. As for the rest, general severe bruising especially round his rib cage, but no cracked ribs by the looks of it. He has a bad bruise on his head too, which is coming out now rather spectacularly, but all told nothing that a good rest and lots of TLC won't put right. We reckon he must be made of rubber, full of bounce you know. So he'll be staying here tonight and we'll operate first thing tomorrow morning. He's still in shock, we'd rather wait till he's feeling better. You can go see him now, but we've given him a sedative to ease the pain so he'll be feeling sleepy.'

Myra thanked him profusely. 'We're so grateful, doctor, thank you very much.'

'Grand little chap, he's a credit to you. So brave.'

When they walked towards Piers' bedside Myra thought she would die. The two of them stood either side of him tenderly looking down at him. The doctor was right: he was sleepy and didn't seem to realise they were there.

Graham touched his shoulder. 'Piers? We're here now.'

Mercifully, to their relief, Piers opened those wonderful blue eyes of his and smiled. 'Hello, Dad. Thanks for coming. I'm going to sleep. I hurt.'

'You must I'm sure,' Graham didn't miss a beat despite Piers' slip of the tongue. 'But the doctor's well pleased with you.'

Piers nodded.

'Myra's here, too.'

'OK.' Long pause. 'Don't leave me will you, Myra?'

Myra couldn't believe that he wanted her to stay. The pleasure of his words flooded over her like a vast gush of hot water, enfolding her, succouring her. It washed away the paralysing guilt. She'd never felt so needed. All these years doing anything she could to avoid hospitals, and now within weeks she'd not only been a patient again herself, but was volunteering to stay in with this brave little lad. 'Goes without saying, Piers, of course I won't leave you.'

She took hold of his good hand to reassure him as his eyes shut again. She turned back to Graham.

'There's Oliver to think about, too. We mustn't forget him. He'll be home soon.'

'Look, if you're staying ... you are, are you?'

Myra nodded emphatically.

'I'll ring the office, go home, wait for Oliver and explain it all to him, then I'll arrange things with Viv, get you some overnight things, see Oliver gets fed and has got her to keep an eye on him. Then I'll pop back to check on the two of you here, but I won't stay long. I'll need to be at home with Oliver tonight, he'll be feeling bad when he hears.'

'He might want to see him.'

'Ah, of course. Yes, he'll be too sleepy for more visitors tonight but we'll make sure he can see him as soon as possible tomorrow. Take care, ring me if needs be.'

Graham turned and spoke to Piers, who nodded vaguely, then Graham kissed his cheek, which appeared to be the only exposed bit of him not bruised, and then kissed Myra's cheek and she kissed him back somewhere round about his ear, so grateful that despite her acknowledging total responsibility for Piers' injuries, Graham had not questioned her further or uttered one word of accusation.

She sat the entire night beside Piers' bed. Occasionally he woke to find her still holding his hand and he squeezed hers as though saying thank you. Dawn broke with Myra still waiting with him, having eaten nothing, drunk nothing, nor moved one inch away from his bedside. Myriad thoughts had filled her mind, a great kaleidoscope of images. About what, she didn't really know, what she did know was that something had changed. She was too tired to work out what had shifted, but she felt different. Throughout the night nurses and doctors had come and gone, easing Piers' pain with tablets, giving him sips of water to freshen his mouth, asking her if she perhaps ought to go home, and all through the night Myra didn't let on that Piers wasn't their son. Of course it said it on the paperwork when they'd been admitted, but she found she was happy to let anyone new assume they were mother and child.

There were voices outside, the door opened and in walked Oliver and Graham. She couldn't remember the last time she'd felt so glad to see Graham, but she knew this was Oliver's moment.

'Oliver! Come up close to the bed and speak to him, he was talking a moment ago.'

But Oliver couldn't. He was afraid he'd make a complete fool of himself by bursting into tears, and in any case the horror he felt at seeing Piers bundled up in bed with that awful rainbow bruising on his forehead and his face, and his arm strapped up, was more than he could bear. He shook his head and declined without even opening his mouth. He thought about his little brother dying in the car accident like their mother did and he couldn't think what on earth he would do. It was all too much.

'He won't bite, you know. Come on.'

But Oliver was having none of it, and Myra couldn't understand.

Graham interrupted the awkward moment by suggesting she went home and showered and had a rest while he and Oliver stayed. She was reluctant to leave.

'I want to be here when he comes back from the operation. In any case, I can't get home, there's no bus for ages. I'll have to stay.'

'There are plenty of taxis, just go. You need a break. Plus I saw Viv last night and she said she'd pop in, too. I've switched my phone off, so leave me a message if you need me and I'll ring you to let you know when he goes in to surgery.' He handed her two twenty-pound notes and opened the door for her. 'Come back the same way, by taxi, when you're ready, but there's no rush.'

He almost reached out a hand towards her in sympathy, but changed his mind and withdrew it. 'Take your time.'

Myra stalked like an automaton out towards the taxi rank, gave her address and sat frozen clutching her bag, hating herself. To make up for what she had done she'd have to ... well, she didn't know what she'd have to do. Be kinder? More understanding? Get back to the hospital as soon as possible? Well, that would be a start. But she couldn't let things slip at home, either. First, get meat out of the freezer for Graham and Oliver ready for tonight. Scrape some potatoes, clean some vegetables ... they could have ice cream to finish, that would be easier.

She was so deep in thought she hadn't realised the driver was holding the door open for her. 'Are you OK?'

Myra nodded and gave him a big tip which she would never normally have done. Once home she felt so grubby she stripped off all her clothes in the utility room, dumped them in front of the washing machine and went stark naked up the stairs and into the shower room. The wetroom shower Graham had insisted on really came into its own that day. She let the water pour over her without a thought as to cost nor global warming. Sometimes there were more important things. Finally, having wasted gallons of water she stepped out, dried herself on a luxuriously hot towel straight off the heated towel rail and went to find clean clothes. She found herself surprisingly disappointed. Did she really wear such drab clothes? This dark lifeless navy suit. This charcoal one with the pinstripe? This awful skirt in a kind of dreary mock tartan. This beige blouse that went with it? And that polo necked jumper in a terrible bottle green.

Standing there beginning to shiver with cold, seeing her clothes as they really were, Myra made a vow. The first day she had a chance to go out she'd buy some new clothes. Definitely. Then Piers' plight and the guilt she'd experienced filled her mind once more. She snatched the first things that came to hand, and covered them with an old-fashioned mac that made her look like an army recruit who'd been kitted out with a coat two sizes too big.

She decided to skip the dinner preparations. They could manage with beans on toast for one night. Or even a takeaway. Usually, she frowned on such extravagance, but she was desperate to get back to Piers.

The taxi driver had given her his business card so she rang the number on it and with money at the ready she leapt out of the taxi at the hospital without a word and went up to the ward. Surely by now the operation would be over.

He was sitting in bed propped up with a multitude of pillows, looking half asleep, the multicoloured bruise even more gloriously technicolour now, and his arm in a plaster that stretched from his wrist to the very top of his arm. But all she truly saw was the fact he looked glad to see her, even when it was all her fault. What a generous-hearted boy he was.

He held up his injured arm. 'Myra! Look!'

'I can see, that's a plaster and a half.'

'I can't come home until tomorrow. How did I get like this? I can't remember.'

'We can always talk about it later. Oliver, are you ready for lunch? The nurses tell me the cafe is excellent. When you're ready.'

Graham looked grim, well aware she was avoiding talking to him, not even looking in his direction and he knew full well why, because Viv had told him what she knew about yesterday morning, not realising Myra hadn't told him about her marching Piers back to school under duress. He wondered how long he would have to wait before Myra told him the full story. Possibly forever.

The next day, Piers was given the all-clear and discharged home, with instructions for caring for his cast. Myra busied herself making a special meal and getting everything ready to make Piers as comfy as possible. It also gave her ample excuse not to talk to Graham properly. But that night when both the boys were in bed and fast asleep the whole story poured out of her, unstoppable, underpinned with guilt and at the end she begged his forgiveness.

'You didn't do it knowingly, you did it thinking it was for the best. Both of us have a lot to learn, Myra, it's sad that it's turned out as it has, but you weren't to know. I can see what Viv meant, Piers is still a very scared little boy. The demon that plagues him is fearing he'll be sent away, he needs enormous amounts of reassurance. And if having a day at home does that very thing then, for now it's OK, isn't it?'

Myra nodded.

'As it turns out he is getting a few days at home now anyway, which is apparently just what he needs.'

'I'm so sorry, Graham, so sorry. I know I didn't want them, don't really want them now even – when I think of how I've messed up already it makes me dread what I'll do wrong next, but I do know I was stupid and I shall be more careful another time.'

'I know you think sometimes Viv is not quite your kind of person but she has brought up five children of her own, and it might be worth listening to her advice?'

'They've not exactly set the world alight, any of her children, though ... ?'

'It's not like we're Mr and Mrs dynamic, are we? Viv's children are all hard-working, married and what's more, they sound happy, from what Viv says. Now, you look very tired, Myra, why not go to bed and I'll bring you a drink up.'

Rather than their usual cup of tea, he decided something

stronger was in order. He broke open a bottle of her favourite red wine and took up a glass of it for himself, too. He sat on the bed while he waited for her to finish in the bathroom. Her nightie lay on the duvet and he thought he remembered it from the days when they slept in the same bed. Surely to goodness she wasn't wearing the same ones from ten years back.

'Ah! there you are.' Embarrassed, he got to his feet. 'I'll go and get ready for bed and then let's drink our wine together.'

Graham scrutinised his face in the bathroom mirror and remembered he'd never got round to that new look he'd promised himself after Oliver's comments. Maybe now might be the time.

Myra was coming out of the boys' bedroom when he crossed the landing.

'Just thought I'd make sure he was all right,' she whispered.

'And is he?'

'Yes. Sleeping soundly.'

She sat up in bed with three pillows behind her, waiting for him to pass the wine to her. 'Being a bit daring aren't we? Oh! It's my favourite.'

'I reckon we've not been daring enough in the past.'

Graham phrased his next sentence very carefully. 'You know, we have plenty of money in the bank. I earn a good salary now, and always have as you know, so if you feel you'd like to have a splurge on clothes or anything at all then please feel free. Yes, we'll be needing to buy things for the boys now, too, but it doesn't mean you have to miss out on anything you might like You have access to our bank account like I have.'

She glanced down at her nightgown. 'You mean this?'

'Well, I seem to remember it.'

Myra blushed. She held up her glass saying, 'To you.'

'To me?'

'For being so patient with me. You could have blown your top and I couldn't have blamed you.'

Graham shrugged. 'We have to be thankful it wasn't any

worse, thankful Piers is back sleeping in his bed in our house, tonight.'

'About his birthday... '

'Let's wait and see how he is. You know he might want to go back to school soon with his plaster on. You never know. If the school are happy with it.'

'He hates it, you know, the plaster.'

'He'll get used to it, but he'll get bored being at home for weeks. Did you notice when he was doped up he called me Dad?'

This was a matter to be ignored as far as Myra was concerned. 'I'm glad he doesn't remember anything about the accident.'

'He will, in time. But we'll just tell him the facts – it doesn't need to be a drama.'

Myra shuddered. If Piers remembered! How on earth could she explain her behaviour to him? She couldn't. It was her being pigheaded like her mother always said she was.

'Drink up,' said Graham. 'Would you like another glass?'

'Let's keep the rest till tomorrow night.'

'As you wish. Goodnight, Myra.' Graham leant forward, and ignoring her retreat into her pillows to avoid him, he kissed her on her mouth. Not a peck, more a lingering kiss with memories of the past in it. She tasted the wine on his breath, and turned away after a moment so he didn't get any ideas in that direction.

Graham picked up her glass from the bedside table, and stood looking at her wondering if he gave in too easily ... should he be more, well, he didn't quite know the word ... flirtatious, attentive, persuasive?

Myra slid down on her pillows, pulling the duvet up around her shoulders to keep out the cold.

'Graham! That's as far as it goes, thank you very much. You remember that.'

But the tone of her voice was not quite so harsh and forceful as usual and didn't match the words she used and Graham, in the darkness on the landing, smiled.

Piers woke twice in the night, thirsty and in pain. Myra saw to him and sat for a while on his bed whispering so as not to disturb Oliver. She gave him some more painkillers as instructed by the hospital, and a drink of that posh apple juice he'd taken a fancy to and waited for him to go back to sleep.

By morning she was exhausted, being unaccustomed to being up in the middle of the night, but Piers was much happier and eager to go downstairs to eat his breakfast.

'Are you sure?'

He nodded so she said he could, but to be careful going down the stairs. All he needed was another fall and then where would they be?

The doorbell rang at ten and Myra went to see who was there. She got a shock when she saw it was Delphine standing there dressed to kill, or so Delphine no doubt thought.

'Why, it's you. Why are you here?'

Delphine adjusted her scarf saying, 'It's almighty cold round here, there's a gale blowing, is it always like this? I've heard about Piers and I've come to see him. It was in the local paper. I'm so worried about him.'

'Ah! Right.'

'Well, can I come in then? I'm not getting any warmer standing out here.'

'Oh!' She had to think fast, she wasn't having this blasted woman interfering or getting ideas about taking him away. Surely it was best not to let her see him. 'He's sleeping.'

'Huh! That doesn't sound like Piers, that doesn't. You're trying to stop me seeing him.'

'Do you care that much?' Myra thought of mentioning the stick but decided against it. She remembered what Graham had said about getting the police involved, and thought it best to see what Delphine had to say for herself, first.

Delphine looked shocked. 'Of course I care, I've been

looking after him and Oliver since Mo died, haven't I? I miss them. They should be mine anyway, but obviously John wanted Graham to have them. How are you coping?'

'You make it sound like they're possessions to be traded rather than two grieving children,' Myra snapped, then moderated her tone – she didn't want Delphine to see how much she had riled her. 'But we're doing very well indeed, thanks. They're a pleasure to have in the house.'

Delphine, her head on one side and a sceptical look on her face, studied Myra. 'I bet. Whose leg do you think you're pulling?'

Myra could have killed her on the spot. What was someone like her doing being so astute? She'd prove she was coping. 'You'd better come in then, you can see for yourself.' She wanted Delphine to see Oliver's collage on the wall, Piers' card in pride of place.

She ushered her into the sitting room, relieved to find that Piers was nowhere to be seen. She sensed rather than saw that he was hiding behind the sofa. 'Like I said, Piers is resting. I'll make us a coffee, it'll warm you up.'

Delphine followed and sat herself down on a kitchen chair without so much as a by-your-leave, but didn't move to take off her coat or rather ridiculous hat. 'Has probate been granted yet?'

Ah, thought Myra, so that's it. 'No, these things always take time.'

'In the meanwhile a person could starve to death. Though I can see from your house that won't be happening here. What is it your Graham does? I've forgotten.'

'He's in charge of waste for the county. It's a fascinating job. Milk? Sugar?'

'Yes. Both. Two teaspoons. I can imagine that, interesting work if you like that kind of thing.'

The slight sneer on Delphne's face angered Myra, but she couldn't think of a cutting reply.

'You're obviously well off and no doubt you're used to your creature comforts, six weeks' holiday a year. Having the boys will clip your wings a bit.'

'Frankly, that's none of your business. Here's your coffee.' She handed Delphine her mug and deliberately refrained from telling her it was very hot.

'Are you sure Piers is all right? Maybe we should go and look in on him.'

'I'd best go see. Won't be a moment.' Myra went to the sitting room and peered straight behind the sofa and she was right, he was hiding. He looked panic-stricken when he saw he'd been discovered. Piers put his finger to his lips and as he did she recognised his fear.

Myra hesitated for a moment and then mimicked him and also smiled. She gave him a thumbs up too to tell him his secret was safe with her and gestured for him to sneak up to his bedroom. She went back to the kitchen, shutting the door so Delphine wouldn't spot Piers. Essentially a truthful person – often too truthful as Graham had found to his cost – she found lying difficult, but persuaded herself that there were times when it was justified.

'He's fast asleep laid on his bed, so I'm sorry I'm not prepared to disturb him not for anybody, he hasn't slept properly since the accident.'

'How did it happen? On the pedestrian refuge it said in the paper.'

'That's immaterial. It happened and we're very upset, but he's being brave. Now, how are you getting along?' Myra almost added 'without John's money every week?'

'Well, that was what I was hoping to ask about. Graham said he'd pay me my expenses, the ones that came up after John went into the hospice, so I've brought a list. It comes to quite a bit.'

Myra's eyes widened when she saw the total. Two thousand,

three hundred and twenty-one pounds thirty-five pence! She was horrified. A lot of it had to be lies. She tried to think what Graham would do and thought ... receipts! They'd be needed. 'If you give me the receipts I'll put them with this list ...'

'John never asked for receipts, he never bothered.'

'Well, you see,' said Myra making it up as she went along, 'the money isn't Graham's, the solicitor will have to pay this bill. Send the receipts in the post to Graham when you get home, it shouldn't be long now before everything's settled. They've got a buyer for the house.'

Delphine looked uncomfortable. 'Do you keep all *your* receipts?'

'No, but then I'm not asking someone else to pay me for what I've done or what I've bought. You've got to provide the evidence, solicitors don't pay money out willy nilly.'

'I see. After all I've done for the boys over the years ...'

Myra's anger finally got the better of her. 'By the way, if you're wanting that stick back, Graham's broken it into little pieces and put it in the bin.'

Delphine lurched to her feet. 'What stick? I don't know anything about a stick.' She jerked her head back and her dreadful hat almost fell off.

'Don't pretend you can't remember! The one you hit Oliver with every night? For what you did to that boy, you don't deserve a penny of this money.' Myra banged her fist down on Delphine's list where it lay on the table.

'I don't know what you're talking about, I never used a stick on Oliver, it's all lies. Boys never tell the truth at that age – they make things up to suit them.'

'So how did he get those stripes on the palm of his hand? Answer me that.'

'He's fibbing. I never did.' She stood there stabbing the air with her finger, looking threatening. But Myra just sat there in silence, letting Delphine dig herself into a hole. 'Wait till you're reduced to hitting him because he won't do as he's told, just you wait and see.'

'It'll never come to that. Hitting him to make him good! You should be taken to court for it, it's abuse that is.'

For a second, Myra could see the panic in Delphine's eyes. Something in her seemed to collapse but she soon gathered herself together. She defiantly declared she wasn't putting up with this and why should she when it was all lies. She prodded the list with a moth-eaten fur-trimmed glove. 'Remember this. I'm owed it and I shall sue, just you wait and see.'

Myra could see Delphine's bluster was an utter sham. She'd never dream of taking them to court – not when she was the one that should be prosecuted for what she'd done to Oliver.

'Anyway, if Piers is still asleep I'll be off.''

Myra stood up to hasten her departure.

Relieved the dreadful woman had gone Myra went to find Piers. He had come downstairs when he heard Myra shut the door behind Delphine.

'I don't like Delphine. Don't want to see her ever again, you won't make me, will you?'

'Not if you don't want to. How about a hot drink and a biscuit?'

Piers nodded and they went to the kitchen.

'Oliver forgot to see to Pete this morning, he was running late so I've fed him. Would you like to have him in the kitchen for a while? To play with. Only the kitchen, he's not house-trained yet so I don't want him on the carpets. Or perhaps he could go in the hall on the wood floor, I suppose.'

'Do you mind?'

Myra didn't let on he'd been in the kitchen almost every day. 'No, we'll try him out, shall we?'

Piers was delighted, then he hesitated. 'But I shouldn't carry him when I can only hold him with one arm, he wriggles such a lot.'

'Never mind, I can do it.'

So Myra carried Pete in, making sure she kissed the top of his head when Piers couldn't see her. She was getting ridiculously attached to this rabbit, she didn't know why, but he was such a sweetie and never threatened to bite her, as she assumed all such creatures would.

To Piers' surprise Pete ran about the kitchen perfectly happily. 'Just look! You'd think he'd been in here before, wouldn't you? He likes it.' He looked up at Myra, his expression happier than she'd ever seen him, and for a moment her heart rejoiced.

'To be honest he's been in once or twice before when I've been on my own.'

Piers laughed so happily Myra almost clutched him to her for a hug, but she didn't, because Myra Butler didn't make gestures of that kind, but briefly she wished she did. The idea came to her that perhaps she could begin with Piers. After all, she'd managed some sort of embrace when he was so sad the previous week. Maybe she could learn how to do it without flinching and tensing – it seemed to come so naturally to most people.

The two of them spent half an hour playing with Pete in the hall and round the kitchen, back and forth until Piers was exhausted by the pain from his bruised body when he moved and he had to lie down.

Myra covered him with his rug, gave him a painkiller, switched the TV on, took Pete back outside and came in to try out a little idea that had been growing in her mind. She would make a chocolate cake. She hadn't made Graham a cake for years; they had shop-bought eccles cakes sometimes if she remembered to buy them, but she would never normally think to bake something herself for the two of them. Of course it wasn't for them, she thought, she was making it for Piers and Oliver.

She had everything ready to start, but before she switched the mixer on she went to see if Piers was happy. He lay fast asleep, the rug had fallen off, those angelic blue eyes of his were closed, his mouth was open and he was snoring slightly. It made her smile. Poor little chap. Guilt crept over her all over again, if only she'd listened to Viv. But she hadn't, had she and she hadn't seen her since. She'd found the mug Viv had taken with her clean washed on the front doorstep the next morning, a silent reminder of her foolishness.

When the cake was in the oven and everything washed and put away, Myra decided it was time to try something else she never normally did: offering an olive branch. She put the kettle on and rang Viv. 'Coffee? Viv?' There was a slight hesitation and then Viv replied, 'Yes. Why not. I'll be over right away.'

Viv came in through the back door calling out 'It's me. There's a lovely smell in here!'

'It's a chocolate cake I've just put in the oven.'

'And who are you making a chocolate cake for?'

Myra didn't answer her question, instead she replied, 'I should have listened to you, Viv, I'm sorry.'

'I don't profess to be the all-time, top-of-the-shop advisor on children, but you must admit I do have some experience. In fact, raising kids is about the only thing I do know! When you think about it, Myra, that little lad is in the most appalling position, his safety net has completely gone in a flash and he's not quite ten yet, so he's bound to feel desperately afraid. What child wouldn't, and Oliver too. They've no one but Graham. And you.' Viv sensed there'd been a sea change in Myra and decided her lecture should cease immediately before she got Myra's back up. 'Thanks for inviting me for coffee, I did so want to know how Piers was getting on.'

They sat down at the table with their mugs of coffee and it felt like old times.

'Well, he has a lot of pain simply because he is so badly bruised all over, his arm doesn't hurt now it's in plaster, only a kind of general ache, and he's been playing with Little Pete in here ...'

Viv thought she must have misunderstood. 'In the garden, you mean?'

'No, not in this cold weather, he runs about in the kitchen.'

'He does? You amaze me,' Viv stuttered.

'Well, I don't allow him on the carpets, that's asking too much. But like you've always said, he's a dear little thing, and I think he even quite likes it when I pick him up. But the effort of playing with him made Piers so tired he's asleep on the sofa. He's being so brave.'

Viv didn't answer for a moment and then said, 'The cake, Myra, is it all right?

'Oh! I'd forgotten.'

It was absolutely splendid, beautifully risen and a serious dark chocolate colour. Soon it stood on the cooling tray on the worktop looking proud of itself.

'That looks wonderful. Is it for something special?'

'Not particularly. I just felt like making one. After all, have you ever met a boy who doesn't like chocolate cake!'

Curious, Viv asked, 'How's Graham coping with it all?'

Before Myra could answer, they heard Piers calling out.

'Can I see him?' asked Viv.

'Of course.'

He was still laid on the sofa, the rug pulled round his shoulders just as Myra had left him.

'Can I have a drink of water, Myra, I'm so thirsty?'

'Of course you can. Viv's come to see you.'

'Hello! Piers. How are you feeling?'

'Better thanks, but it hurts to move about.'

'Of course it will. You take your painkillers like a good chap, make you feel better.'

'Yes. I will.'

Viv leaned closer. 'Don't let on you know but your Auntie Myra has made the most beautiful chocolate cake!'

Piers' eyes lit up.

'I suspect it's for supper. I wish I could look forward to a slice of it.'

Piers grinned. 'Good. The food's not half bad here.'

'I'm glad. Just what you need to get you better, before you know where you are you'll be wanting to go back to school, and they'll all be asking to sign your plaster.'

'I'm all right at home.'

Myra came in with his glass of water.

Viv was glad to hear Piers saying it was all right at home. It seemed like a good omen and she thought to herself, though of course she wouldn't dare say it to Myra, that Myra was perhaps making a better job of being a mother than she, Viv, had ever expected. Nor had Myra ever expected either. And it wasn't just the boys that she seemed to be warming to – letting the rabbit in the house, she could barely believe it. Maybe Myra was finally thawing.

'Well, Piers, I'll let you get some more sleep, you look as though your eyes are ready for closing. Sleep's the best thing for healing. Bye, darling. Any time you fancy a change come across and see me, I'd enjoy that.'

'Thank you. I will.'

Myra walked to the door with Viv who, just as she was leaving turned back to say, 'I meant what I said to Piers any time you feel in need of a break send Piers across to me for an hour. I'd enjoy his company.' Myra closed the door behind her and went to see if Piers had had enough of his glass of water.

Halfway through finishing it Piers broke off to speak. He burst out with, 'Why can't everyone be lovely, like Viv? I hate Delphine, she's horrid. I hope she never comes here again. She gave us soya milk and cream crackers with no cheese and no butter, said they'd do us good but she knew we didn't like them and Oliver told her but she took no notice. In the winter it was always so cold in her house. She said she couldn't afford to heat it properly, but Dad gave her lots of money I used to watch him give it to her. Notes and notes and notes. Piles of them. Every week.'

'Well, now look here, Piers,' then, as though she was two quite separate people she heard herself telling him that he'd no need to fear, she wanted him and Oliver to live with their Uncle Graham and he'd no need to worry about Delphine, he was absolutely safe. But how could she say those words when in her heart of hearts she still wanted them to go? She longed for the peace the silent empty house gave her, so what on earth had she said that for? She was lying all over again. Didn't she know any longer what honesty was when she'd prided herself all her life that she always spoke the truth? Into her mind sprang that feeling of needing to avoid Graham when he'd bent down to kiss her goodnight; for one single second just as she pressed back into her pillows to escape him, she'd wanted his kiss more than anything in the world. There again she was two persons. One the old, controlled, safe Myra and the other a new Myra that had emerged unbeckoned. She'd have to put a stop to this new person as of *now*.

Chapter 10

That afternoon, Myra decorated the cake helped by Piers who sat on a chair supervising and offering suggestions. Between them they covered it in vanilla butter icing, stroked the top with the back of a big fork to make a kind of basket work pattern on the top, put big fat whole glacé cherries right round the edge and flakes of chocolate all over the top.

'You are good at doing cakes, Myra. Do you enjoy making them?'

'I haven't made one for ages, could even be years, in fact I think it is. Uncle Graham likes to keep slim, you see, and chocolate cake like this has no respect for slimness.'

'I think a cake like this is loving.'

Myra clattered the bowl and the grater and the spoons and the palette knife into the sink and turned to ask him what he meant.

'It's all covered in love, that's why you did it, for love.'

Myra had never equated love with cake, in fact she no longer equated love with anything at all. 'I don't know, perhaps you're right.'

'It's two weeks to my birthday. A cake like this with candles on would be amazing. I've only ever had shop cakes for my birthday, you see.'

The new Myra emerged again. 'In that case then Piers Butler shall have a cake like this for his tenth birthday. And that's a promise.'

Piers went to the kitchen door. Did she really, really mean it, or was she saying that just to please him? He so hoped she did mean it.

'Thank you very much. I'm going to get bumper cars out now, will you have a go with me?'

'Of course, you set it up while I wash these things. Are you sure you feel up to it?'

'For a while anyway.'

So when Oliver came home from school dispirited after a day when everything he did seemed to go wrong, he found Myra on her knees playing bumper cars, and for some unknown reason his spirits lifted. They lifted even more when Piers took him in the kitchen to see the cake he'd helped to decorate. 'Isn't it lovely?'

'Is it for tonight, Myra?'

'It certainly is, Oliver.' He stood lost in admiration and then unwittingly made a similar remark to Piers' own comment.

'It's beautiful. The best cake ever. I bet you two have loved making it, haven't you? There's love in that fancy icing.'

Myra flushed red, and she had to turn away so they couldn't see. When had she ever been praised like this before? Graham used to do it, but she snapped at him so often for it he gave up. These two boys were so sensitive. They'd get that from their dad, John had always been careful about feelings.

By the time they got round to eating the cake that evening, they were so excited that they didn't seem like the solemn quiet boys they'd been ever since they'd arrived. They were bubbly and happy and Graham caught her eye and smiled in gratitude.

When they'd each finished a slice and Myra had enjoyed it better than any food for years Piers said, 'Viv would love a slice of this, she said so when she was here. Would it be rude to ask for a slice to take across to her? Say no if you want, if it's not all right.' She heard the longing in his voice and couldn't say no.

'I like children to be generous. Yes, why not, but it's from you, not me. Right?'

Graham stood by the front door to watch Piers walk across to Viv's and realised too late that with one hand virtually unusable Piers wouldn't be able to hold the plate and ring the doorbell at the same time. 'Hold on there, Piers, I'm coming!' But he was too late, the plate, the cake and the napkin ended upside down on the doorstep.

'Don't worry, we'll get another piece, it's all right, don't panic.'

But Piers did. He'd struggled to be brave ever since the accident and just when he tried to do something nice, he completely ruined Viv's surprise.

'I'm so sorry, so sorry.'

Graham whispered, 'Look, she hasn't heard us, we can go home, get a fresh slice and come back as if we've just arrived. Come on quick.'

So the pair of them slipped back across the road, put the cake he'd dropped into the bin and went back with a fresh slice and a spanking new paper napkin to ring Viv's doorbell.

Graham pressed the bell and left Piers to wait for her to answer the door, thinking it would be better for Piers' confidence if he coped by himself.

Viv was delighted. 'Oh! Piers, how wonderful! Thank you so much. Come in.'

So he went in to Viv's comfy kitchen and sat with her while she ate her cake.

'This is beautiful. Really beautiful. Myra is clever, isn't she? I make cakes but I'm sure they're never as good as this.'

'She says she's going to make me one just like it for my birthday.' Piers hesitated and then added, hardly daring to ask for confirmation, 'Do you think she will?'

'I'll make sure she does. It would be lovely, wouldn't it?'

'I told her I'd always had shop birthday cakes, you see, having no mum . . .' Without warning, just as Viv had put a huge lump of cake in her mouth and was unable to speak, Piers broke down. It seemed as though a dam had opened and the tears flooded down his face completely out of control. Viv passed him a tissue and made no attempt to stop the torrent of tears coming down his cheeks because she sensed he needed to let all his upset come out. She washed up Myra's plate, put the crumpled napkin in the bin, and then took him on to her knee, put her arms round him and hugged him tight. When the tears slowed down she wiped his face with a tissue, and began to sympathise with him. 'You've been such a brave boy all this time, you did right to have a good cry. We won't tell anyone, you and I. OK? Feeling better now?'

Piers nodded. 'It's comfy sitting here.'

'Well, that's 'cos I'm well padded. I never have been thin though I've always wanted to be.'

'Well, don't, you're all right.'

'If that's the case then I'll stay as I am. Your Auntie Myra is what I have always wanted to look like, slim, able to wear anything at all.' She gave him an extra squeeze and he smiled back. 'She's doing all right, isn't she, Myra?'

'Oh! Yes. She's getting better. We're going to have Little Pete in the kitchen for a while each day. He's very good, he doesn't do a poo or anything and we haven't trained him. I'm getting a rabbit too for my birthday and then he'll have a friend.'

'What will you call it?'

'Haven't thought about that. I could call it Viv, couldn't I?'

'If it's a girl.'

'If it is will they have babies? I'd love to have baby rabbits.'

'Well, I don't know about that, better ask your Uncle Graham.'

'He's all right is Uncle Graham, you know, he tries so hard to be a dad. He isn't, but he does try.'

'It's hard work being a dad when you have never been one.'

'I suppose so. Myra's getting better at being a mum. She was hopeless to start with, she got it all wrong. I wanted to stay at home that day, you know,' he raised his broken arm to show her what he was talking about, 'but she made me go back to school and I screamed and yelled all the way, but she made me go, then for just a teeny weeny second she almost let go of me and I turned to run home and that was when I hit the car. Don't tell her I've said, will you? I haven't been cross about it, she really didn't want me to have an accident.'

'Of course she didn't, she may seem like a dry old stick, but she wouldn't have wanted that. Now, I think it's time you went home, it'll be your bedtime soon and you're looking tired. Wash your face under the tap then no one will guess about ... you know ... here, dry it on this hand towel. Now I'm going to see you across the road, just in case. Anytime you want a chat come over, but mind you tell Myra where you're going else she'll worry.'

So she watched him across the road and called, 'Goodnight, thanks for the cake.'

Back at home, Uncle Graham helped Piers have a shower with his plastered arm wrapped in a sheet of plastic he had brought home from work. The hot water felt lovely on his bruises.

Oliver came upstairs when he'd finished his homework and they had a chat before lights-out.

'How's the arm today?'

'Not bad. I think I'll go to school next week. It's nice being at home but it'll be nice see my friends. I suppose they wouldn't let me go out at playtime though. Will my arm be better by my birthday, Oliver? Do you think I might have a birthday party? A proper birthday party? Or perhaps a trip to the cinema and then a birthday tea at home with a cake? Like that one Myra made today.'

Oliver honestly didn't know if birthday parties figured large in the Graham and Myra household so he had to be tactful. 'I'll ask Uncle Graham for you, man to man.'

'Yes please. I think I need to go to sleep now.'

Piers was asleep almost before Oliver had left the room. In Oliver's mind there was nothing like going straight for the jugular as soon as an idea hit you, so he said as he walked into the sitting room, 'When it's Piers' birthday on the twenty-fifth, could we have a party or something to celebrate? He'd love that, especially after his broken arm and everything.'

Myra had one of her shocked moments, something the old Myra was good at, but before she could get a word out Graham had said, 'I don't see why not. It would be good for him to have something to look forward to, wouldn't it, Myra?'

'I'll have to think about it.' Her mind raced through what would be expected of her, balloons, food, invitations, food, cake, games, food. She couldn't face it, she really couldn't. A host of boys running about all over the house whooping and fighting. Certainly not.

Graham reassured Oliver. 'Leave it with us, Oliver, it's a very thoughtful idea and well worth doing. You'd help, wouldn't you?'

'Yes, I would. But we'd need cake like the chocolate one we've had tonight ... with candles. That would be great. He'll be so pleased.' Before Myra could naysay the idea, he turned back to the door. 'I've some revising to do for a test tomorrow so I'm going to do that before bed. OK? Goodnight.'

Myra, sitting in her favourite easy chair, was too preoccupied to reply. She wasn't doing a party and she didn't care what they tried to do to persuade her. They could scream and cry, trash the house, do what they liked but she wasn't going to give in. Definitely not. 'I'm not doing a party and that's that.'

'If it was on a Saturday, I'd be here.' Graham recognised the resistance in that grim expression of hers, he'd seen it all too often these last years. But even Graham had reservations about it. He knew nothing about what ten-year-old boys wanted these days. Party games for a start, what did kids play at parties nowadays?

'You've organised boys' birthday parties before have you?'

'Well, no, but we could try.'

'And make fools of ourselves.'

'Not necessarily, we might surprise ourselves.'

'We're not party people, Graham, never have been and never will be. A party we organised would be a crashing failure and then where would his image be? We'd be a laughing stock and not just amongst the boys, their parents too. No, it's not on.'

'He's had a rough time these last few months and I very much want to make things up to him. A successful party would improve our street cred enormously in the boys' eyes.'

Myra shook her head. 'I'm afraid he'll have to do without. Put another couple of logs on the fire will you, I'm cold.'

She settled down to watch TV, dismissing the party idea as a non-starter. Her giving a party for a load of boys? Not likely. She wouldn't know where to begin. How could she? She glanced across at Graham and read his mind.

'You're still thinking about it, I can tell, well, you can stop as of now. I'm not having it. Absolutely not and if you organise it without me agreeing to it I shall go out all day on the day, not lift a finger towards anything and leave you with the lot. Food. Games. Whatever.' She folded her arms to emphasise her decision. He might think he'd got the hint of an upper hand at the moment just because she'd been more accepting of the boys these last few days, but he was very, very mistaken.

'But we need to do something for him. Just going to a restaurant the four of us isn't a celebration now, is it? Not for a boy of ten.'

'It's more than we do for my birthday,' said Myra, indignantly.

'Because you refuse to go anywhere. I've tried booking a weekend away, or even just the theatre but you won't go. So I buy you a present, that's all.'

She held up her hand. 'Stop there. So that's what we'll do for Piers. A present.'

'It's not enough, Myra.'

'It has to be enough for me.'

'But you're a grown-up and you haven't been recently orphaned and been in a road accident. He needs something special. I'm not saying we have to do the full works every year but you must see that this year he could really do with a bit of a fuss.'

'No, I'm sorry.' Pause. 'No, actually, I'm not sorry. I'm not doing a party. Full stop. Now don't mention it again.'

'I shall if I choose to.'

Myra boiled at this unheard-of outright flaunting of her authority. 'You heard me. I said *no*.'

'For once, Myra, you don't get the last word on this. If push comes to shove I shall have to do it all myself because I insist he has a party of some sort.'

'I shan't allow it. You might think you're in charge here, Graham Butler, because you bring the money in, but you are not. *I* am.'

She glared at him and her rage almost turned to amusement as she thought how short-lived Graham's rebellion had been. They'd managed this long with Myra ruling the roost and she wasn't going to let that change. Then she noticed a steely look in his eyes, she'd only ever seen it before at John's house on the morning of the funeral.

Graham took a deep breath and said, 'I have never in my life laid a finger on you in anger and never would, but I am at my limit, Myra, I really am. I am this close,' he held his index finger and his thumb a hair's breadth apart, 'to saying something I might regret. Your kind of stubborn arrogance has no place in this house *any more*. I will not be controlled like this. I've had it up to here.' He leapt to his feet, his hand raised on a level with his face, and for one terrifying moment Myra actually believed he was going to hit her, despite his fine words. But he didn't, he lifted her gently to her feet and with his eyes centimetres away from hers he said quietly now, 'You've had your own way for far too long and it's embittered you, Myra. You must understand and get it right, in there, in your head, that these two boys are not just mine, but because we're married they are yours too, and I shall make sure we do treat them as they should be treated, with thoughtfulness and consideration and respect until ... until it turns to love on everyone's part. Right?' He loosened his grip on her arms and she sank back on the sofa as he stalked out. All she could hear above the noise of her pounding heart was his footsteps thudding up the stairs, one, two, three ...

Thoroughly wound up by Myra's intransigence, Graham couldn't sleep. As the hours rolled by he went inch by inch over the deterioration of their relationship and saw clearly how it had all come about. Tonight he'd accused her of being arrogant, maybe he used the wrong word but it all came to the same thing. She'd had her own way because she had been too wrapped in her own misery to accept support from him, let alone see that he needed support from her, as well. Progressively their lives had become more bleak as the years went by and the operation she under-went which finally finished any hope of future children had been the final blow. He recollected the loving relationship there'd been between his brother John and Mo, and envied them with a depth of feeling he'd almost forgotten he possessed. But then the loss of John hit him afresh. He couldn't afford self-pity. He knew John would have given anything for some more time with his boys, and Graham had to make the most of that time, he had to do John proud.

He turned over and thought about the boys. He and Myra would have to sort out their differences, but that could wait. Right now, it was the boys that needed their time. Oliver was

so like himself at his age, intelligent, highly motivated, ten-
acious, it was a pleasure to witness. He'd found an envelope,
while he'd been collecting things from John's house, full of the
boys' school reports, and he saw in Oliver's reports the same
remarks he used to get in his. Odd that. A matter of genes,
he supposed. Except Oliver was artistic too and that wasn't a
Butler trait at all. As for Piers, from his reports he seemed to
be a happy popular boy who talked too much. Graham smiled
at that, he could well believe it. He finally settled to sleep with
the problem of Piers' birthday still foremost in his mind, but
determined to solve it by asking for ideas at the office.

Myra, thinking the whole idea of a party had been dropped
after what she'd said, got a surprise the following night when
Graham came home from the office, because as soon as they sat
down to eat, Graham said to Piers, 'I've been thinking about
your birthday.'

Unfortunately for Myra, the thought of a party had niggled
away at Graham all day and would not let his mind rest. He
said he had asked at work what others did for a boy's tenth
birthday party and was overwhelmed with suggestions from the
downright dreadful to the highly impossible.

Oh, have you, thought Myra and as she looked at him a
flicker of anger ran through her. Whatever he might be going
to suggest she did towards this so-called party, she would shoot
down in flames. But – and it took her a moment to work it
out – that flicker of anger came very unexpectedly mixed with
a stirring of desire for him. He was full of enthusiasm, as he
always used to be, she thought – and full of determination, even
if that was directed against her wishes.

'How about, seeing as you don't know many boys at school
yet, being new, if you asked say two boys to go to the cinema
with us and then come home for tea and one of Myra's stunning cakes ... with candles of course. I'd suggest bowling or

iceskating or something if you were fit, but your plaster won't be off, will it, so you wouldn't enjoy that as much as the cinema. Any film you like. Two boys would fill the car up with Oliver and you and me, so Myra wouldn't be able to go with us, but I'm sure she'd rather be at home making a nice tea for us all for when we get back, wouldn't you, Myra?'

Piers looked as though a huge fluorescent tube had been switched on in his body; he glowed from head to foot with joy. The change in him was Graham's reward.

'That would be fab, Uncle Graham, just fab, perhaps another year we could do the ice-skating or something when I haven't broken my arm.'

'Exactly. So the cinema it is.'

'We'll need invitations won't we, Myra?'

Her immediate instinct to always say no was pushed aside by Piers' hopeful face and instead of saying 'No! I'll ring their mothers, we can do without the expense of invitations', she saw how important they were to him and said instead, 'Of course, it wouldn't be a party without invitations, we'll go and buy them tomorrow.'

Oliver reminded her about the birthday cake.

'Yes, and a birthday cake. With ten candles.'

Myra felt she had been outmanoeuvred by Graham because she'd finished up with a kind of a party, but doing the one thing she could quite enjoy, in the house all alone getting the tea organised. And for only two extra guests – which also thankfully meant no games and everyone delivered home once the candles were blown out. Some kind of a reasonable compromise, she supposed.

She'd laid awake for half the previous night dwelling on Graham's surprising reaction to what he called her stubbornness. It was the first time in fifteen years of marriage that he'd behaved like that, when his backbone had manifested itself and he'd said what he wanted to say and not what she had planned

143

for him to say. He was wrong though, she thought, she was neither arrogant nor stubborn. Well, perhaps a bit stubborn on occasion – her mother always said she was, too. But never arrogant, she was humble really if anything at all, yes, humble, but determined, she decided.

The next morning Piers was watching children's TV with Oliver while he waited to go shopping for the invitations, and Myra had gone upstairs to change Graham's bed linen. But now she knew they were there, she couldn't resist climbing up to get the baby vests out of the wardrobe for a second look. She unstuck the adhesive flap straight away and slipped them out, held one to one cheek, another to the other cheek and loved the cuddliness of them. They could have been Piers' vests. Ones he'd worn perhaps and she'd kept in a sentimental moment of yearning for him to be a baby again. For a few minutes she lost herself in her imagination, Piers newborn, Piers beginning to crawl, Piers taking his first steps, Piers starting to talk. Or Oliver, she imagined herself brushing his beautiful baby curls, in her mind, she wound them round her fingers, every single one of them, held his hand, kissed his rosy cheeks.

She heard Piers calling from downstairs, 'Are we nearly ready to go shopping, Myra?'

'Five minutes.' Graham's sheets would have to last another day.

'We can get the candles in the same shop, couldn't we, Myra?'

Myra shouted down the stairs, 'Yes, of course.'

So she went out to buy the invitations with a real boy who lived and breathed and wanted *her*, not some faceless person in a shop, but *her* to make him a birthday cake.

Chapter 11

Graham picked up Carl and Aidan from their homes en route to the cinema so Myra did not see them until they arrived at 12 Spring Gardens after the film. She knew little about children, she was the first to admit, but as soon as she saw them she knew they were the same kind of boys as Piers. Well-meaning, well-mannered and thoroughly nice to know. They all gasped, Graham included, when they saw the dining table ready for the tea.

Myra had bought the paper tablecloth with the same emblems on it as the invitations, the paper napkins matched too and smack in the centre of the table surrounded by a glorious array of savouries and sandwiches and ham rolls, delicious-looking glass dishes with individual desserts topped with cream and flakes of chocolate, was a birthday cake fit for a prince. Piers counted the candles to make sure she'd got exactly ten, and satisfied it passed the test, that fluorescent tube inside him lit up again. Even the sceptical Oliver had to admit she'd made a hit. 'Myra! It's fantastic!'

Piers was speechless and as for Aidan and Carl they rubbed their hands together and said, 'Thank you so much, Mrs Butler. The film was good but this ...' They looked at her with admiration.

'Well, then you'd better sit down, but I should like it best if you washed your hands first. Piers, you lead the way.'

Miraculously there were no groans and all four of the boys did as she said without a murmur.

While they were taking turns in the downstairs loo, Graham looked at her.

He had such admiration in his face she blushed, and that feeling of desire for him, which she'd no intention of doing anything about, sidled into her again. 'Is it all right?'

'You know it is.' As the boys came back into the dining room he mouthed 'Thank you' to her. Then came the task of getting everyone seated and busy eating. But it was no problem because it all looked so tempting and the horrific idea that they'd begin throwing food and spilling drinks and causing mayhem quickly faded, so Myra found herself actually enjoying sitting down at this all-male party and for once enjoying herself. She even managed to eat a lot which is exactly what all four of the boys did too, and Graham.

Then came the moment Piers had been waiting for; blowing out the candles and then finally at last Piers James Butler would be so old he'd reached two digits; no longer nine but ten!

He was almost too tired to blow them out in one go, but he did and collapsed back on his chair filled to the brim with satisfaction. Myra didn't know who looked the most delighted, Graham, Oliver or Piers. The slices of cake Myra cut were huge and delicious, the icing just right, the sponge moist and tasty and the glacé cherries shining.

Graham had asked the parents of Carl and Aidan to come at half past seven to collect them and sure enough, as half past seven struck, they heard the doorbell. She'd forgotten about the parents and went into an immediate panic. Were they coming in? The house wasn't tidy, the boys had the bumper cars out in the hall, the dining room looked as though a chimps' tea party had been held in there and as for the kitchen ... but Graham stepped in and took charge with an air of confidence Myra didn't know he possessed.

'Please go through into the sitting room, we'll have a drink in there if you've got time.'

Myra wondered if she'd heard him correctly. 'Have a drink in there'? This she was not prepared for at all. They had nothing in. She thought she'd managed to throw a party without failing all these secret social codes she had no clue about and now she was about to fall at the final hurdle. Always ready to imagine the worst-case scenario, Myra was already imagining these parents gossiping at the school gates – telling their friends how the Butlers hadn't even offered them a proper drink.

But Graham stepped into the breach with the kind of aplomb that made her full of admiration for him. He'd obviously been aware that this might happen and was already in the kitchen calling out to see if they wanted beer or wine. She'd been so busy preparing the party tea that she hadn't even noticed Graham must have stocked the fridge in anticipation. That Graham! Doing all this. He played the part of the host so suavely she began to wonder where on earth he learned to do it, because they'd never had a party in this house before. Ever.

She even managed to chat a bit to the mothers and drink her orange juice at the same time. Then tiredness hit her and she looked across at Piers and saw it had hit him too, his face was flushed and he was sitting on the floor just watching the other three playing with the bumper cars.

Maybe the time had come to give out the going home party bags that Piers knew nothing about. Nor did Graham. I can do surprises, too, she thought to herself. While Piers had been at school she'd gone back to the *Smart Party* shop where they'd bought the invitations and asked about party bags and what you put in them. They'd cost rather more than she'd expected, but being determined to do things right for Piers she paid up without a murmur.

The parents took the hint and swept up their boys full of profuse thank-yous and departed calling out 'Goodnight, see you soon' to them from outside in the street and Myra blushed.

The neighbours would think she and Graham had gone mad – they never had guests.

Piers was ready for bed almost as soon as everyone left. Graham had said he would do all the clearing up while Myra saw the birthday boy to bed. Piers was exhausted and had little to say about his party except a hug for Myra as she leant over him to pull the duvet up.

'Thank you so much for my party, it was the best.'

'I'm sure your dad did good ones too.'

'Yes, he did, but not like this one. Being ten is the best.'

He scuffled himself onto his good side as best he could, his plastered arm making it tricky to get comfy. 'Now I can't wait for next year, I think I'll choose ice-skating. No, maybe not, I'll think about it. Oliver could have a party too, couldn't he, when he's thirteen? Anyway … I'm so tired. Goodnight, Myra.'

'See you in the morning. So glad you enjoyed the party.'

'Yes. I did. So much. Thank you.'

Oliver had a programme he wanted to watch so it was almost ten before he headed to bed.

'Thanks for the cinema and the great tea, Piers loved it, and so did I. I really wanted him to have a special day, and he did, didn't he?' said Oliver as he got up.

Myra was dropping asleep by this point and had to rouse herself to answer him.

'It turned out OK, didn't it? You know, considering it was the first one we've done.'

'It did. You're getting better at it.'

'What d'you mean?'

Oliver grinned. 'At being parents.' He saluted the two of them, shut the door and they heard his 'Goodnight' through the closed door.

'I fancy a drink, Myra, to round off the day. How about it? One for you?'

'I won't have anything, you know I'm not much of a drinker.'

'Be a devil, just this once, you've got to help me get through all those bottles I got in for Aidan and Carl's parents. It seemed best to have something in for them, just in case.'

She felt so full of triumph at the success of the party that she decided to have a vodka and tonic. 'You were right, weren't you, they did hope for a drink. I can't imagine what the neighbours will think, them shouting goodnights and thank yous out in the street. We're meant to be the quiet house.'

'It doesn't matter what they think, it's not a crime, not yet anyway, to shout goodnight in the street. Here's your vodka and tonic.' He held his own drink up to clink her glass with his. 'A toast. To birthday parties and may we have lots of them.'

'Well, Piers is already planning Oliver's thirteenth.'

'And why not. A big thank you for everything you did for the party, it's made him so happy, and the party bags ... inspiration on your part.'

'Where did you learn about being such a suave host, anyway?'

The word 'suave' amused Graham but he kept his face straight. 'At the office. There's always something to celebrate in waste.'

'Really?'

'Oh! Yes. Births. Marriages. Deaths. Divorces. New contracts. New member of staff. It seems barely a week goes by without a little office get-together for some reason. If it keeps them happy, who am I to complain, it costs me nothing. You should come sometime.'

The vodka meant Myra was off her guard.

'Perhaps I shall one day. Leave the boys with Viv after school, she wouldn't mind.' A rosy hue coloured Myra's cheeks. Graham toasted her. 'To the boss's wife.'

'To the boss.'

'Another one?'

149

'Why not?'

An hour and three vodkas later and Graham realised that Myra would be incapable of getting up the stairs. Graham knew he had a problem when she muttered, 'I feel really odd-d-d. I'd better get t'bed. It's 'ar' work havin'... party.'

He gently took her empty glass from her hand and stooped to pick her up. She was no weight at all and he wondered why he'd never noticed how thin she was. It was like carrying a child.

He laid her on her bed and began to undress her. 'Sorry, Myra, it's got to be done.' Layer by layer he unclothed her until she had nothing on at all. He hadn't seen her like this for ten years. She was as beautiful to him as always, though he knew time had aged them both. Her skin was still beautifully silky, with a rare sheen almost pearl-like, her breasts were small as they had always been except when she was pregnant. He choked back a sob as he remembered how pleased she'd been to find her breasts swelling because of the baby. He traced the small operation scars on her stomach with a gentle finger. It was the first time he'd seen them and he felt ashamed of how easily he'd allowed her to carry the burden of the operation with scarcely a sympathetic word, so afraid was he to cross the great divide she'd established. He'd been the world's biggest fool.

Graham got her night things out from under the pillow and found a pair of pyjamas she'd worn before they married. He tried to hitch them onto her body but she resisted him even in her drunken sleep, so he covered her with her duvet. He was beginning to feel uncomfortably like a voyeur, almost ashamed of himself. He sat for a long time on her bedside chair, studying her while she slept. Was there perhaps after today, a way back opening up for them? He'd need to tread so carefully. Slowly, considerately. Were they both equally to blame? Perhaps so. Into his mind came the memory of a perfume he bought her not long after they married, a rich perfume that had made him think of summer evenings. She'd left all that kind of thing behind, had Myra, such a pity. Maybe he'd buy her some as a thank you for the party.

Before he went to bed Graham checked the boys were OK. A naked, drunken wife in one room, and two sons loaned to him to check on in the next room. He'd scarcely have imagined it a few months ago. But this was life in all its glory. Hallelujah! Should he sleep next to Myra tonight? No, that was neither slow nor considerate, he reprimanded himself immediately.

Staring into the bathroom mirror, he recalled again his promise to himself about his image overhaul. The chunk of hair at the front that inevitably fell over his forehead and had done all his life would have to go. He rather fancied something a bit spiky. He'd book an appointment. This week. Put an end to fuddy-duddy old man Graham.

Chapter 12

On the Monday morning, having got permission from the head teacher at Piers' school for him to attend school with his arm still in plaster, Myra had to face crossing the pedestrian refuge where he'd had his accident. He couldn't get to school if she didn't and he was keen to get back to his new friends, plus a day on her own in the house felt very appealing, so she reminded herself it was Piers and not herself who'd been injured and for his sake she must be confident.

So they set off, the two of them each with their own demons to face. But in the end the traffic was not as heavy as usual so they crossed the main road without having to pause on the refuge, so all Myra had to face was speaking to the headmistress about the arrangements they had made for Piers to be at school with an arm in plaster.

'Like I said, I'm afraid I can't take responsibility for him to be in the playground at break time, but he can stay in and read comics that we keep for wet days and someone will always be about to make sure he's OK. Will that do?'

'Of course. I'm glad you feel able to cope with him. There's nothing wrong now, except for a few fading bruises and his arm still in plaster. Keep his mind busy, won't it?'

'Indeed. He's a very good boy in class, no problems there.'

'Thank you for allowing him to come to school.'

'It's a pleasure, Mrs Butler. Say bye-bye, Piers, and off you go.'

All the way home Myra felt this strange loneliness coming

over her. She'd thought that being at home by herself would be lovely but her footsteps echoed on the parquet flooring and the stillness closed in on her and she found the reality of being alone didn't appeal as much as she had expected. When the doorbell rang she was delighted but surprised; knowing it couldn't be Viv because she always came round the back, she rushed to answer it.

Standing on the doorstep clutching a huge box which appeared too heavy for her was Betty Bannister. Though she was her next-door neighbour this was the closest view of her Myra had had in fifteen years.

'Can you take this, it's awfully heavy for me.'

'Of course.' It was reasonably heavy but not too difficult for Myra and as Betty didn't add any more to her original statement Myra found herself asking her in to fill the silence. 'And this is ...'

Betty followed Myra in and shut the front door. 'It's a train set.'

'Oh, right!'

'It's for your boys. Your two new boys.'

'That's extremely kind, too kind in fact.' She stood it on the hall table and waited for an explanation.

'May I sit down?'

'Of course, we'll go in the sitting room.'

'Oh! This is a lovely room, so much nicer than ours, it's strange how they've made the houses in the cul-de-sac so different from one another. Ours is narrower, and it's got a funny extra bit making it L-shaped.'

'Do sit down.'

Myra noticed Betty was dressed rather oddly. Nothing matched, in fact the colours she'd chosen clashed: a yellow shirt with a purple jumper and a thick green jacket with brass buttons. Brown shoes and a rather curious woolly black hat pulled down over her ears completed the ensemble.

'So tell me about this train set? It's awfully thoughtful of you.'

'Well, if you don't mind second-hand, it's a lovely thing, Myra. Do you mind if I call you Myra? I'm afraid I don't know your surname.'

'It's Butler but yes, please call me Myra. I can't believe we've been neighbours all these years without having a proper chat. But you were saying, about the train set?'

'Ah, yes. I've been thinking about it since I saw the boys arrive. It needs to be played with so it's not on loan, it's for keeps. And before you say anything, I don't want any money for it.'

'It's very kind of you.'

'No, you're doing me the favour. It's been gathering dust in our house for years and it's time it got some use. It was our Col's. Our son. You won't have seen him coming and going because he doesn't, he hasn't for twenty years.' She crossed her ankles and sighed.

'Has he been abroad then?'

'No. We had a big falling out when ...' She fell into silence and looked at the floor.

'I'm sorry. Is he your only child?'

Betty nodded.

'That's very sad for you and your husband ... Roland, isn't it?'

Betty nodded. 'It was when he told us he was ... not what his father expected.'

Tired of beating about the bush and Myra inquired rather brutally, 'What do you mean – had he changed job, or moved away? He's not ill, is he?'

'No, no, he's in perfect health as far as I know. We get a card at Christmas and he's doing well in his job, but ... Roland said some dreadful things and I was caught between them – I should have said something.'

'You just wish he'd come and visit, I'm sure.'

'No, not as things are. It would only lead to rows and I've had enough of those. They make Roland even more furious.' Betty paused. 'He's gay. That's all.' She smiled, relieved to have spoken freely at last. 'But Roland is dreadfully old-fashioned you know, limp-wristed he calls it.'

'Oh! I see.'

'But he's still our son, isn't he?'

'Of course and I expect you'd like to see him and make sure he knows you support him.'

Betty nodded.

'Why don't you go to see him then?'

'But Roland wouldn't want to go.'

'Go yourself then.'

'Oh no! Not by myself, Roland wouldn't want me to. He likes to know where I am at all times.'

'It's up to you. He'll always be your son no matter what. If you want to see him just go one day while your husband's out at work.'

Betty rapidly changed the subject. 'How are you getting on with these two boys of yours? They are so much like your hubby. The older one even walks like him.'

'Well, they are his brother's boys so they have the same genes.'

'Yes, Graham told me what happened when I called round with the flowers when you were in hospital. It's not easy bring-ing up children. But it makes life worthwhile, doesn't it?'

'It's early days yet, I'm still getting used to it all.'

Betty stood up to go. 'Well, I mustn't keep you. The train set is complete and I hope they have as much pleasure in it as our Col had when he was a boy.'

'Will he mind? You giving it to the boys?'

'I don't expect he thinks we've still got it.'

'It's very kind of you to give it to us, thank you very much.'

'It's a pleasure. And do come round any time, Roland usually has his head in a book, he'll never notice you're there, but I'd be glad to see you.'

Myra stood in the sitting-room window watching her trotting back home. Poor old stick. Afraid of her own shadow. If she wanted to see her son why didn't she just go? She would. She'd been so used to laying down the law at home, and until his recent attempts at defiance, Graham had always bowed to her wishes. But she thought of how Betty had spoken about her husband, assuming his word was law, and how miserable it made her. Was that what she did to Graham? It made her seem like some kind of monster. Surely he'd always been happy to go along with her choices until now, hadn't he? And anyway, maybe Roland wasn't as bad as Betty made out. She'd only seen him when he worked in his garden or occasionally out at the local shops, but always without Betty. Perhaps if Betty saw him as others saw him, chatting with ladies in the precinct, sometimes surrounded by four or even five all laughing at his jokes, she might see a different aspect of her husband. He appeared a very sociable chap from what she saw. But perhaps he displayed a whole different side of his character at home. Just as she'd seen a different side to Graham the day of Piers' party. She thought about all those times since John had died when Graham had exerted his authority and gone completely against what she had planned. Which then was the real Graham? Did she want to know? Had she dominated him to the point of him having no personality beyond what she allowed him to have, no decison-making capacity, no independence of mind? Deep down somewhere buried very deep she acknowledged it wasn't right to stifle someone like she had done. It was only his kindness of heart that had stopped a rift developing that would have ended in divorce. Was that what she wanted?

Determined not to let her mind wander any farther down that

dangerous path, Myra turned away from the window, straightened her shoulders and dragged the ironing board out from the cupboard in the kitchen. How many shirts was it nowadays? Seven a week had suddenly turned into seventeen plus the boys' weekend T-shirts. She couldn't face it right now so instead she went to investigate the box Betty had brought.

The set was complete right down to little figures of men and women and children to stand on the platform as though waiting for a train. A signal box carefully wrapped in tissue, signals, lines, a bridge, trees and bushes, a waiting room and ticket office, even a man with a trolley loaded with suitcases. And beautifully detailed engines and little carriages. Everything was absolutely pristine as though it had never been out of the box, except for one man whose right leg had been snapped off. The money this must have cost when it was new, surely Betty and Roland should have some recompense for all this. As Myra began stowing it away again so the boys could open it for themselves and have all the pleasure of discovery, she thought about the memories there must be within it and how sad Betty was about never seeing her son. With the lid safely replaced Myra stood up and went to begin the ironing.

This state-of-the-art iron Graham had bought for her glided its way through the piles of ironing so quickly and so easily she felt really grateful to him for choosing it. Her old one he had consigned to the bin, saying it came from the dark ages, and when she protested he jammed the lid on tightly so she couldn't rescue it. He was right, but she hated losing an old friend. She didn't like trying new things and it had taken some persuasion for her to try the new iron and admit Graham was right – it made things much easier. She recalled Graham remembering the nightie she wore the night Piers came home from hospital. He was right about that nightie too, she'd worn it those early stolen nights together when they'd anticipated their marriage and she'd felt guilty about it all and yet exultant.

Exultant? Myra thought about that word and decided it was the right one for that particular feeling. Then the new shop in the High Street sprang to mind – the one that specialised in women's underwear and nightwear. When it first opened, she'd taken one look at the window display and decided it wasn't for her, it was for women in their teens and twenties. But she thought of that nightie again and realised even when she was young she'd never have dared wear something like those little wisps of silk and satin she'd seen in the window.

Then completely without warning she switched off the iron, stood it up on the kitchen worktop, dug her coat out from the hall cupboard, checked in her bag for her purse, picked up her keys and left.

Viv happened to see her leaving and noticed the determination in her stride.

No stoop, no plodding feet, she didn't even have her old shopping bag with her. She obviously had an unusual mission in mind and Viv longed to know what it was.

Secrets was the name of the shop and it was written in fancy handwriting above the window in shining chrome. The window was filled with daring underwear and nightwear; after one brief moment of hesitation she opened the door and marched in. The inside was even glossier than the outside and she was dazzled by the choice. A man emerged from the back. 'Good morning, madam, how may I help?'

'Do you have a lady assistant?'

'I do but she's just gone to the bank. Can I be of any assistance?'

'I see. Right. I want some pyjamas.'

'For yourself, madam?'

No doubt he'd taken one look at her, thought Myra, and clocked her dowdy coat and practical clothes and decided she was not his normal kind of customer.

'Well, yes.'

'Very well, madam. We have these satin ones here in some gorgeous jewel colours.'

As he reached up to bring her some to examine she said to her great surprise, 'No, I've changed my mind.'

The manager assumed she'd decided to leave so he was shocked by the unexpectedness of her reply.

'A nightgown, actually, with lace if you have it.'

'Do you have a particular colour in mind, madam?'

'Black.'

His smooth face almost broke into a grin but he kept it contained. He loved those moments when he helped people find their inner vixen. That was the joy of lingerie – you never knew what secrets people were hiding under their sensible clothes. So she wanted a black nightie. What was she up to? An unexpected lover? Or more likely a husband who needed sparking up a bit? Well, he'd the very thing.

'I have two or three for you to choose from.'

The first was very plain – more of a nightshirt in fact, with long sleeves and buttons right up to the neck. Gaining confidence, Myra rejected it and chose instead a comparatively flimsy one with black lace at the V-neck and at the hem, and low at the back and clinging.

When he told her the price she almost died from shock and it showed in her face. 'You see, madam, it's designer lingerie, so you pay for the exclusivity. Would madam care to try it on?'

Myra wished the floor would open up and she could disappear. Certainly not, especially with only a man in the shop. She held it up against herself and decided this was definitely the one. 'No, thank you, I'll take it. I shall be paying by card.' After all, in the last ten years she'd hadn't bought one new nightie so she wasn't going to feel guilty about the price.

The carrier he put it in shouted extravagance and it unnerved Myra. She'd be sure to meet someone she knew, you could guarantee it. If they commented on it she'd say it was a present for someone, she decided. But she didn't meet anyone she knew, and she sighed with relief as she pushed open their garden gate. Safely home and no one the wiser.

But she hadn't seen Viv shielded by her cherry tree picking up rubbish the bin men had spilt on her front path. She spotted the unmistakable magenta pink of Myra's carrier and hiding behind the tree she raised her clenched fists in the air and shouted 'Hallelujah!' to herself.

In the house Myra raced upstairs and put the nightgown right at the back of the drawer where she kept her miserly collection of pyjamas. Back downstairs she went, opened the back door, finding to her horror she'd never locked it before leaving the house, and went out to bring Little Pete in. He wasn't nearly so little as when she'd first brought him in to the kitchen but he was still as charming and cuddly as always. She cut half a carrot into little squares and gave him it in a little dish by the boiler where he loved to sit.

She couldn't stop thinking about the nightie stashed upstairs. She was being silly. No one knew, least of all Graham, whom she intended to surprise with it. But when? A nightie like that was an open invitation to ... *sex*. She said the word out loud hoping Little Pete wouldn't know what she meant. She laughed out loud at herself. The older she got the dafter she became. Honestly! She turned back to the ironing. Three shirts later she decided her new purchase would come out on display when she was good and ready and not before. Heaven alone knew when that would be. The question was, having rejected not just sex but any kind of intimacy so emphatically for so long, would she ever be ready? Did she want it? And for that matter, did Graham?

The doorbell rang. Standing there was Roland Bannister looking furious, his face dark red, his breath coming in great forceful gasps. 'Betty had no business to bring our Col's train set round for your boys. I'm sorry, very sorry, but I've come to take it back.'

'That's your prerogative. I had thought we should pay something for it, it must have cost a lot when it was new.'

Roland shook his head. 'It's not that, not the money. It's more that Col might very well need it sometime, when he has children of his own. He just needs to find the right girl.'

'Oh! I see.' Myra opened the door wider. 'Well, here it is just as Betty brought it. Do come in.'

Roland did and bent to pick it up from the floor. His temper and his big fat stomach almost did for him; he simply couldn't pick it up.

'Here, let me pick it up for you.' Myra handed it to him saying, 'If any time you decide to pass it on, Graham and I would be glad to pay you something for it. Mind how you go.' He trundled awkwardly down the front path in imminent danger of dropping the whole lot, but managed to get back home without Myra hearing an almighty crash. The poor man deluding himself about Col being in need of a wife.

'Well, really,' she said to Little Pete, 'did you ever?'

The day wore on with Myra having to find things to keep her occupied; she was delighted to be setting off to collect Piers from school and find out how he'd managed and even more delighted when Oliver got home. Then there was supper to supervise followed by the welcome sound of Graham letting himself in.

Oliver gasped, 'Uncle Graham!'

Piers said, 'Oh! I say!'

Myra said, 'Sit down, Graham, I'm just serving. Boys go wash your hands, please.'

She heard their laughter but took no notice because she'd just remembered the nightgown she'd bought and was blushing at the thought, never mind the deed.

As she was putting Graham's plate on the table she glanced up at him and almost dropped it.

Chapter 13

Sitting there in a sharp new suit – most definitely not the one he had left the house in that morning – and a crisp new open-necked shirt, Graham looked ten years younger. Or maybe it was his hair – or what was left of it. Where was the lock of hair that always fell across his forehead? His hair was short and spikey all over and looked shiny. The flecks of grey coming through at the temples looked distinguished, rather than ageing, as they had done as part of his old, shaggy hairdo. There was also something different about his face, it was brighter and younger-looking.

Oliver broke the silence. 'Uncle Graham, you've been in for a refit! Now you don't even look forty-three. He looks great, doesn't he, Myra?'

'He's like a new man,' said Piers. 'A new uncle. I can't believe it.'

It was the first time in years that Graham had been out and bought clothes that she hadn't first approved or insisted he needed. Had he taken leave of his senses?

'Well, what do you think, Myra?' Graham asked.

Myra dropped to her chair unable to comment. Oliver was right, he had been in for a refit. She swallowed hard and said in a soft voice, 'I'm amazed. Now, Piers, will you put our plates on the table for me?'

Graham, secretly amused by Myra's reaction said, 'Seeing as it's casserole let's have wine with it. That favourite red you like, Myra. You boys can have a drop too, watered down like they do for children in France.'

The wine went straight to Myra's head so she had to concentrate on her food otherwise she would miss her mouth and make a good stab at her cheek. He'd been out and modernised himself! What did it mean? In particular what did it mean for her? What made him do it? It wasn't because of her daring purchase, he didn't know about that. She determined to ask him tonight when the boys were in bed. Then a thought struck her – what if all this effort wasn't for her and the boys? What if her own secret attempt at a change of image had come too late? She shook her head – Graham would never dream of looking at another woman. Would he?

'Where did you go for your refit?' said Oliver.

'Not telling, Oliver.' Graham tapped the side of his nose with his forefinger.

'It wasn't that new place that's opened in Trinity Street, was it?'

Graham kind of half acknowledged it was.

Oliver pretended to wipe the sweat from his forehead. 'Whew! That place is *the* place to go. All the kids in school are talking about it. But it's seventy-five pounds for a haircut!'

Piers whistled loudly.

'All the girls at the office will be after you. Watch out, Myra!' Oliver said, not realising he was tapping into Myra's fears.

Myra gave Graham a speculative look from under her eyelashes and decided that perhaps the boys had a point. This was a new Graham, a Graham she hadn't seen in years, if ever. It looked like he'd even had a manicure too at this fancy barbers. She'd never had one in her life. Divorcees from all over town would be finding him attractive. It wouldn't do. Good old reliable Graham had taken a step out of his comfort zone and it was hard for her to stomach. The new nightie was a step in the right direction but nowhere near far enough. She had some catching up to do.

She ate the casserole which she'd been so looking forward

to without even tasting it, her mind was in such a whirl. The same with the fruits-of-the-forest sponge she'd made, even smothered in cream she couldn't take pleasure in it. Finally she asked Graham for more wine and he filled her glass nearly to the top. Her biggest mistake was drinking the whole lot inside five minutes. Accustomed as she was to being virtually teetotal the wine hit her square between the eyes.

Piers began to giggle when she tried to stand up and didn't.

Graham winked at Piers and went to put a firm grip on Myra's elbow and hoisted her to her feet. 'I'll be back to clear the kitchen, could the two of you make a start?'

Oliver sensed there was something going on he and Piers knew nothing about but he really rather approved of whatever it was. The two of them were becoming almost human.

Graham laid Myra on the sofa, with two cushions under her head, facing the TV despite the fact that she was dozing. She wouldn't be for long, she'd soon wake up. He looked down at her and considered the situation she'd found herself in. Her fuddy-duddy husband of fifteen years coming home transformed must have been quite a shock. He thought about the old pyjamas he'd dragged out from under the pillow the last time she drank too much and wondered if he should go out and buy something glamorous to set the ball rolling for her. For now, when the boys were safely in bed he'd give her the perfume he'd bought that afternoon, the one she used to wear that he knew and loved. That might well be the start of something bigger.

Oliver had just disappeared upstairs when Myra awoke. She'd a bad head but decided not to say a word about it. She swung her legs off the sofa, sat up, straightened her skirt, ran her fingers through her hair as if nothing had happened, and said, 'Tell me then.'

'Tell you? What?'

'The reason for the new clothes and the new hairstyle and the manicure and so on. All of a sudden, not a word to me about it.'

'If I'd told you, it wouldn't have been a surprise would it?'

'But *why*?'

'If you really want to know, it was because Oliver was amazed when I told him how old I was, he thought I was at least in my fifties. When I took a proper look at myself in the mirror that night I knew I looked a lot older than I needed to and so I did something about it.'

Myra didn't answer him for a few minutes. 'I know I'm old-fashioned, too. I've known for a while.'

'There's plenty of money in the bank, like I've always said. If you want to treat yourself, you know it's our money, not my money,' Graham said. 'Not that you have to change anything for my sake, I just think you might find you like it. And if you're anything like me, once you get started, you might do more than you planned. After all, what's the use in me working hard if we never spend anything. The latest bank statement came today, this is the balance in our savings account.'

He unfolded a sheet of paper and gave it to her. She almost trembled with shock.

'That much? I'd no idea. £167,500.'

'That doesn't include shares and bonds that we have. You can go mad if you like. It's not just because of my work that we've got that saved up – it's just as much down to you working so hard to look after our home all these years without ever spending a penny more than needed. You've always said no to holidays, moving house, new cars. You've been scrupulously careful with money so if you want to let loose occasionally, you should. You've earned it.'

She looked at him and liked what she saw. So where had he been all these years, this smart up-to-the-minute man she was married to? Maybe she would do what he said, not tomorrow necessarily but in her own time. No good being impulsive – her trip to *Secrets* today had shown she should probably think a bit more about what she really wanted before venturing out on a spending spree. Otherwise she'd end up repeating old habits – another bottle-green polo neck jumper or another grey striped suit she could have bought twenty years ago. What did women like her wear nowadays? But that wasn't right to say 'women like her' – she wanted to be new like Graham had become.

'Was all this really because of what Oliver said?'

Graham nodded. It wasn't quite the absolute truth because partly it was his desire to regain his respect for himself. Too long he'd allowed Myra to dominate him and he'd realised that for her sake as much as anything he had to take hold of his life and *exist*.

'And while we're talking about breaking our old habits, I've been thinking, this Christmas I thought we'd invite Mum to come here for the day. Not overnight, just the day itself. I can't stand another of those ghastly Christmas dinners at hers – half-cooked or burnt, take your choice, tiny portions more fit for a sparrow and that terrible Christmas pudding she makes which we have to pretend is wonderful. I bet they had nicer ones in the war.'

Myra was on red alert. 'Here? We never host Christmas.'

'But it will be different this year – this is the boys' home now. They'll want Christmas here and we can make it a special one for them. We could invite Mr and Mrs Stewart, too, because they'll have no one to invite with John not being around. Then they can all spend Christmas with their grandsons.'

Myra's heart began pounding. Sweat broke out on her forehead and in that moment she felt that death would be an easier option than facing Christmas with the Butlers and the Stewarts. If this was what happened when Graham found his voice, well it could stop right now.

'It's only six weeks to Christmas, there isn't time.'

'Myra! Of course there is. You've proved yourself in the catering department with that wonderful spread you did for Piers' birthday so ...'

'This is not the same.'

'Christmas Day is a Sunday this year so I shall be home all day Saturday to give a hand with all the preparations, and the boys will love not having to go to their Grandma Butler's, won't they? They can stay at home and play with their toys seeing as she won't let them take any toys with them to her house.'

She was about to put her foot down when she thought of Betty telling her how Roland controlled her life. Maybe she didn't always have to have the last word.

'The best I can say is I'll think about it.'

'Lovely! I know you'll come round to it.'

'I meant to tell you, Betty from next door came round with a train set that belonged to their son, Col. Said she wanted the boys to have it, I had a look at it and it was beautiful.'

'Really? Where is it? I always wanted a train set when I was small.'

'Believe it or not, Roland came round and took it back home.'

'Oh.'

'I suggested we paid something for it but he said no, Col might want it for his children.'

'And he took it back?'

'Yes, very angry he was.'

'We could buy one for the boys for Christmas, couldn't we?'

'If we wait long enough, Graham, the train set might well come back again,' Myra said. When Graham looked puzzled she filled him on what Betty had told her. Even if he had children one day, she said, Col certainly wasn't in the market for a wife. She even did an impression of Roland struggling to carry the box.

The two of them burst out laughing and once started they

couldn't stop. All kinds of ridiculous suggestions surfaced which made them laugh more than ever, including an idea that the track could go from their house to Roland's through the back garden fence so they could all have a turn with it.

Eventually Myra dried her eyes, saying, 'I shall have to stop laughing, I've got the most terrible stitch in my side. But yes to what you said before: it would be a good idea to buy one for Christmas. I'm sure they'd love it.'

Graham stood up, bent over Myra and kissed her cheek and this time she didn't shrink away from him. 'Hot chocolate, before we go to bed? Biscuit?'

Myra nodded. It was lovely to be waited on for once. She might even take quite a liking to this new Graham. They hadn't laughed like that for years and it felt good. But she wasn't sure she could stretch to playing hostess at Christmas, there was a limit to what she could put up with.

The telephone rang the following morning. She'd only just got back from seeing Piers to school. It was the secretary from Piers' school asking her to go to school fifteen minutes early this afternoon as the head teacher wished to see her.

'Is there a particular reason she wants to see me?'

'I'm afraid the matter is for the head teacher to discuss privately with you, Mrs Butler. We have a teacher ill today so the head is teaching all day so can't see you any sooner.'

'Oh, right. Should my husband come too?'

'No, that won't be necessary, unless he particularly wants to. Good morning, Mrs Butler, we'll see you later.'

Myra rang Graham immediately but his PA told her he'd gone out on business and wouldn't be back in the office until about four o'clock.

Myra returned the phone to its cradle and sat down to worry. What on earth had happened? What had he done? She couldn't wait all day to find out. But there was no alternative. Maybe the school had decided they couldn't cope any longer with him with his plaster on. That would be it! Well, if so she wouldn't mind, to have him at home meant at least she had company. Still, it would be a long hard day worrying about what she would be told.

'Come in, Mrs Butler. Thank you for being so prompt.'

Myra didn't tell her she'd been lurking behind some trees close to the school gates because she'd got there far too early in her anxiety to find out what had gone wrong.

'Now, do sit down. I do hope you haven't been worrying all day about this.'

'Of course not.'

'Good. First I need to ask you, did you know that Piers has not been doing his homework?'

'No. He said he hadn't been given any.'

'Well, he has and he hasn't done any of it since he started. Is there a reason for this that you can think of?'

Myra shook her head, appalled by her own lack of attention to Piers and his homework.

'We thought that maybe it was a kind of settling-in problem but it's not getting any better.'

'It's my fault, I thought he was speaking the truth. I never thought to question it.'

'Well, children in his year get on average a solid half an hour of homework every night. But the other thing I wanted to discuss is his behaviour, or rather misbehaviour. He was a model pupil before his accident and while he's been here with his arm in plaster he's been defiant, difficult, truculent and cheeky. Has he been like that at home?'

'No, he's quite the jolliest of boys at home, easy to get on with, you know. I'm appalled to hear he's been misbehaving.'

'Don't be, it could just be a phase.'

'Is he being bullied, do you think?'

'I don't think so. If anything, any bullying is being done by Piers.'

'Piers? Oh dear. We'd no idea.'

'Perhaps when he gets his plaster off he'll feel better.' The head teacher fiddled with a pen for a moment as though searching for the right words. 'I know he's new to the school, but we run a well-disciplined happy school here and I like to think there are few children who won't thrive in such circumstances. I know Piers came to us in the saddest of circumstances, but I would like to think school might be a place where he can get away from his grief. Do you mind if I ask how things are at home?'

Myra hadn't an answer to that and panicked. She was going to have to tell her the truth. Tell her that they were all still learning how to be a family.

'I don't know what to say. This is all new to us. We have no children of our own and it's been hard learning how to manage things. But we are doing our best. We've had rows, we've had mix-ups, we've had tears. But we've also had a lot of laughter, learnt a lot about each other and worked out that most things can be helped by tea and cake. I know Social Services will ask how things are going, and I don't want you to make anything up – but I'd like them to know we are trying our best, and I think it might be getting easier – for all of us.'

It was a big revealing speech for Myra and such a long out-burst of the unvarnished truth played havoc with her nerves. What surprised her was how lucid she'd been about the whole thing. No hiding in long silent gaps, but straight out with it no messing. She'd surprised herself, and she pulled at the fingers of her gloves while she waited for the head to respond. 'It's been a big change for the two of them.'

'And for you. Thank you for being so honest with me, it explains a lot. Can I recommend that you treat him with gentle-ness? We will make sure that happens here. He still has a lot of adjusting to do, and will need a great deal of understanding. I admire you for taking them on, it was a brave decision. It can't have been an easy one.'

Myra's head came up from the study of her gloves. 'I didn't know if I could cope. I really didn't. Didn't know how I could manage two boys. I still don't, but I am trying. But what else can you do? Put them in a home? Piers is terrified that will happen to him, he just can't believe he's safe where he is.'

The head teacher got to her feet. 'That's the bell, you'd better go to where you usually pick him up. Any time you need help, please feel free to come and see me. And thank you for being open with me. We'll solve it, you and I, between us.'

She followed Myra out in order to witness Piers greeting her. She watched as Myra pulled his scarf into order and checked he had his gloves on, then saw Piers show her a picture he'd done that day and watched the pleasure she showed when she looked at it. She was right, they were trying. Poor Piers though, he must have had some desolate moments.

Having been treated with such sympathy by the head, Myra's nerves had vanished by the time they got near home, and with it any anger she might have felt towards Piers for hiding his homework. Gentleness was the word the head teacher used. She tried to remember that.

'Now Piers, I had a word with one of your teachers today. She mentioned you were a bit behind on your homework. When we get home shall we sit down and get today's out of the way? I know that Oliver gets help because he asks for it from Graham, but you don't ask and perhaps you should. You can always ask me or Graham if you need help. What is it tonight?'

Piers hesitated momentarily – amazed Myra had found out his guilty secret and hadn't blown her top. 'A story,' he said in a quiet voice.

'About what? Anything in particular?'

'No.'

'Has it got a title?'

'No, we have to think of one.'

'Well, then perhaps I could help with that. I was hopeless at school and no one took any interest in my school work so I just gave up. Is that how you feel?'

'No. I just don't want to do it.'

'Can I ask why?'

'Don't know. Have you baked today?'

'No, but I soon can. We could make fairy cakes for after supper.'

'Right, in those paper case things?'

'Yes. That's what you could write about, if you'd like.'

'I'd like that. Then everyone at school will know how yummy your cakes are.'

Myra didn't really want to bake, but if it got him going then why not. Someone, somewhere had to make an effort and right now, it seemed it had to be her. Never in all her life had she put herself out so much for another human being. Any effort had always been for herself, but she had to admit she found the experience of not just caring about Piers and his problems, but actually doing something to help them made her feel lighter, somehow.

He set to with a will to start the baking and showed a real enthusiasm for doing his share, and when the fairy cakes went in the oven he even offered to help to wash up the mixing bowl. 'I could scrape that before we wash it up, can I?'

'Go on, it's best when you lick it off your finger like this.' Myra demonstrated and Piers followed suit.

As she watched him it occurred to her that perhaps he'd reached the age of ten years and never done it before, so she asked him and he said no he hadn't, and she felt desolate at the thought. All this because a cruel trick of fate had robbed him of his mother before he even had time to know her.

Myra reached out and squeezed his shoulder and turned away

before he saw her eyes full of tears. When eventually they'd cleared up and the fairy cakes were out of the oven, she said to Piers, 'I must start the supper, why don't you sit at the table in here and start that story homework, then if you get stuck I could help?'

Perhaps hers and Piers' happiest half an hour since they'd come to live with them followed. While she did the vegetables and got the chops in the oven Piers laboured away at his homework, occasionally asking for help with a spelling, and he wrote a whole page before he put down his pen. Myra didn't ask to read it, just hoped he'd offer, but he didn't. At one time she'd have insisted he showed her but with time she was becoming wiser and left it to him. She'd once read about people needing 'space' sometimes and this was the first time she realised what that phrase truly meant. She'd always thought it meant her old way of having as little to do with other people as possible, but now she saw it could mean just letting people do what they want – giving people room to be themselves, letting them come to you when they were ready. Maybe at last she was getting the hang of this parent business.

Graham had office work to concentrate on straight after supper with being out of the office most of the day, so she didn't trouble him with her interview with the head teacher. It could wait for another day – especially since for once, she felt she was handling it well. But he knocked on her bedroom door about half an hour after she went to bed.

'Oh good, you're still awake. Sorry I've not been much company for you this evening, has everything been all right today?'

Myra propped her pillows against the bedhead and sat up. 'Fine. Piers and I made those fairy cakes we had and he's written a story about it for his homework.'

'I thought he didn't get homework right now?'

'Well, he has been given it but he's not been doing it. The

head teacher asked to see me today and told me. So ... I had to tell her about ... things not being plain sailing at home. She's very sympathetic and admires me ... well, us ... for taking them on.'

Graham sat down on the bed and rubbed his eyes. 'I'm pleased you were open with her – most of the time people want to help rather than criticise, but I think we all forget that sometimes.'

'Well, we're still learning this parent business, aren't we? Both of us.'

Graham smiled at her and for a single moment their eyes met and neither of them dropped their glance. Graham bent forward to kiss her cheek.

'Thank you for everything you do, you've been an absolute stalwart and I know it's been hard for you, too,' said Myra.

'You're right, it has been hard and still is, but it's getting quite rewarding, isn't it?' Graham answered.

'I've an idea we're not out of the woods yet ...'

'But if we both try hard ...?'

A long silence followed. Myra wasn't sure what Graham was expecting her to say.

'It's late. I should get to bed,' Graham eventually said.

Myra agreed, although as he got up, she realised what it was she felt – rather than her usual sense of relief at the end of another day, tonight she felt disappointed at the thought of being left alone.

Myra had the sense of a moment slipping away from her. She acknowledged deep inside herself it would be nice if he'd stayed and slept in the other half of her bed. Indeed, it wasn't *her* bed, it used to be *theirs* – a fact she'd ignored for far too long. Just to touch him, properly, would be ... an excited shudder went through her body at the prospect of such close contact. She'd thought the other day that she wasn't ready to share a bed again, but now she realised she had to start somewhere. Knowing she was running the risk of being rejected, she held up the bedclothes so he could slide into bed with her. As he climbed in, Myra could feel herself tense up, making sure she kept her body away from touching his, but Graham seemed to know what a big step this was, and didn't expect anything of her, just lay on his side letting his breathing settle into a sleepy rhythm. As she watched her husband drift off, Myra felt herself relax. She even wished she was wearing that new nightie. Soon, she thought, soon she would.

Chapter 14

Next morning, almost as soon as she was back from the school run, the shout of 'Myra, it's me!' from the back door heralded the arrival of Viv. She came dashing in bursting for information. 'I saw Graham in town the other afternoon coming out of a shop, I scarcely recognised him. What's he been up to?'

Myra filled the kettle and with her back to Viv she said cautiously, 'He gave us all a surprise. The boys were very impressed.'

'Well, what has he had done?'

'New clothes, a hair cut, the works. Oliver said now he finally does look the age he should. Which, I must admit, is true.'

'You approve then?'

Myra leant against the sink and looked directly at Viv. 'Yes, I do.'

'Is he pleased with the result?'

'I do believe he is.'

The kettle boiled, she made the coffee for the two of them and handed a mug to Viv. 'I was very surprised, believe me.'

'Well, he certainly looked terrific. If I was twenty years younger, I'd quite fancy him myself.'

'Viv! Honestly! Though if you must know, Piers said all the ladies would be after him.'

'He's not wrong. I would have been in yesterday to catch up with you, but Sally and Bill are having money troubles and I had to go see them. Bill's been put on a four day week and it simply isn't enough money when they've two children to feed and clothe. I don't know, children seem to be so expensive to bring up nowadays, so demanding, I blame TV giving them all ideas. I gave them a bit of a helping hand but there's a limit for me as a widow.'

'Of course there is. Be careful, Viv, you could live another twenty-five, thirty-five years and you'll need your money.'

'You sound like the Grim Reaper, Myra! But enough of me. What I want to know is if you fancy trying some of what Graham's been up to?'

'Me?'

'Yes, why not, maybe he's telling you something. Maybe he'd like you to add a little sparkle like he's done. Come on, Myra, why ever not? Step right out of the box and do something spectacular so he gets a surprise when he comes home. Just like you had with him. What do you say? Haven't you thought about that?'

Myra denied any such thoughts, but Viv had caught a glint in her eye.

'I can tell you've been thinking about it. I mean, let's be honest, how long have you had this checked skirt and bottle-green polo neck? They don't even use that word now for green. Forest green, I reckon they'd call it. It's the perfect excuse for a spot of shopping. Like Piers said, they'll all be after him and he's quite a catch in those new clothes. But I think you could give any woman a run for their money – if you just gave yourself a chance.'

After last night when she'd had that unexpected feeling of wanting Graham to sleep beside her, Myra turned away blushing. She focussed instead on watching Little Pete scampering into his hutch out of the cold wind, just in case Viv read her mind.

'I don't mean you have to dress like a lady of the night or leap into bed with him tonight, you could just treat yourself a bit and see how it makes you feel.' She grinned wickedly at

Myra but Myra didn't see her because she was still looking out at the garden.

'Viv. Did you ever know Colin Bannister? From next door.'

'Of course. Nice chap. Always very friendly unlike his dad, who can be a pig if he chooses. He's had more than a few words with me about my boys playing football in the street when they were little. "How about them going to the park to play, there's plenty of space there." I used to tell him they were too young to be playing in a park on their own. You should have heard him going on about lazy mothers. He was a nasty old man even then. She's alright, Betty, I don't know how she puts up with him. He keeps control of all the shopping, all the housekeeping money, and I bet in thirty years I've only seen them out together about five times and that was on the way to their dentist for check-ups. Colin was a nice lad but I don't wonder he left home as soon as he could.'

'Apparently Roland has disowned him for being gay.'

'How do you know that?' Viv was clearly surprised that Myra knew any gossip that she didn't.

'Betty told me when she came round with a train set the other day. She said it was their Col's and he didn't want it and we could have it for Oliver and Piers. Half an hour later Roland came round and took it back home.'

Viv laughed so loudly and so delightedly at the thought of him coming round to take it back that Myra thought she might do herself an injury. Finally she drew breath and managed to say, 'Typical of him, absolutely typical. Oh dear! But be careful of him, Myra, he once was up in court for attacking a chap who cast aspersions on his virility, some road rage thing I think it was, but he got off on a technicality. It was so disappointing. All a long time before you moved in. Right, must go.'

She twinkled her fingers at Myra, dumped her mug in the sink and left, leaving behind her usual trail of destruction, but somehow today Myra didn't mind. She didn't even pause to wipe off the dried coffee rings on the table, but sat down to finish her coffee and thought about following Graham's lead.

Better not. He'd spent enough money for two; four fancy shirts, two very expensive suits, new socks and underpants, new pyjamas to say nothing of the trendy haircut. No, two of them spending money needlessly would be extravagance taken to the extreme. He did look younger though.

She went in the sitting room to look at their wedding photo in the silver frame her mother had bought for her, about the only decent gesture she'd ever made. In the light of the big bay window he did look quite stunning in that picture. She didn't look bad herself, she supposed. But that was then. She remembered that even on her wedding day she wished it had been John she was marrying. But Graham had to do, he enabled her to escape her barren, miserable existence with her mother. Myra had always felt her mother had never really wanted a child – and then when her father died young and left her with Myra to raise on her own, she'd just felt in the way. She'd never had enough money to break out and live away from home, bound in by a school with hopelessly low expectations, followed by a rotten job with low pay, sick to death of her mother's grumbling. Marrying Graham seemed like entering paradise even if he wasn't her real love. Even if it hadn't been a grand passion, they'd always got along. They had the prospect of children to look forward to, and before that she discovered that sex suited her very nicely, Graham was good at it and she got pregnant so easily she could have had a houseful of children, she thought. No problem.

That was when the tears began. They ran silently, steadily down her cheeks dripping on to her polo neck. Not tears of regret for the babies she never held, but regret that she was such a fool as to reject Graham. There was every chance she could have had all the babies in the world if she'd been prepared to try again but she'd deliberately turned her back on that glorious opportunity.

All these wasted bare years, locked away in her grief, shutting everyone out, excluding friendship, hating the human race, loathing physical contact with people, scornful of every decent motive, even barely tolerating Viv who was kindness itself and full of goodness towards her. Was Viv right? Was Graham more interesting to other women now? She had to admit he was. And he was working in an office full of smart well-groomed, good-looking up-to-the minute women who cared not one jot whether a man was married or not. Any man was fair game to some of them, she imagined.

Like that consultant had said to her, she had the children she wanted now, not in the way she would have liked, but she had got them. She rubbed her cheeks vigorously to dry the tears. For the first time in months she got out her make-up bag and stood in front of the hall mirror to apply it. She took one appraising look at her reflection in the hall mirror and seeing the improvement in her appearance gave her enough resolve to put her coat on and head out of the door with her handbag in less than five minutes of making her decision.

She went home in a taxi. It was half past five and soon time for Graham to be home. She'd rung Viv earlier and asked her to collect Piers and make sure Oliver went to her house when he got home from school. With an afternoon all to herself, she had done what she should have done years ago: thrust herself into the twenty-first century. She stacked all her purchases in her bedroom then rang Viv. The phone was still ringing when she heard Viv at the back door.

She burst into the kitchen and Myra knew instantly that something was terribly wrong. Viv looked distraught.

'Myra! It's Oliver! He hasn't come home.'

Myra's heart thudded. 'But is it his late night? No, it isn't, is it?'

'If he misses the school coach how does he get home?'

'He never has before now. Where's Piers, doesn't he know?'

'He's come over with me but he's absolutely terrified, and he's shut up like a clam.'

Myra went into the hall. 'Piers! Come here, please.'

There came the slow dragging of footsteps into the hall and there he stood, his face streaked with tears.

'Where is Oliver? Do you know?'

Piers shook his head.

'Has he said anything to you about staying at school for something special?'

Piers shook his head.

'Let's see. It's half past five so he's almost an hour late. The coach will have broken down, that'll be it. Or maybe there's a crash on the by-pass. We mustn't panic.'

But Myra was panicking. Before she could think what to do next Graham walked through the door and Myra expelled the breath she'd been holding. Graham would know what to do.

He was instantly on the telephone to the school and surprisingly someone answered his call. Myra stood behind him hands twisting and turning in her fright. She learned nothing from the one side of the conversation she could hear.

'Well?'

'As far as the school is concerned all the coaches are back at the garage, the last one has just reported in. Piers, did Oliver have money on him? His spending money for instance?'

Piers shrugged and looked anywhere but at Graham.

'You remember how I told you only a few weeks ago that I was adamant about speaking the truth. Telling fibs is not right whatever the circumstances and we need to have some idea of what might be in Oliver's mind. Now I'm going to ask you again. Do you know if Oliver had money on him? So he could get on public transport if he needed to?'

They could see from Piers' face that he was making up his mind. 'I promised I wouldn't tell.'

'Oliver's safety might be involved here.'

Piers studied the carpet closely. 'He ... we have money hidden away just in case.'

'Do you know where?'

Piers nodded.

'Show me.'

Piers reluctantly trailed upstairs, going more and more slowly
the nearer to the top he got. 'I'm not supposed to say, we
agreed.'

'Today you have to. For Oliver's sake.'

Piers pointed to the top shelf of the wardrobe. 'I haven't *told*
you, have I?'

Graham ignored him. He found the pair of socks, squeezed
them and heard the rustle of paper money. Inside was fifteen
pounds.

'How much did you expect I would find?'

'We had forty five pounds in there on Saturday. He'll kill me
if he thinks I've told.'

'He won't, because I shan't let him. So he actually has thirty
pounds on him.'

Piers looked thoroughly unhappy.

'So has he said to you where he's going? Delphine's? His
Grandma Stewart? Grandma Butler?'

'No.'

'Do you know *why* he's gone?'

'He said something about a school letter, and he was angry
and he wouldn't tell me more. He wanted me to go with him
but I daren't, but now I wish I had.' He looked pleadingly at
Myra and she put an arm round his shoulders.

'Never mind, Graham will sort it, you'll see.'

Viv was standing to one side almost writhing with the anxiety
of it all. 'It's most likely a storm in a teacup, you know, it can
happen.' She said this with far less confidence than she truly felt.

'He always comes straight home. Always. If there's something from the shops he needs he comes home first, leaves his schoolbag and tells me before he goes out again. Without fail.' Myra said.

Graham rubbed his face with both hands as though it helped to clear his head. 'We'll give him another half an hour and then I'll ring the police.'

'I'll go home. If you need me to have Piers I will, while you ... whatever. Shall I take him home anyway and give him his supper? I've enough for two.'

'Piers?' Graham looked at him.

'Yes.' He looked relieved to have somewhere to go to avoid any more of Graham and Myra's questions.

Piers was glad Orlando, Viv's friendly cat, rushed over to him as soon as he arrived. He played with a furry mouse on the end of a piece of elastic and a ping pong ball till the supper was ready, all the time worrying about Oliver. He so wished Oliver hadn't done what he said he would do.

Gobbling his supper down, comfortably seated in Viv's sitting room watching TV, with a tray on a little table in front of him he felt safe.

'Poor Oliver, I wonder what he's having for his supper?' Viv pondered between forkfuls of mashed potato.

'He'll be all right.'

'You sound very sure. Delphine will have a nice surprise, won't she?'

Piers didn't even answer.

'He hasn't gone there then?'

'No.'

'Grandma Stewart?'

'No.'

'Grandma Butler?'

'No.'

'You wouldn't say even if you knew he had, would you?'

'It's the brotherhood.'

184

'The brotherhood? What's that? The English Mafia?'

Piers laughed for the first time since he realised Oliver really had gone and done it, lived up to his threats, and by doing so, put everything at risk. 'No. It's our pact, the two Butler brothers' pact to be loyal.'

'Ah! Loyal to whom?'

'To each other of course.'

'Sometimes where safety is concerned ... for the other person's safety in the pact, you have to say what you know.'

Piers thought about this but decided to stay silent. She wasn't going to dig any of Oliver's plan out of him no matter what, even if she fell out with him forever.

They had ice cream to finish, strawberry with bits of real strawberry in it. He loved it. There'd be no more of this if Uncle Graham and Myra took a dislike to him over him keeping quiet about Oliver. He wished he'd agreed to go with him, but he couldn't go with him because of her cats and his asthma. He could just about cope with Orlando, but any more than that and he started to wheeze. Just thinking of it, he felt that familiar pressure in his chest, the mounting feeling of not being able to stop the panic. He felt in his pocket for his inhaler and it wasn't there. 'I'll have to go home ... it's my asthma.'

Viv, having no experience of it, immediately set off towards the door. 'Come on then, I'll see you over the road.'

Piers, torn between avoiding Myra and Uncle Graham and needing his inhaler, dragged along behind her. Viv took him in by the back door calling out, 'Piers needs his inhaler.'

Myra didn't think anything else could go wrong. Piers had only had one mild episode of his asthma since he'd come to live with them and it had frightened her to death. She was already scared beyond endurance and now this. 'It's on the end of your bed, it must have fallen out of your pocket before school.' She saw his chest noticably heaving and added, 'I'll get it, you sit down.'

She raced back downstairs and handed it to him. She put a cold wet piece of kitchen roll on his forehead and kept him still while he used the inhaler. Immediately his breathing began to flow more easily. Once his chest had stopped straining, Viv winked at Myra and nodded her head towards the hall.

Mystified, Myra followed her and shut the kitchen door behind her.

'Yes?'

'I'm sure he knows where Oliver has gone but he's determined not to let on. I've asked him and tried the usual possibilities, but he refused to answer. Something about being loyal to Oliver. The Brotherhood he called it.'

'I'll Brotherhood him. Just you wait and see.'

'Careful, Myra, remember his asthma. And it's terribly important to boys to be loyal, especially when they've only got each other.'

'If he knows, he should tell. I thought he and I were being honest with each other.'

Myra marched back towards the kitchen determined to get the truth out of Piers. Forgetting her new role of being an understanding parent, forgetting what the head teacher had said about gentleness, she stormed immediately into action.

'Now see here, young man, you know where Oliver has gone, don't you? I can see from your face you do, now tell me and Uncle Graham where he is.'

Piers' lips clamped together and he avoided her eyes.

'Right. In that case Uncle Graham will ring the police and *they* can ask you where he is. And believe me, they'll get it out of you.'

'Myra! Myra!'

'Don't Myra me, Graham. We've no alternative.'

Viv had never seen Myra so angry, she was alarming to an adult, never mind a boy of ten. The grim aspect of her face, the twisted lips reminded her of the old Myra before the boys came. 'Myra, you'll make things worse.'

'They couldn't be worse and I don't know what you're still doing here, just leave this to me and Graham.' Her temper was getting the better of her and she began to shake, from head to foot. When Viv stayed rooted to the spot she grew angrier still. 'Go on, get out and don't come here ever again. We can sort it ourselves, we don't need you or any other of our neighbours poking their noses in!'

Graham was speechless, he was already having the gravest difficulty in keeping control of himself and this was making it harder still. How could she speak like this to the only person in the road who bothered about her? He mouthed 'sorry' to Viv and nodded his head towards the back door. Viv left on the brink of tears.

Once she'd gone, Myra broke down. 'I can't bear it, not knowing. It's nothing we've done, is it? It isn't. I've tried so hard. I really have.'

Graham put a hand on her shoulder. 'Whatever it is, he must have a serious reason – he's not a fool. A letter from school you say, Piers?'

He got a nod in reply because Piers was using his inhaler again. When Piers had calmed down some more Graham said very, very gently, 'I think in the circumstances, Oliver is in need of help. Tell us where he's gone, that's if you know. We want him back home so we know he's safe, not to get him into trouble.'

'Cousin Susan's,' Piers spluttered, then burst into tears frightened by his disloyalty.

Graham was on the phone in a moment, but got no reply. 'Maybe she's bringing him home right now.'

'Have you got her mobile number?'

'No, I've never had a need to. I'll keep trying.'

It must have been the longest half an hour in the history of the world. The three of them sat in the kitchen not daring to catch anyone's eye, not wanting to speak, and unable to draw strength from each other because all three were so distraught. Finally, when the journey from Susan's to their house would easily have been accomplished, Graham spoke. 'We'll go to Susan's in the car. That's what we'll do. Perhaps her phone is out of order.'

'One of us will have to stay here in case someone brings him home.'

'Good thinking, Myra. Piers and I will go. Bring your inhaler Piers, just in case. I've got my mobile so if in the meantime he comes back home ring me, Myra. Don't bother about food for me, I don't feel like any.'

'Neither do I. Just go. Please.'

Myra paced the house from room to room, especially Oliver's, hoping against hope that something might occur to her and she'd realise why he'd gone. Even if he'd told Piers he was going to Susan's, they had no way of knowing if he'd made it there.

The silly boy. A letter from school! Had he done something very wrong, opened the letter and then not dared to let Graham know, neither what he'd done or the fact he'd opened a letter addressed to his uncle? Whatever it was, he couldn't possibly have done something so bad that they wouldn't want him any more. He was a very dear boy, she could admit to herself, and Graham said very gifted.

Finally, with no word from Graham for over an hour, she huddled in a chair in the sitting room wishing she could do something, anything to help. It must have been exhaustion or shock that caused her to eventually fall fast asleep, a deeper sleep than she ever had even at night in bed. So when the telephone rang she jerked awake and leapt to her feet all in the same moment.

The phone, where was the phone? If only Graham hadn't

bought this new cordless phone then at least she would have known where it was. Then she remembered it had been in her hand when she sat down. Here it was! Down the side of the chair cushion. 'Yes?'

'Susan's just got back from work.'

'And ...?'

'She's not seen him.'

'Oh God! No.'

'She stayed on late at the office, for a leaving party. So we don't know if he's been here or not. We're coming home, Piers is exhausted. We'd better keep the line clear in case Oliver rings and when I get back, if we haven't heard from him then I really will ring the police. Sit tight, Myra, we'll get things sorted somehow.'

'We're fast losing time when we should be acting.'

'I know. I know. We'll be about twenty minutes.'

Myra checked her watch, it was only seven o'clock. Seven o'clock? She thought it must be at least ten or even eleven. So they hadn't lost as much time as she thought. But where was Oliver? He must have been devastated when Susan didn't come home. Good thing Susan hadn't taken the boys on if this was what she did, out drinking on a work night. They were best where they were, with her and Graham.

She'd make a cup of tea in case Oliver came home and needed a hot drink. Or for Graham when he came back. The phone went again. It was Graham calling from outside the police station.

'Have you heard anything?'

'No. Not a word.'

'I'm going in then, they'll want to speak to Piers anyway so they can do that at the same time. Don't worry too much, Myra, it could all be something very simple that we haven't thought of. I'll be as quick as I can.'

A whole hour and a half later the two of them arrived home, by which time Myra was out of her mind.

'Well?'

'I've told them all I can. I happened to have those photos we took last time we went kite flying, they were still in the car, so I've left a good one of him and in the morning if there's no news they'll circulate it. They took it very calmly which was annoying. They didn't seem to realise that he is not a boy who normally goes exactly where he pleases without telling us. I think good parents must be thin on the ground.'

Piers had seated himself on a chair and looked completely drained.

'I think, Piers, a mug of hot chocolate would be a good idea, do you?'

He nodded.

'With a chocolate biscuit?'

Another nod.

'I'm asking you one more time, do you have even the smallest possible suspicion where else he might have gone?'

A shake of his head.

'Better have your hot chocolate and then be off to bed.' Graham sat back in the chair and almost overbalanced in it. He grabbed the edge of the table to save himself and was forced to laugh because he spotted a hint of a smile on Piers' face. 'We'll find him, son, he's a sensible chap, he won't have done anything completely silly. Did he tell you about the letter? What was in it?'

'Something to do with money and it wasn't him and he didn't want you to know.'

'I see. You drink up and then off to bed.'

Piers was too tired to cry but he wanted to. 'When he comes back, will we have to go?'

Myra swung round shouting vehemently, 'No, you will not have to go. This is where you live and where you're staying. Right?'

Piers, startled by her loud voice, knocked his mug over and the chocolate spread all across the table. This was the final straw.

He fled upstairs, his hysterical sobs ricocheting off the walls. Graham leapt up to go after him but Myra put a restraining hand on his arm. 'You drink your tea, and eat that ham roll I've just made for you. I'll see to him.'

Every shred of mothering instinct that Myra had came to the fore for the next half an hour. She didn't know she had it in her. He even allowed her to undress him and go with him to the bathroom for clean pyjamas. She reassured him time and again that he was safe where he was and finally she appeared to have convinced him. 'I shan't ask you again, this is the last time, do you really not know where he went?'

'He said he would go to Cousin Susan's and sleep in that box room. I didn't want to go. The cats and that, you know.'

'I'm glad you didn't go, you're a bit young for gallivanting. Now you try to sleep, Uncle Graham will sort it all out. He's clever is Uncle Graham, you see. Goodnight, Piers, thanks for being such a good boy.'

She stood at the door and switched off the light. 'Perhaps you'd like the night light on on the landing?'

'Yes, please. Sorry about the mess in the kitchen.'

'That's nothing, it won't take a minute to clear up.'

Myra sat on the top step worried sick. She'd put on a calm front for Piers' sake but under it all she was terrified something appalling would have happened to Oliver. She'd visions of his broken body being found in a ditch somewhere, of him drawing his last breath with no one to care. Of being caught up in one of those dreadful situations you saw on TV or read about in the papers; evil twisted minds that preyed on young children. She had to race for the lavatory where she fetched up nothing but bile as it was so long since she'd eaten. Her stomach in torment with fear she staggered down the stairs to Graham.

His hands were locked together resting on the table and she grabbed them with both her own. 'Graham, what are we going to *do*?'

'You're staying here and I'm going to visit the two late-night cafes I can think of. I'll take a photo, see if anyone recognises him or he might even be there when I go in. It's probably pointless I know but ...'

'Of course, if he has money he'll want to keep warm and get something to eat. If only Susan had just gone straight home from the office.'

'Well, she didn't, she wasn't to know, we can't blame her. I'm off. Don't put the bolts on the front door, will you, by mistake?' He released his hands and went without another word.

To the world Graham appeared worried but positive, however, inside himself he was sick beyond endurance. The ham roll Myra had made him he'd wrapped in a piece of kitchen roll and dumped in the bin, which fortunately was almost full so he could push it down where a casual observer wouldn't notice it. Just thinking of Oliver without support out in this cold dark night feeling abandoned and afraid crucified him.

Like in a film where the hero can always find a parking space right outside his target building, Graham pulled in outside the first of the cafes he intended to visit and sat for a moment thinking how he would approach this terrible situation.

The cafe was well lit with ranks of fluorescent tubes so every person sitting in there was visible. No dark corners for hiding one's identity should one wish to. Taking the plunge Graham whipped out of his car and into the cafe and went to the counter.

'Cup o' tea, mister? Full English? Coffee with hot milk? No?'

Graham showed him the photo. 'Has this boy been in here tonight?'

'Run away 'as 'e?'

'Something like that.'

'I've been here since tea, not seen him. There was a young lad in here but he had black hair in a pony tail so it wasn't him. Sorry.'

'Thanks for your help.'

He couldn't allow himself to be disappointed, common sense told him he wouldn't find him the first place he tried, but he was, nevertheless. He walked to the other late-night cafe round the corner, down the alley and across the road. This was pokier, less well lit and definitely scruffier. Surely to goodness he wasn't in here?

He was right. Oliver was nowhere to be seen, for which he was glad, as the clientele, sparse though it was, looked like the kind that would have no sympathy for a boy his age, rather the opposite. As a last resort he showed the photo of Oliver to the man behind the counter. 'No mate, not been in here, not tonight. Not ever.'

As he walked back he heard footsteps and swung about to see who was following him but whoever it was must have slipped into a doorway because there was no one visible. He checked he'd locked the car and went to walk along the river where once in the past he'd seen homeless people sleeping the night away. He slowed his pace as he passed but there was no heap of person on a seat that looked remotely like a boy of twelve with blond curly hair.

He walked round the town peering in shop doorways and down alleyways, anywhere that Oliver might have found refuge, but there was no sign of him. He could walk about all night and not find him, it was all futile, but at least he'd tried.

It was hours later when he finally came back home, having run out of places to try. He softly bolted the front door, went into the kitchen and drank a whole glass of water, thought about food but changed his mind, knowing he'd never keep it down; turned off the lights and went up to the bathroom. There was some comfort to be had going through his nightly routine but all of it was tainted by his crushing anxiety.

He didn't even switch his bedroom light on because Myra had switched on the night light on the landing for Piers who didn't like the dark.

He put on his new pyjamas and climbed into bed, exhausted. This was what worry did—

'No luck then?'

His scalp prickled with the shock. It was Myra in his bed.

'Myra?'

'Who did you expect? I couldn't bear to sleep on my own. Oh, Graham, what are we going to do?' She felt round for his hand and gripped it tightly. 'I'm at my wits end, what if he gets spirited away by ... well, you know, men with designs on young children. It's too terrible to contemplate. What if ... he's already ... dead? Tell me, what are we going to *do*?'

'We could talk all night and not find an answer. Come daylight we'll contact the police again. Maybe they'll have some idea where he is, they must have had countless boys who've done this before, he's not the first.'

'I don't suppose he is, but this one is *ours*, Graham.'

He knew better than to comment on her remark but in his heart a small part of him rejoiced, hardly daring to believe how much she had changed.

'Let's try to get some sleep shall we?'

'Sleep? I can't sleep. I shall stay awake all night in case the phone rings. Were the cafes busy?'

'Oh! Yes. Very busy. I never thought ...'

'What?'

'I should've left a phone number with the cafe people then they could have phoned me if he came in.'

'What time do they open in the morning?'

'The better one opens at six.'

'Set the alarm then and you could ring at six.'

'I will.'

'We shan't sleep, but just in case.'

'Right.' So he altered it to six instead of seven, turned on his side and found Myra had tucked in behind him. Was this the beginning of what had been? Turning to him in her desperate anxiety? If Oliver had disappeared six weeks ago she would have been glad and sent Piers after him. It had taken the two of them, Oliver and Piers, to bring out the love in her. They had succeeded where his meekness had miserably failed. He found her hand and tucked it under his arm and she snuggled closer.

They woke instantly at the sound of the doorbell ringing furiously. Graham snatched up his dressing gown and fled downstairs. Myra leaned over the banister hardly daring to listen.

Graham almost had heart failure because all he could see in the beam of the outside light were two police officers and no Oliver.

'Mr Butler! I can see you're worried, but don't be. We've found him, you'll be pleased to hear. He's sitting in the car scared to death about coming in. He wants to know if you still want him.'

'My God! Of course we do. Bring him in.'

'Oliver!' Myra shouted from upstairs. She ran to get her dressing gown and was down in the hall before Oliver got out of the police car. 'Oliver! Hurry up!'

He was enveloped in her arms and squeezed so hard he could scarcely breathe. 'Oh! Oliver I've been so worried, you foolish boy, it doesn't matter what's happened we just want you home.' She ran her fingers through his curls and kissed him hard, several times. 'Come in. You need a shower and a hot drink. Have you had anything to eat?'

Oliver nodded, speechless with exhaustion and worry. He couldn't believe the reception he'd got, fearing the anger and bitterness he always faced with Myra and here she was cuddling him. Better get her to let go or the police would be thinking he was a little kid. Which he wasn't, except right at this moment it felt good to have her cuddling and kissing him.

He could hear the police talking to Uncle Graham and guessed they were telling him how they found him. Sod that man behind the counter in that dirty cafe for phoning the police, the only reason he liked it was because it was warm and dark enough that he wouldn't be easily recognised. But the talk the police gave him had made him decide he'd never run away again, and that was for certain.

Showered and sitting downstairs in the kitchen in fresh pyjamas, eating a massive ham roll which he didn't want, and drinking Myra's speciality hot chocolate with plenty of sugar, he had to explain himself. Uncle Graham had asked him and he knew he needed to tell them everything for his own sake, too.

'The school trip to London, the one we all had to take £20 in for? The last day for the money was Friday. Everyone except one boy who'd been off ill had paid, but on Monday he brought his money and the history teacher, Mr Blacker, put the money in his desk till he had time to see to it. At lunchtime I realised I'd left a book behind and went back to the classroom to get it. That was all I did, picked up the textbook off the teacher's desk where he'd put it for safekeeping, and as I left the classroom the Hicks twins came in, I don't know what for because I didn't stay to find out. Next thing I hear, the money is missing from Mr Blacker's desk. The twins said they'd seen me in there near his desk when they went in to pick up a pile of exercise books for Mr Blacker. So he sent for me. The rest you know.'

'No, we don't. Piers said you'd been given a letter from school.'

'That was on Tuesday because they said they needed to investigate who'd taken the money, and wanted to talk to you.'

Myra gasped. 'But there could have been dozens of boys who'd gone in there. You weren't the only one to know it was there. Why pick on you?'

Oliver shrugged. 'I did not take the money. Honestly, Uncle Graham.'

'You know that, I know that and so does Myra, but why didn't you come home and give me the letter? Then I could have gone to school and sorted it out.'

Oliver didn't answer for a moment, because he didn't know

it. 'I panicked. Dad would have known I hadn't taken the money but you don't know me.'

'I see what you mean. You've heard me say about telling the truth whatever the consequences ...'

'I have but I didn't know if you would *know* I was telling the truth. So I went. I thought if I disappeared they couldn't accuse me of it. Which now I see is daft. I even saw you, looking for me and that only made me feel worse. But you know I didn't need the money because Piers and I had plenty with what we brought with us and the spending money you gave us. And I wouldn't steal, anyway.'

'I don't understand why you've been saving all your pocket money. You mustn't be cross with Piers, but he showed us where you've been keeping it.'

While frantically trying to think of a convincing reason, Oliver took a long drink of his hot chocolate. 'Don't know.'

Graham tapped the hand that held the mug. 'I think you do. I think it was your insurance in case things didn't work out here.'

Oliver's pale exhausted face flushed suddenly.

Myra realised that Graham was absolutely right and she felt ashamed of herself. Oliver's fear of the consequences of this false accusation was entirely down to her. She knew Piers was very anxious about living with her and Graham but she had never given a thought to Oliver feeling the same but not giving off signals like Piers had. Children, she saw now, had deeper worries than she had ever imagined.

'Can I be honest?' When Oliver nodded she carried on. 'I am ashamed to admit it but you know I had my doubts about taking on you two boys. Too much work, too much trouble, too disturbing to my routine and worst of all, I didn't know how to speak to boys. And I might not have learnt how to speak to boys properly yet – but I realise I was wrong about everything else. Honestly, I want you to stay with us, more than I can say. You really must believe that. Graham will get this school matter sorted and then we can begin to think about Christmas and your grandparents coming and presents and things. So don't you be concerned about anything, with Uncle Graham batting on your side nothing will go wrong, will it Graham?'

Graham, not quite himself after their traumatic night, wasn't up to the plate with his reactions. Could she really be saying those words out loud to Oliver? And could he possibly be this invincible person Myra was suggesting? Batting on the side of the boys ... and her? Well, if she believed in him, he'd better not let them down.

'Of course we'll sort it out. There isn't much left of the night but we'll sleep for a while and then we'll go to school in my car and get this whole matter settled. I could ask to keep you at home the rest of the day while they get to the bottom of it, or you could stay if you feel that's what you want to do.'

How clever of Graham to give Oliver options so he could decide for himself what was best, thought Myra. There was far more to Graham than she had imagined all these years. No, that wasn't accurate — there was far more to him than she would *permit* him to be. What on earth had been the matter with her? Why hadn't she realised sooner and asked for help? Instead she'd locked herself away with only tea cosies for company. Her skin prickled at her foolishness. A new idea had come into her mind the other day. She might not have had any creative spark for years — but she did have once, and it might just have been waiting for someone like Oliver to reignite it.

Chapter 15

Graham rang Myra from the office. 'I've been to school, Oliver wants to stay there for the day so you can expect him home at the usual time. The headmaster is investigating further, they're not accusing anyone of anything yet, just gathering facts and nothing more will be said to Oliver without my permission. I've given him my office number too.'

'Thank goodness.'

'Myra ...'

'Yes?'

'Have a nice day,' he finished off, rather lamely.

Myra sensed there was something else he'd wanted to say and replied with a warm tone in her voice, 'And you, Graham, and thanks for dealing with the school, that's the kind of support Oliver needs. See you later on.'

Having tidied the kitchen, put the first load of washing in and generally cleared up, Myra knew exactly where she was going next, somewhere she'd never been before despite the fact that Viv came across to their house so frequently.

She took in a deep breath and rang the doorbell. Viv opened it with difficulty, as hers was the kind of house where everyone, including the window cleaner and the milkman, always went to the back door.

'Yes?' said Viv, arms folded across her chest in a defensive attitude.

'I'm here to apologise most sincerely for speaking to you like

I did. There was no need for it, but I was so upset. The police brought him home during the night.'

Viv's warm heart responded to the apology immediately because she knew what it had cost Myra to say it.

She opened the door wider, saying, 'I'm so glad he's safe. Come in, all is forgiven. Tell me all about it.'

Myra was so pleased that when she stepped inside she surprised even herself and hugged Viv, twice for good measure. Myra was not normally a hugging sort person, not the slightest bit touchy-feely. But here she was trying new things every day, it seemed.

Viv's house wasn't as immaculate as her own, her furniture was battered but welcoming and her kitchen not even close to being as smart as hers, but for once it didn't bother Myra, she was just so glad to be back on friendly terms with Viv. They sat down at her tiny kitchen table and Viv put the kettle on.

'Well, go on then, tell me why and where.' She handed Myra her mug of coffee and sat down opposite her, eager to hear the story.

'So things are better over at number twelve then?' Viv said, choosing her words with the greatest care, when she was up to date.

'Better?'

'Yes.' Viv took a sip of her coffee. 'Well, you made no secret of the fact that you didn't want the boys at first. But now it seems ... different.'

Myra studied Viv's kitchen curtains intently and didn't speak for a minute or so. 'I've been the biggest fool.'

'You have?'

Myra nodded, she got up to look out at the back garden. Being winter there wasn't much life in it but it was well tended all the same, with a lot of promise of spring in its neat flower beds carefully raked and free of weeds, and the climbing plants pruned and slumbering until the warmth of the sun would wake them. It seemed to reflect Myra's mood. 'My life's like your garden; waiting to be enjoyed.'

Profound statements of this nature were not Myra's modus operandi at all, so Viv remained silent and let her carry on.

'I'm realising that though I missed my chance to have children myself, in a roundabout way I've got some and it's best if I get on with life and enjoy them. They've had enough grief in their short lives – why should they have to suffer mine as well? If they can be happy after all they've lost, I need to look at myself. I've missed so much all these years of being ... a misery.'

Viv daren't answer. She looked at Myra's back and waited still and silent.

'I was so devastated when I lost that second baby, when it was so close to life and yet so far. I couldn't imagine a future for me. It poisoned me, through and through. Last night thinking we'd lost Oliver ... I clung to Graham, relying on him to get Oliver back for us. Silly really when I haven't relied on Graham for anything emotional all these years since ... but last night I did. Last night I was *glad* to have him to hold on to. He's a pillar of strength in truth and I should have relied on him when we lost the baby, then things might have been diffferent.'

'It's difficult to be sensible when you're badly hurt.'

Myra turned back from the window and sat down again. 'My coffee's going cold.'

'I'll heat it up for you.'

While she waited Myra said, 'Thanks for sticking with me while I've been a misery.'

'I just felt you needed someone.'

'I did, but I didn't acknowledge it.'

'Well, you have now. Here you are.'

'Thanks.'

They sat in companionable silence until Myra said, 'How about lunch in town, just the two of us? Have you got time? Say no if you don't want to. Perhaps you're too busy?'

'I've always got time for enjoying myself. I'll need to get changed.'

'So will I and I must get another load of washing in too, I've a huge pile. Back here in an hour?'

'Let's go in the car in case we shop.'

'Right, you're on.'

And they laughed like two naughty children planning an exciting secret escapade.

Chapter 16

Myra hurried to get the evening meal in the oven. Dressed in some of the clothes she'd bought just before Oliver went missing, she felt like she was starting her new life, her new beginning. The red sweater she wore was brighter than anything she'd owned in years, and the straight navy skirt was stretchy and fitted, unlike the others she owned that could quite easily have hung in her mother's wardrobe rather than her own. Over the top she'd put on one of her old aprons so as not to drip anything on her new outfit. This was her first plunge into being a modern mother. Well, not exactly, she still had a long way to go. But to the world, to the people she saw in town, in the shops or the cafe where they ate, she now *looked* like a mother of two young sons, not a dowdy faded old misery-guts, beaten by life as she had been. She caught a glimpse of herself as she passed the hall mirror and paused to take stock.

It was a good start, but instantly she knew that the hairdressers was the next move. First thing tomorrow morning after she'd taken Piers to school, she wouldn't come straight home and tackle the ironing, she'd get her hair done. Myra turned sideways to examine her shoes. Ten years in flats and now she had her first pair of heels in a decade. Small enough to walk in easily, the heels did a lot towards making her legs look almost elegant. Tomorrow she'd go back to the same shoe shop, she thought and buy another pair – with heels perhaps a little higher than these navy ones. Black patent perhaps. Then she'd go back to the department store and choose another outfit for every day.

And perhaps even something to wear in case they went out in the evening. But before all that she couldn't wait for Graham to get home. Tonight it would be a small surprise, but tomorrow night a big one.

Piers hadn't seen her new skirt and sweater until she took off her coat when they got home. He was delighted. 'Oh Myra! You do look nice. You nearly match Uncle Graham now.'

Myra forgot herself and almost asked for more approval. 'Only nearly?'

'Yes. Because he had a fancy haircut to match his new clothes and that means you can have one, too. If you want to, of course.'

Myra knew he was right. 'I'll see to that tomorrow. It'll be a new Auntie Myra tomorrow night waiting outside school. You won't know me. I promise.' She heard Oliver opening the front door and put her finger to her lips and winked. She hadn't winked for years, consequently it was verging on grotesque, but Piers sensed she was trying hard and winked back without a comment.

Oliver had been equally as impressed as Piers and the two boys couldn't wait for Graham to get home. Graham walked in just as the casserole was placed on the kitchen table. Having missed lunch he was longing for food. The sight of his wife smiling, in a bright colour she'd not worn for years, and the two boys beaming with delight at his arrival, filled him with deep pleasure. This, he thought, is what coming home really means.

'My word! Myra, you look great!' Graham leaned towards her and kissed her with an enthusiasm that both the boys realised was different from before. This time they could sense he meant the kiss, he wasn't just being polite.

Myra blushed and waved the soup ladle in the air, saying, 'Beef casserole?'

Oliver managed to smother his grin and Piers remembered to keep quiet about the surprises Myra was organising for tomorrow.

But their joy did not last for very long. Something happened that night which threw the Butler world into chaos yet again.

The two boys were preparing to go to bed. Oliver wanted to watch a programme about rugby but Myra had said it was a school night and he needed to get his sleep so he agreed to get ready for bed with Piers and then go as soon as the programme finished.

Piers called out from the bathroom, 'There's someone crying outside! Uncle Graham, did you hear me? They're in the garden.'

Graham went outside to see for himself. Turning on the outside light, Graham peered into the shadows. Right there beside the greenhouse was a small dog. A black and tan terrier, laid on its side and obviously in pain. Tentatively, Graham extended a hand to him, thinking he might bite. He'd no experience with dogs whatsoever, never having been allowed to have one when he lived at home and Myra had always thought pets were unhygienic – until she met Little Pete.

The dog couldn't get to his feet, he tried but didn't succeed. 'Myra! Bring me a torch. Please.' He waited but Myra didn't come. He shouted louder. 'A torch, Myra, please!'

Eventually Myra came. When she shone the torch on the dog she said, 'Don't bring him in the house. I don't want it. If it's a stray it'll be riddled with fleas and worms and things. Don't let it in. Do you hear me?'

'But ...'

'I mean it. I don't like dogs.' She never had. All her life she never had and this one was not coming into the house. 'No buts about it.'

'Myra! The poor thing's in pain,' Graham protested.

All the changes wrought in her by the two boys had disappeared in a flash and the old Myra returned. Full strength. 'Leave it out here till tomorrow, perhaps then it will be dead – which would be a mercy, then you can bury it.'

She hadn't noticed the children had followed her out and Piers wept painful searing howls of despair at her words.

Oliver, close to tears himself, felt the agony of the little dog's pain. In a strangulated voice he whispered, 'He's only a baby. A little baby. Please, Myra. We can't leave him to die, not on our own doorstep. He's a puppy. He needs his mum.' Inside himself he knew how that felt. Oliver Butler needed his mum even if he'd no memories of her. 'Please, Myra. Please, let's take him in.'

Graham once again became the man of the moment. 'The vet's have an all-night clinic in case of emergencies, I know someone at work had to get them up in the night because their dog was terribly ill. They're just off the High Street. They've got the works, operating theatres and everything apparently. I'll ring them up and take him. Or her. I can't tell in the dark. Myra, can you bring an old blanket and that cardboard box the new microwave came in. Right now. Please.'

Myra didn't move an inch. The three men in her life waited for her to move. But she didn't. Oliver said, 'I know where the box is.'

Graham said softly to Myra, 'Right now, Myra, please. Please.'

'I'm not coming near it.'

'I know you're not, I'll pick him up if you can just get a blanket. Oliver, you and Piers stay close to him, talk softly to comfort him, keep him still. I'll phone the vet's and let them know we're coming.'

Myra scorned his suggestion. 'It's a waste of time. They won't be open for animals all night, Graham, they're not human beings, are they now?'

'I'm telling you they do. We can't leave him crying all night with the pain he's in.'

The puppy made absolutely sure they knew he was in pain because he howled as he struggled to get more comfortable. Piers shed even more tears if that was possible, murmuring,

'Please, Myra, I'll go and get the blanket. Where do you keep them?'

Though it choked her to say it, she admitted there was one in the top of the blanket box on the landing. 'The purple one, that's the tattiest.'

Piers had raced off inside the house almost before she'd finished speaking. Oliver found the cardboared box in the garage and rushed back as Piers came down with the purple blanket.

'Now,' said Graham using his you-can-rely-on-me voice, 'they perhaps won't be able to operate or whatever they want to do for him at this time of night, but one thing's for certain, they will give him pain relief and make him comfortable. So you boys must go to bed right now and get some sleep. Myra will stay here, won't you, and I'll let you both know everything that happens in the morning.'

Reluctantly Myra nodded her agreement and winced just as much as the boys did when the puppy howled as Graham gently lifted him into the box.

She made more hot chocolate for the boys and persuaded them they must sleep because the puppy was in the very best place he could be right now. 'Where better than a vet's for a sick dog?' she asked.

She went to bed angry and disappointed with herself. She'd thought that anger, that fear, had left her. But it turned out it was still there, waiting. How could she be such a crazy mixed-up person all wrapped into one? This new Myra with the two boys and Pete the rabbit and the new clothes was what people saw, but there right under the surface was the old Myra lying in wait. How could that be? She thought about all the ways in which she'd changed – and not just the big things, like how she felt about the boys and Graham, but the little things like hugging Viv or letting a rabbit play in the house. So why had this puppy somehow changed her back to the old Myra in an instant? Before she knew it, there was that fearful, isolated, withdrawn Myra in all her terrible self-righteous glory.

Unnerved by her outburst, she'd gone to bed in Graham's bed. Quite why she didn't know. She wanted to talk to him when he got back, but it was more than that. It was comforting. For herself, she didn't really want to know what had become of the puppy. But she was concerned for the boys' sake. They'd be upset when the vet's found out who it belonged to and with any luck, they'd return it directly and that would be it.

She'd just check to see if the boys had got to sleep yet. Myra crept into their bedroom. Piers was asleep, his face tear-stained but at least he slept. She bent over him and placed a very gentle kiss on his forehead, pulled the duvet closely round his neck and tucked one of his bare feet back under the bottom edge of the duvet too. Then she stood smiling at him. Remembering the happy time they'd spent together when he'd come home from school earlier in the day.

'I need tucking in too.'

Myra jumped with fright. Oh, it was Oliver. She hurriedly pulled herself together. 'I was just coming to do that very thing.' And she did. His duvet needed straightening, and in the half light she thought she'd give him a kiss too. On his forehead like with Piers, or was he too old for kisses? Then she recalled the night the police brought him home when he'd run away and how she'd hugged him, so she impulsively kissed his forehead.

'Goodnight, Oliver.'

'That little dog was desolate, wasn't it? It needs a good home like Piers and I have, doesn't it? Goodnight, Myra.' In the half light Myra couldn't see the slight smile on Oliver's face as he settled down to sleep.

An hour later she heard Graham turning his key in the front door. At last! In the time she'd spent thinking after kissing the two boys she'd decided that first of all they'd do their level best to find to whom the puppy belonged, because surely to good-ness the owners would be distraught. If he was truly homeless then she'd make sure the vet would find a deserving home for the poor thing. That was the kindest thing to do, because Myra Butler definitely did not want a dog. It was obvious Piers and Oliver were both taken with the little beggar. They didn't need to say a word. She just knew they wanted to keep him. She thought she was getting better at this motherhood business but to add in a dog, and a young one at that, would set her back to square one.

Graham got into bed, exhausted. He'd been right, they did have an all-night service and they'd treated that little scrap with such care, he was mightily impressed. If it had been his own grandmother being examined she couldn't have had better treatment. Under the bright lights at the vet's, it was obvious even to Graham that one of the puppy's back legs was strangely twisted into quite the wrong shape. They had decided to give an injection to relieve the pain but to leave X-rays until the morning to give the dog a chance to rest and recuperate.

Graham was taken aback by the close questioning he received as to how the puppy had ended up with such a damaged leg. Keen to make it clear he had nothing to do with the injury, he gave a detailed account of finding the dog.

'The first we knew about it was hearing it yelping and we found him in our back garden in this dreadful state. Our two boys were terribly concerned for him. I decided that because of his obvious pain I'd ring you. I'll call again in the morning about ten and ask what you've decided to do about him. Will that be OK?'

'We might need to ring you before then. Please leave us your mobile number. And your address and of course, your name.'

Finally he'd been allowed to leave. No doubt they wanted the name and address so they could bill him. They'd checked whether the puppy had a microchip and found he hadn't so the vet's wanted to know who would be paying before they'd proceed. Thinking of the boys waiting anxiously for news, Graham said he was more than willing to pay. Before he'd left Graham had gently stroked the puppy's head, but got no response as he was already under the influence of the injection they'd given him.

Lying in bed trying to get some sleep, he remembered how much he and his brother John had wanted a dog when they were boys, and how their longing had been scoffed at by their parents. 'Absolutely not. We are not having a dog. Blessed smelly nuisances they are, and the expense ...' That had been the end of their hopes.

Myra, the old Myra, certainly wouldn't have wanted a dog, but maybe the new Myra might be persuaded. He recalled how vulnerable the little dog had looked knocked out by the injection, how badly shaped its back leg was, it needed such a lot of care. His bedroom door quietly opened and there in the soft glow of the night light on the landing he saw it was Myra. He pretended to be asleep – he wasn't ready for a tirade about why they couldn't have a dog.

She brought a coldness to his bed that he had only just warmed but he didn't complain, aware that this newly revived habit of sharing a room was still delicate and strange to them both. 'Are you awake?' she asked.

Graham didn't reply.

'I thought you might be thinking about the dog.' Getting no reply from Graham, she carried on nevertheless as she desperately needed to hear how he stood on the question. 'I don't want him, you know. I really don't. The rabbit, yes I can cope with him because he's locked up most of the day but you can't do that to a dog. He'll need exercise and playing with like dogs do and I know I can't do that. Think of the mess, the mud, the hair. I honestly couldn't cope.' Graham still didn't respond; she shuffled nearer to him. Foremost in her mind was a picture that wouldn't go away: Graham tenderly lifting the little dog onto the blanket and wrapping him carefully to make sure he kept warm. 'Do you want him?'

Despite herself, Myra found herself beginning to relax into sleep. The heat of Graham's body was warming her up and it felt comforting and pleasant on this cold winter night. Almost asleep now and genuinely wanting to be close to him, Myra fell asleep with one arm around his waist.

Graham, silently enjoying the pressure of Myra's arm around his waist, lay there consumed by the sensation of togetherness. He'd longed for this closeness all the long, futile years of Myra's pain. He thought about the changes the boys had triggered in both of them. Perhaps having the little dog to care about might be the last piece in the puzzle. He didn't want to push Myra too far, but maybe she just needed some time to get used to the idea. And he knew how much it would mean to the boys. Oliver and Piers had got used to everyone tiptoeing around them, treating them as if they were damaged – it would do them the power of good to be the ones giving the care and helping the puppy heal. They all in their different ways needed big hugs and to give big hugs to others at this moment in time. Was a father hugging you the same as a mother hugging you? You could briefly turn into a small child when your mother hugged you, but if Dad hugged then you had to measure up to the man and be older and braver than you really were. Or maybe he'd got that wrong – he knew he was from a different generation – his parents had always been old-fashioned in their views, and he had never had the need to see what all of this 'modern dad' stuff meant that some of his work colleagues talked about. He was pretty sure Myra was as oblivious as he was to the mores of modern parenting. He fell asleep wondering what the two of them would say to each other when they woke in the morning. Would she be stuck being old Myra again, or would her anger have vanished with the night?

★

Being Saturday morning there was no need to scurry about getting organised for the office or for school for which Graham was grateful, but Myra was up and on the go long before he woke. Immediately he'd eaten breakfast he intended ringing the vet, to ask if the little chap had lasted the night. Little chap. He didn't even have a name and everyone deserved their own name. What were some of the names he and John had intended calling the puppy they longed for so desperately? Roscoe, after that lovely man who lived two doors down and was so kind to them. Beano, after the comic he and John enjoyed so much. Then he remembered the name John chose for the imaginary puppy the two used to pretend to own. Tyke. A good Yorkshire name. But he was getting ahead of himself – an owner might already have come forward.

He glanced at Myra as he took his place at the breakfast table, better get this over with before the boys woke up, he thought. 'We're paying for the medical attention that dog is getting for his leg, that's if they can do something for it. I thought you ought to know.'

Myra didn't even look at him when she answered. 'It won't be cheap. I wonder who owns him. They'll be worried to death, him being so young. Still, the vet might know who he belongs to, and if he doesn't he might know someone who would take him on.'

So that's the way the land lies, thought Graham while chewing on his Shredded Wheat, realising it tasted even more like old straw than it normally did. 'If he belongs to no one at all then we really should adopt him.'

Myra slapped her spoon down in her cereal bowl and splashed milk all over the tablecloth. 'There now, look what you've made me do. I do not want a dog. How many times have I to say it before it sinks in!'

'I heard the first time. You didn't want a rabbit. Remember? You wanted me to leave Little Pete behind and leave the door open so he would hop away. Now you're bringing him into the house all by yourself.'

Myra had to bite her tongue as Piers had just walked in the kitchen, his head full of names for the dog. 'I've been thinking. How about Ben for a name? Or Mack? Or better still we could call him Duke or something else very dignified, like Prince, couldn't we, Myra? Prince Butler. That sounds good.'

She swallowed hard. 'Don't think about him too much, Piers, he may belong to someone and they've probably spent all night worrying about him. We'd have to hand him back to them, wouldn't we?'

Piers fell apart but tried to be hopeful. 'Maybe. But ...'

Graham caught his eye and gave him a small shake of his head; it spoke volumes to Piers and he decided to leave the whole matter to the grown-ups. He felt he could rely on Uncle Graham.

'Just saying, if he doesn't have an owner, Oliver and I would love a puppy and I've found just the right place for his bed, where he'll feel safe and and not afraid the whole night long. You see, I think he's been hurt on purpose by somebody. That funny twisted leg, you know?'

Myra didn't even inquire how he'd come to that conclusion. She wasn't having him and Oliver trying to persuade her otherwise. She glanced at Graham and he looked back at her, an innocent look on his face, as though all he cared about was his breakfast cereal.

She buttered Piers' toast for him as otherwise, as the plaster came halfway down his hand, they would have the problem of getting it free of butter. He looked at her and those gentian blue eyes so like Mo's stole her heart. But, no, this time she wasn't giving in, not like with Little Pete, and she vigorously pushed away that soft bit of her heart that Piers could always reach.

'What are we all doing today?' asked Myra brightly.

Graham said, 'Well, what I shall be doing is going to the vet's to find out what plans they have for Tyke.'

Piers' face lit up. 'Tyke? You've given him a name? Oh Myra, I like that, don't you?' He paused. 'What does it mean, Graham?'

'Well, it doesn't mean he's ours because we don't know that yet but Tyke means a naughty, mischievous person that you can't help but smile at him, and I think that when he's fit and well he is mischievous.'

Myra steamed into action yet again. 'Did you not hear? I said no and no means no, it does not mean *perhaps.*'

She saw the light go out in Piers' eyes and they began to fill with tears.

'I know perhaps he truly belongs to someone, but if he doesn't what are we going to do?'

She comfortingly patted Piers' nearest hand, saying, 'Don't worry, someone is bound to want him ...'

At the thought of another family taking the puppy in, Piers leapt from his chair and shot out of the kitchen. They heard him clattering clumsily up the stairs and the bedroom door slammed shut.

Graham and Myra continued eating their breakfast in silence.

'There's no need to look like that,' Myra eventually said, all doleful. 'I told you I didn't want a dog but you didn't listen. Who is it who would be looking after the dog all day every day? Who will have to buy its food, wash the kitchen floor every day because of it running in and out of the garden? Walk it? Tell me. If you can't I can.' Her voice rose to a crescendo. 'Me!' She stood up, her chair fell over backwards with an enormous crash and she stormed out.

Graham drank the last of his tea, placed his cup quietly down in its saucer and put his head in his hands. It wasn't until Myra said that final word that he knew what he hadn't faced all night: he wanted that puppy with the same intensity as Piers and Oliver. Why? He knew not, but he did. For some reason he knew the puppy would bring all four of them together in a way that was not happening right now. *Beginning* to happen but not yet quite. It would give the boys a break from being the focus of everything. He could visualise him and the children striding over the hills, the wind blowing them along, Tyke rushing about loving the scents he picked up. He could buy a ball and throw it for Tyke to chase … He stopped himself. There was no point imagining all of this without checking to see how Tyke actually was, if an owner had been found. He'd go to the vet's right now to hear the latest on Tyke, how badly he'd been hurt, would the operation to straighten his hind leg work? He had a thousand questions and he didn't care what it cost to put Tyke in order.

'Oliver! Oliver! Come and get your breakfast. Now! That's an order. We need to get to the vet's to see Tyke! Hurry up.'

The urgency in Graham's voice drew Oliver out of his bed in a moment, but for Myra, lying on her bed, hands clenched, seething internally, his words sounded like a death knell. All the effort she'd put in to making things right for those two boys – and for Graham for that matter – was unravelling before her eyes. She'd just begun to discover she might be able to care for these boys in the way she deserved, it was as though the right words had been there all the time but she'd never realised and now that blasted dog was ruining everything. Graham didn't even trouble to knock on her bedroom door, he simply walked in and stood there looking at her. Sometimes on Saturdays she didn't get dressed until after breakfast, she was glad she was fully dressed this morning because she felt like she needed the armour. He was looking at her so, well, so intently. Not speaking. Just looking. For a split second she wondered if he had something else on his mind – the way his eyes bored into her reminded her of those early days – and nights. But he wouldn't be thinking anything like that, would he? Not with the boys around. She tried to dismiss her flight of fancy as he finally started to speak.

'You were asking what we were all doing with it being Saturday? After Oliver's had his breakfast, the boys and I are going to see the puppy. You are welcome to join us. I shall pay whatever has to be paid to get him well. I promised I would.'

The intensity of his gaze still alarmed Myra. She wished he wouldn't look at her like that, all kind of hot under the collar and determined. Even if now definitely wasn't the moment, she realised something had definitely reawoken in her. How could she let him know without actually saying it that she really wouldn't mind if he wanted her. After all these years? Did you have to *ask*?

Somehow, the heat of her hidden desire eclipsed all her anger about the puppy. Was she really going to destroy her second chance at love, at being a family by fighting about a dog? She shrugged her shoulders as though she'd no alternative but to give in.

As had happened several times these last few weeks since the boys came, she said words she had never intended and didn't even know were in her head. 'I'll come with you,' Myra blurted out. 'We'll go together, it's a family thing is buying … a dog.' There! It had happened again, as though inside herself there was another nicer person driving her on to do the right thing.

As she passed him on her way to her en suite to clean her teeth she almost kissed him on the mouth but decided against it at the last moment. Not yet, she thought. Not yet. But yes. Soon.

She was mightily impressed by the wonderfully clean antiseptic aroma in the vet's reception area. It gave her hope that there might actually be dogs and cats that didn't smell. Graham explained why they'd come.

'Oh! Yes. Mr …?'

'Butler.'

'That's right. Yes. We are going to operate on him this morning, he's being prepared right now. His right hind leg, isn't it?'

'To tell the truth I don't know if it's his right or his left.' Graham felt foolish. 'You can do something for him then? He'll be OK?'

'It's very complicated but yes, fingers crossed, Mr Bush is confident. I think the best is for you all to go home, or shopping or whatever and ring back in about three hours. He should be coming round by then. You boys don't worry, Mr Bush is an excellent surgeon, he'll put him right.'

Myra was standing behind the two boys keeping a low profile, she might have given in to the idea of visiting Tyke, but she still felt anxious at the prospect of owning him. Perhaps there was still a chance his real owner would be found. She clung on to this thought as she heard her voice asking when he'd be fit to go home.

'We'll keep him here for a day or two, I don't know how many as yet, we'll see how he recovers, then he'll be back home with you on a strict exercise regime.' She leaned over the counter and patted Myra's arm. 'Don't worry, we'll take good care of him. That's our speciality.'

She could only give the receptionist the briefest of smiles. 'You've still no idea who he belongs to then?' she heard herself ask.

'You mean he's not yours?'

Graham answered for her. 'No, we found him hurt and crying with pain in our garden. He's not ours, but we are concerned about him. And I've promised to pay for his operation if you don't find his owner. And yes, we would very much like to give him a home if he doesn't appear to have one.'

She checked her notes about him. 'Ah! Right, yes. I didn't know. It's very kind of you. I see from the file that the puppy is down to be included in our regular piece we have in the local paper – his owner might see that, if they want him back, that is. But like I said, ring in about three hours and we'll see how he is. But he definitely will not be going home today.' She hesitated and then added, 'Wherever that is.'

★

The Butler family went home. Oliver and Piers talked all the way back about how much they hoped no one would come to claim him.

Graham chanced his arm, finding the courage to say, 'I cannot say he's ours because we don't know for certain but if he *can* be ours would you like that idea?'

He was in truth only asking the boys, but Myra assumed she was included and didn't want to waste an opportunity to voice her concern. 'I'm still not sure. Not sure at all.'

'But,' said Piers, 'you love Pete.'

When she glanced at him she saw the light in Piers' eyes had dimmed.

They counted the hours. After two and three quarter hours Piers could stand it no longer.

'Uncle Graham, can we ring now?'

'No.'

'One more game of bumper cars and then we can, can't we, Graham?' Oliver suggested.

'Oliver, you and Piers have one more game and then we'll go. Coming, Myra?'

The two boys waited with bated breath, desperate for Myra to show willing about the dog.

Graham caught her eye and she saw the message in his eyes. But there was more than just asking about the dog in his eyes and foolishly she agreed she was going with them. She even got changed into one of her new outfits. The coat that looked as if she'd been issued with an army coat two sizes too large had been abandoned now, she was wearing a bright red warm jacket with slim trousers, new furry knee-high black boots and a big shiny handbag. There was scarcely anything in the handbag but that didn't matter – no one else used it except herself. It would fill up in time with her bits and pieces.

★

The practice was very quiet. In the reception there was one over-anxious lady with a yowling cat in a basket and that was all. The four of them sat down to wait. They waited until the boys' patience was almost at fever pitch.

'Uncle Graham!'

'Piers! It won't be long now. Honestly.'

Through the door came Mr Bush. 'Good morning, every-one. I'm pleased to say that your puppy has come through the operation very well indeed. It's been difficult putting it right but I do believe we've been successful. I've every hope that eventually he will be walking normally. He's not quite come round properly yet from the anaesthetic, but come in and see him.'

Myra said urgently, 'Gently, boys, don't alarm him.' Just as a mother should.

Tyke was in a cage wrapped in a special blanket to keep him warm and comfortable. His face was close to the wire and Piers couldn't resist poking a finger through and touching his nose. Tyke opened his eyes and looked to see who was there. The vet began talking to the boys about how they would need to treat him when they got him home, and Myra, following some instinct she didn't know she possessed, put a finger through the bars and tickled him under his chin. Tyke licked her hand three times, looked up at her and then closed his eyes in sleep again.

Emotionally, Myra was in pieces. She was glad she was used to hiding her feelings as it would be impossible to explain why she was so moved by such innocent friendship from a *dog*? This was ridiculous. Totally ridiculous! She was obviously going mad. There was no other explanation for it. Trying to act normal, she asked Mr Bush the same question she'd asked of the receptionist. Before anything else, they had to know if the vet's had found an owner for him.

'He's never been to this practice before, Mrs Butler, and as yet no one has inquired about him. It will be another few days before he will be well enough to go home, so if you are interested ... now's the time to say so.'

Graham intended to speak out on this subject but Myra very softly spoke up first. 'On the understanding there's no real owner for him wondering where on earth he is, we'd like to have him. He's healthy other than his twisted leg, is he?'

Piers and Oliver froze with shock. Graham opened his mouth to speak, but didn't say a word because he sensed more than any of them in that clinic that this was a critical moment for Myra.

'He's just what we need, the four of us,' Myra continued. 'How old do you think he is?'

'Difficult to say with me not seeing him in full health, I would think nowhere near fully grown, about four months old I should estimate, judging by his teeth, that's all. He seems to have been well cared for wherever he's been until this last injury. Although one of my nurses has suggested that his twisted leg could be due to cruelty by persons unknown. And that is a serious possibility. I can guarantee *nothing* about his personality if that is the case. But loving care can do miracles.'

Piers spoke up using an indignant tone of voice. 'We're not cruel, are we, Oliver? We'd love him. All of us.'

Mr Bush smiled. 'With parents like yours, I'm sure you wouldn't be. Think about it. I have another emergency operation to do right now, so I'll leave it to you. Come again tomorrow if you wish, he'll be more lively then.' Mr Bush shook hands with each of them in turn and left at speed.

Myra couldn't believe it. That other nicer Myra had done it again. Now, not only was she saddled with two boys and a rabbit, but now possibly a dog too. Tyke! She liked that name, she admitted to herself. Before Graham had turned the ignition key she said, 'So ... if no one claims him, Tyke is coming home to 12 Spring Gardens. Good thing we've got a big garden, isn't it boys?'

Both Oliver and Piers were speechless with excitement. They

dared not utter a single word at first, in case by mistake, they shattered their dreams. But Oliver remembered his manners. 'Thank you, Myra, for deciding about Tyke. Thank you very much.' He nudged Piers.

'And I want to say thank you too. I've got all my fingers and my toes crossed because I don't want anyone else to turn up. He's meant to be ours, I'm sure he is. Otherwise why would he turn up in our garden? He knew we'd help him.'

Graham, so filled with delight he was unable to find the right words to say, gripped Myra's knee for a moment. If Tyke was reunited with his owner then they'd have to buy another dog. Black and tan, as like Tyke as possible. They definitely would. He felt as though he was a young boy again, desperately longing for a puppy. A huge balloon of delight arose somewhere inside him and he wished they were collecting him right there and then. They passed a pet shop and he was in two minds whether to rush in and buy a bed and a bowl with 'dog' written on it. Perhaps not yet – he didn't want to tempt fate. But what else would Tyke need? Another bowl for his water. Toys! Yes, toys to play with. An identification disc, of course. He was so intent on thinking of what they needed to buy that he drove straight past Spring Gardens and it was Myra who brought him back down to earth.

'Graham! You've missed the turning!'

'My word! I have.' He pulled up and began to laugh. Oliver began laughing too and then Piers and then Myra. They sat there, all four of them laughing like lunatics.

Oliver complained of a stitch, Piers really didn't know what he was doing, laughing or crying, he didn't mind either. But what he did know was that just at this moment, they all belonged to each other. Normally wary of his Auntie Myra even at her happiest, because he knew if he got turned out one day it would be her who would do it, he glanced at her, but she was laughing too, helplessly roaring with laughter and it sounded to Piers that it was the nicest sound in all the world.

'It must be Tyke living up to his name, being mischievous even before he's ours!' chuckled Myra

It took a week before Mr Bush decided Tyke was fit to go to a home. It was surely the longest week ever. Graham wouldn't allow anyone to buy anything Tyke might need before they actually got the word that he was theirs.

Only Piers knew about the toy he'd secretly bought when Myra ran out of bread one day but the pudding she was tending in the oven was too critical for her to leave and go herself, so she had allowed him out on his own to buy a loaf. The bakers was just round the corner from Spring Gardens, flanked by a few other shops, one of which Piers knew had a small section for pets.

It was a miniature tennis ball that he couldn't resist. Bright yellow and bouncy. He could picture himself in the garden throwing it for Tyke and in his imagination he could see him chasing the ball and bringing it back to him time and time again. He went to sleep seeing him and woke up seeing him. He was so completely possessed by the whole idea of a puppy that he realised one day as he sat down for his evening meal that he hadn't grieved all day for his dad. Guilt flooded over him and before he knew it, he was crying. He couldn't explain because he felt so ashamed and so choked by his emotions.

Myra was putting out the plates, serving the food, calling for Oliver to come and wash his hands and welcoming Graham home all at the same time. Piers weeping was the very last straw. Stung by his distress, Myra quite simply did not know what to do except hug him as hard as she could.

Graham often missed out on lunch if work was hectic, and therefore came home in serious need of food. She normally prided herself on having it ready as he came through the door, but she couldn't serve Graham now she was hugging Piers. He was clinging to her and wouldn't let go. No one could eat because she hadn't served everything and the lamb chops would be burning to a crisp in the oven, the sliced green beans would be going cold now she'd strained them ...

So this was what happened when you had a family? Everything went pear-shaped all at the same critical moment.

But not everyone had a man called Graham Butler who would step into the breach and save the day. In a trice he had the chops out of the oven, the potatoes served and the green beans saved from going cold by being briskly served onto the hot plates. He even remembered the mint jelly.

'Now, Piers, stop crying, if you please. Myra wants to eat and so do I because apart from a ginger biscuit around eleven o'clock, I haven't eaten a thing since breakfast and I'm starving.' He picked up his knife, and pointing directly at Piers' dinner plate with it, instructed him to eat. 'Go on, pick up your knife and fork and begin. We'll talk after you've eaten. Whatever it is, you'll feel better after a good meal. You'd better get cracking, too, Oliver,' Graham added as Oliver dashed in.

'Sorry. I've been doing homework, I've got so much to do, I'll never get it all done tonight.'

'I'll have a look at it then when we've finished eating, I might be able to help. There's a limit to what they can expect you to do.'

Myra sank onto her chair and began to eat. This confident, decisive Graham was not only refreshing but surprising too. In a trice he'd restored calm. Even Piers' crying ceased, and Oliver was getting stuck into his food. And so was she. For years she'd only pecked at her food and here she was actually enjoying it. Really enjoying it. What had happened to her? And the pudding! She was looking forward to it so much. How long was it since they had trifle? Proper trifle: no jelly, just sponge spread with raspberry jam, sherry (just a small amount because of the boys) leaked carefully and evenly over the sponge, tinned peaches, custard, double cream beaten into thickness on top and then lastly cherries spaced out over the layer of cream. If taking care made it good, then this trifle should be extra special.

All four of them ate their trifle in greedy silence and when they'd finished, first the boys and then Graham acknowledged how wonderful it had tasted.

'It was gorgeous, Myra,' said Piers. 'Just gorgeous. Thank you very much.'

Graham said nothing but he did do a thumbs-up.

Oliver laughed. 'If my homework goes horribly wrong I shall blame it on the sherry in my Auntie Myra's trifle. Mr Cox will like that. He's a brilliant teacher, strict and clever but he does enjoy a joke.'

Graham asked what his subject was, aware he still had so much to learn about Oliver's teachers, and which subjects he thrived at and which he needed a little more help with.

'Physics. And even if you're not that way inclined he gets you interested.'

'Does the trifle bowl need scraping out?' asked Piers.

'I intended to finish it off tomorrow night. There's enough for all four of us for tomorrow.'

'OK. I can wait. Do puppies eat trifle?'

'Absolutely not,' Graham replied. 'They have a strict diet so as not to upset their tummies and no feeding them from the table. Right? That is a law that must not be broken. Four meals a day they have when they're growing fast.'

'Four meals a day? Four *proper* dinners a day?' Piers' eyes were enormous with the surprise he experienced. 'Did I get four meals a day when I was little, Myra?'

'At least, more like five or six.' She'd said it before she knew what she was saying. She wasn't his mother. How could she possibly know, she was only guessing really. What a fool she was – she felt the curious glances of the boys resting on her, and sensed even Graham had paused, mid-trifle, to see how she'd go on. 'All babies get that many, they grow so fast, it's to be expected.'

The moment passed. Oliver smiled at her, Graham's spoon scraped up the last of his trifle and Piers licked his spoon, saying as he put it down in his dish, 'You'll have to keep your eye on the clock, Myra, won't you? Four meals a day! I guess he'll do a lot of poo, won't he, Dad?'

Graham saw the shock-horror on Myra's face and the vision of a puppy quickly faded away. He couldn't, he wouldn't allow that to happen. Too much depended on this puppy to permit a small matter of dog poo to interfere. 'I think the gentlemen in this household would have to be responsible for that department. We'll take it in turns clearing up the lawn, it won't be too onerous and then as Tyke gets older he'll learn to always do it in the fields when he's out.'

Myra smiled one of her rare smiles at her husband's quick-thinking. Graham asked for another helping of trifle and got it.

Sensing an opportunity, Oliver also asked and so did Piers. So, as one helping was no good to man nor beast when there were four of you at the table, Myra ate the remains of the trifle and felt completely full. She said she wouldn't need to eat anything at all for at least a day, but was amazed to find herself munching a chocolate digestive along with her bedtime drink.

'Looking forward to it, Myra?' Graham asked.

There was only a moment's hesitation before Myra replied, 'Yes. I think I am.'

'I'm glad.'

'He licked my hand in the vet's – did you see? Three times. To a dog that's the human equivalent to three kisses, isn't it? Yes?' She almost begged for his reassurance.

'It is. Tyke, I think, will be very loving, and it's up to us to make the most of it.' He paused for a moment. 'The boys are thrilled, aren't they?'

'Absolutely. Both Oliver and Piers. You saw Piers' tears to-night, but I don't think we can expect his grieving for his dad to stop any time soon, can we? It just kind of comes over him, and he can't stop it. Tyke will be a great distraction for him.'

'And for Oliver, too.'

'Yes, and it's made you smile properly, as well. You haven't done that for a long time.'

Graham protested. 'I often smile.'

'Not a real smile, it's been forced and has been for a long time. I see that now.'

He sat looking at her, taking in what she'd said, finding it painful. Was this her being like she'd been for the last ten years – mean, withdrawn, unhappy, unkind? But no it wasn't, it dawned on him that she was being honest. And perhaps he hadn't realised how much of a front he'd been putting on, too. But if they were being truthful now, well, that was the first step to looking forward, being hopeful. In fact, as he looked at Myra now, she almost looked contented. Graham had forgotten what she'd looked like when she was happy.

'Time for bed.' He picked up her empty mug from the coffee table and she smiled at him, saying, 'I'm glad we're smiling properly now, that's so good for Piers and for Oliver, they need people who smile a lot, grieving as they are.'

'You're amazing, Myra. I know you've found it hard adapt-ing, and it's not been plain sailing, but even after everything you go and come out with some pearl of wisdom like that and I know you're going to be the best parent for those boys. I know you didn't want them, but what else could I do? Leave them with Delphine? I think not. And you're giving them something special – they're used to having their dad around, but they've never had a mum they can remember. I've said before we're not trying to replace their parents – and we'll always help them remember them and how special they were – but we get to be something new. We, the four of us, get to make up the rules about this patchwork family. Because that's what we are: a family. For life. And I reckon that is spectacular.' He paused for a moment and then added, 'For you, and for me. And for them.'

'It'll be a while yet before it feels normal. Perhaps never.'

'One day it'll happen all unawares. There will be a day when things don't feel new or different, when grief isn't the boys' first thought on waking, when you don't feel lost or I don't feel like I'm not doing as good as a job as my brother hoped. That day will come, just when we least expect it. Things like that take time, you know.'

'Well … I am trying, but I don't have much faith in it happening, I don't really feel like a mum. And I don't behave like one.'

'Yes, you do, Myra. Often. Piers didn't realise the significance of what he'd said when he asked you about how many meals he had as a small baby, but you managed it very well indeed, I felt proud.'

Suddenly Myra sensed a strange warmth flooding through her body. Was this how you felt as a mother? More likely she was kidding herself. She could never feel like a mother because she wasn't one. And never would be. But the warm feeling persisted all evening, and though it had gone by morning, she remained hopeful that there was a possibility it would return.

Chapter 17

'Now Myra, I've got the lead we bought, we've made up his bed, we've organised the food, the boys have got his toys wrapped up ready to give him, you've got the rug to wrap him in seeing as it's very cold today, all that's missing is the boys. Oliver! Piers! Come along – it's time!'

Piers stood at the top of the stairs looking down at the two of them. He was almost trembling with anticipation. Oliver was beaming. Piers opened his mouth to speak but couldn't, so left it to Oliver.'We're going then, it's true? We can collect him today?'

Myra answered him. 'Yes. We've rung again this morning to confirm it and we can go and collect him. He's ours. Graham's got his debit card out ready and we just have to sign a few papers then it's done.'

'I thought after yesterday when that man turned up saying Tyke was his, that was it. No Tyke.' Piers hastily brushed away a tear that he felt on his lashes. 'I'm so glad. I'll get his bag of toys out then, shall I?'

The four of them paused for a moment remembering about the shock they'd got yesterday. Mr Bush had agreed they'd go in about nine a.m. to pay for Tyke's treatment and collect him and then whilst they were at the clinic, agog with excitement, a man had appeared and said Tyke was definitely his. He'd seen his picture in the paper and was so glad he'd been found. Four months old, he said he was, and his name was Clarence.

'Come along, Clarence, there's a good boy,' he'd said in a

wheedling tone. 'Come, good boy. Come.' He'd reached out to take hold of Tyke's new collar and fasten on an old scruffy lead he'd brought with him, but Tyke wouldn't even look at him, he was shuddering from head to toe.

Graham had squatted down to bring himself on a level with Tyke and, clever dog that he was, Tyke retreated to the safety of Graham's arms as best he could with his bad leg.

'Come on, then,' the man had said again in his most persuasive voice. He'd clicked his tongue trying to entice Tyke, but that didn't work. He rooted in his trouser pocket and brought out a broken biscuit to tempt him with.

But Tyke refused to respond.

To the surprise of the three men in her life Myra spoke up. 'We offered a lot of money for Tyke's operation and the care he's had for almost a week here in the clinic. We have yet to pay that money over so perhaps you've arrived just in time. If you'd like to settle the bill, I'm sure Mr Bush will be happy to reunite you. That is, as long as you can convince him you had nothing to do with how his leg got hurt. We gave him our word that we would pay whatever it took to give him the chance of a normal life and a safe and happy home after if he was in need of one.' Something about the man's shifty look inspired Myra to make a challenging accusation. 'Do you know who damaged his leg? Is that it? What did they do, stamp on it? Or beat him with a stick till his leg broke? Whichever it was it was cruel beyond belief. So you can take your grubby lead and go home.'

The man ignored her and snarled at Graham. 'Can't you keep this woman of yours in order? The boss, is she? Accusing me of torture? You miserable old cow! Of course it wasn't me. As if I'm daft enough to stand here waiting to take him home when all the time it was me torturing him. I'm not a complete idiot.'

'No? But you do know who did it, don't you, and you're trying to shield them from getting into trouble.' Myra stepped startlingly quickly towards him, saying, 'Get out or I shall report this incident to the police and don't think I daren't. You will take Tyke over my dead body, and I mean that. I most certainly do. You deserve horse whipping for what you've allowed to happen to this innocent little dog.'

A spontaneous murmur of approval came from the assembled pet owners waiting their turns.

Myra went to the main door and opened it wide.

'Out! Right now! Go on! Out!'

The man couldn't scuttle out of the clinic fast enough. Oliver and Piers were so proud of Myra that their instinct was to give her a hug and a kiss for saving Tyke. But they changed their minds as everyone in the clinic was staring. 'I know where he lives. If you want that man's address, I can give it to yer. Don't know his name but I do know his house and I for one shall be delighted to tell you. It's time the police got on to him, he's a nasty piece of goods he is. His whole family, each and every one are cursed, believe me.' In one way or another everyone joined in the argument, when all the boys wanted was to go home and keep Tyke safe.

Graham asked Mr Bush if he could pay his dues, but the vet was shaking his head apologetically.

'I'm afraid we have to take all claims of ownership very seriously. As well as any allegations of abuse.' When Mr Bush saw how anxious the boys looked, he leaned in a little closer. 'But between you and me, this should just be a formality. Anyone can see the best home for this little chap is with you. Come back tomorrow morning and he'll be ready to go – for real this time.'

What a difference a day made. This time they had a joyful reunion with Tyke without a hitch. Myra took Tyke's lead out and fastened it to the new collar and identification disc they'd just put on him. She picked up the painkillers Tyke had been prescribed, handed them to Oliver for safe-keeping and, keen to be home before anyone else could interfere, she, accompanied by Piers and Oliver, proudly led Tyke out of the clinic, leaving the paperwork to Graham.

Tyke needed carrying, really, and Oliver reminded Myra what the vet had said so she gently picked him up and walked towards their car. She got in, holding Tyke firmly but gently on her knee, and bent over and kissed him on his forehead just as he decided to lick her hand. Tears filled her eyes but neither Oliver nor Piers dared comment. The change in their Auntie Myra was miraculous in their eyes. Just miraculous.

She cleared her throat and spoke so softly they could barely hear what she said. 'We are going to give Tyke all the love he deserves. That's what you do in a family.' She paused. 'I'm sorry that I was horrid, extremely horrid, when you first came. I'm ashamed of what I said and did. I don't think I really knew what a proper family was. On my school report I would have had written "Must try harder" and it would have been justified. Sorry.' She raised her eyes and looked at each of them in turn, intending to say more, but saw Graham striding across the car park towards the car; relieved, she said, 'Ah! Here's Uncle Graham.'

Myra was sitting in the back because of having Tyke on her knee, so Graham reached in and patted his head. 'Your name is Tyke. Remember that. You're part of the Butler family now.'

They drove home with every single one of them bursting with excitement. Oliver sitting in the front seat where Myra normally sat, wishing he was in the back and able to stroke Tyke, and Piers – to his delight – sitting next to Tyke and Myra. Piers was thrilled right from his toes all the way up to the top of his head and it was all he could do to control himself and not be continuously patting Tyke or squeezing his foot or stroking his ears, just to let him know that Piers Butler already loved him.

The first week of Tyke's sojourn in the house was the most exciting any of them could remember, and Tyke, the receiver of all their attention, lapped up every ounce of the loving care they gave him. He had a lot to learn, they realised, but so had they – like shutting doors carefully behind them so he didn't get out on the road. They borrowed a child safety gate from Viv so he couldn't try to climb the stairs and damage his bad leg, and they soon learned not to leave anything at all within his reach because he would chew it to bits. Drawers had to be closed firmly and any food put safely away, because as far as Tyke was concerned food, all food, was meant for him. The list was endless. But so too was the excitement of having a young dog, still a puppy, living with them.

Graham could feel the atmosphere in the house had changed almost overnight. Consumed by caring for Tyke, they had little time left to think of their own worries. Everyone had to make allowances for this energetic, happy, enthusiastic creature they had living in their space. His progress regarding his injured leg was excellent. He went from stumbling along, to walking crooked, to walking almost correctly in a matter of days, and before they knew it the time had come for a visit to Mr Bush to assess his progress.

Very soon, Mr Bush said, in fact next week, he could be taken off the lead and allowed five minutes of free running about in their garden, then back on the lead once more. It might seem they were being unfair to a young dog like Tyke, said Mr Bush, but he needed to take things steadily, too much exercise too soon would slow down his improvement. 'I know I must seem an old fuddy-duddy to you two boys, but believe me *excessive* exercise will not improve his walking one jot. You would not be doing him a kindness allowing him free running about, that leg was badly damaged and it needs time. But you are doing a good job with him and never fear, he will be walking normally very, very soon.' He patted Tyke's head and gave him a treat which Tyke, being Tyke, eagerly grabbed, chewed and swallowed in moments.

Chapter 18

It was one evening just as they were finishing eating a delicious pudding Myra had invented that she said, 'Do you remember the picture you did, Oliver, of the sea and the sailing boat and that wicked octopus and the cheeky mermaid? It set me thinking.'

They waited in complete silence while she scraped her dish totally clean and could speak without her mouth full of pudding.

'You remember I cut up all those dreadful tea cosies I used to make, every single blessed one of them and all the material waiting to be used?'

The three of them nodded somewhat hesitantly, wary of what she might be going to say and also because they knew how painful it had all been for her.

'I have to admit that for years I have had no new design ideas, but ... there's something exceptional about the expression in the octopus's eyes and that cheeky look the mermaid has, it's made me want to get sewing again. It's made me have new ideas – and that's all because of your genius, Oliver.'

Oliver's jaw dropped at such unprecedented praise from Myra.

'What is it you've been thinking about?' Graham asked.

'Something I could pour my heart into, but something I could also perhaps even sell, eventually – if people like them. Do you remember that quilt I made when we first married, Graham? All those different materials, all those patterns? Well, Oliver's collage reminded me of how much I used to love it. It made

234

me think that perhaps it was time to make another quilt. And this first one, to get me back in the habit, would be a special one – it would be a memory quilt. While you've been at school and work, I've not just been walking Tyke. I've been looking at all the bags we brought from your old house, boys. There are all sorts of things in there – old baby clothes, some of your dad's shirts, even a dress or two of your mum's. They're mostly too worn out to be reused as they are, but there's enough fabric to be made into a quilt – all your history, all the people that have loved you, we could even design it together.'

Everyone was quiet for a moment. 'It would be like having a hug from all those people,' said Piers. 'I'd love it.'

Ideas and questions tumbled from their mouths, in quick succession.

'I could help you choose colours,' said Oliver. 'Help cut the pieces out once we have a design ...'

'Someone at school brought in a teddy bear made from their old school uniform – we could make those, too, couldn't we?' Piers added excitedly.

'Or what about other cuddly animals, too – all made out of people's special old clothes and memories? We could give them really funny and cheeky expressions, too!' said Oliver, fired up with enthusiasm.

Myra stopped coming up with ideas and waited for their responses.

'We could even make one for Tyke!' This from Graham who was carried away with the idea.

Myra said to Oliver, 'We could share the money we make – and it would be money, that's if we did well at it, you could keep for university, let it pile up, you know. If it was successful.'

Oliver said nothing. His mind was racing around the idea so intensely he couldn't find time to say anything. Was this the answer for Myra? Was this the answer for him and Piers? Something to work on together – something to make a bit of money for the future – even thinking of that many years ahead felt amazing to him. Did this mean Piers and him definitely had a permanent home? He knew Graham and Myra *said* this was their permanent home, but he'd still feared they could be out in a flash until this last week or two. First Tyke joining the family and now thinking of the future in terms of years, not just days. Then his head spun back to thoughts of all the animals they could make, the designs they could do, and he was fascinated, completely grabbed by the prospect.

'It sounds like a very good idea. But where would we sell them?'

'To begin with I'd get a stall at this year's Christmas Fair again. I know I cancelled my stall but they've always had spare stalls. I'll ring her tonight.'

Oliver panicked. 'No! No! Let's sleep on it. It needs a lot of thinking about it. It would mean a lot of work between now and Christmas and don't forget you've got our grandparents coming.'

A mischievous smile flitted across Myra's face. 'I haven't invited them ... yet. I should have done but I haven't. So I won't. I know you boys weren't keen on having Granny Butler here and I know full well she'll be mightily relieved to be free of toys and mayhem and noise on Christmas Day. And Granny and Grandpa Stewart live so far away they'll probably be glad to avoid the travel. We could plan a trip to see them in the new year, instead perhaps?'

'Very well,' said Graham. 'It'll be just the four of us on Christmas Day. A real family Christmas. And that will leave you with more time to work on the memory quilt before the fair in December.'

'Myra! Shall I be able to help? I don't know what I could do. On the stall perhaps, taking the money?'

'You'll need to help, Piers, we couldn't manage without him, could we, Oliver? Especially if you're going to get money from it for your savings account. Now I'll clear the table and the kitchen, the two of you get stuck into making a list of animals. We'll need smart leaflets and logos too. It all helps to sell things does smart design, especially as we shall be taking orders for Christmas presents to start with. Or … maybe … I know! We should make one or two bears, as well the memory quilt, so that will give people more of an idea of what they're ordering. They'll see the quality and get an idea of all the different things they could send to us to include. We'll have to have a big think about it, won't we?'

The kitchen table didn't get cleared until half past eight and Piers was still coming up with ideas while he was under the shower. He stepped out twice to shout downstairs about a new idea he'd had and left a trail of decidedly wet footprints right across the bathroom floor. But back under the water, tears rolled down his cheeks. At least mixed with shower water no one would realise. Why he kept crying even in the middle of this wonderful time planning things for Myra he did not know and he called out to his dad, 'Dad! Stop making me cry. Just please stop me, Dad!'

Unbeknown to him Graham had come into the bathroom to hurry him up and help him get dried, and had overheard him begging his dad. Graham hastily vacated the bathroom, stood on the landing for a minute or two, and then re-entered noisily.

'Finished yet, Piers? Time you were in bed even if it is Sunday tomorrow.' Piers switched off the shower and Graham handed him his bath towel as Piers emerged from between the curtains. 'I'll go get your pyjamas, right? While you get dry. Cracking idea of Myra's, isn't it?'

When he was tucked up in bed, Graham smoothed his hair down gently. 'You mustn't be surprised if you still get sad about your dad. You know that, don't you? You're allowed to miss him – even when you're having fun with Tyke or thinking about Christmas with us. The people we've lost never really leave us – they're always in our thoughts.'

Piers was quiet for a moment. 'You knew my mum, didn't you, Graham?'

'Of course. She was a beautiful lady. Not just in how she looked because she was beautiful, but inside herself, a very lovely lady. I'm just sorry you were never able to know her. She would have been so proud of you.'

'Was my dad proud of me?'

Graham didn't hesitate for one single moment. 'My word, yes he was. People used to ask when your mum was waiting for you to arrive, "Do you hope it's a girl this time?" but your dad said "I'd like another boy, I'm sure that's what it is." And he was right.'

'Good. Thank you. Would you rather I was a girl? One of each, you know.'

'Not a bit of it. I wouldn't change anything about you or your brother for the world.'

'I forgot to say goodnight to Tyke, will you say it for me to him?'

'I shall be delighted to do that very thing. Goodnight, Piers.'

'Goodnight, Dad. See you in the morning.' He rolled over, closed his eyes and switched off before he began crying again and then remembered he'd said 'Goodnight, *Dad.*' To his Uncle Graham. And felt a fool. Best keep his eyes shut. Sometimes he did wonder about himself. About everything really. About growing up without his mum and now no dad. Would it make him peculiar? He was the only boy in his class with neither mother nor father. The only one. Two boys had no dad because they'd left their mums. One boy's dad had been killed in Afghanistan, so that made four of them without dads. But at least the other three had their mums. Maybe one day Graham and Myra might change into Dad and Mum, then he'd be like the others and could talk about *his* dad and *his* mum so when he moved to Oliver's school no one would know he was really an orphan. Ah! But then they would know Oliver had no mum and no dad, wouldn't they? He'd ask Oliver if he'd told anyone about them being orphans. Piers practised saying Mum, and Dad, and it felt funny. Mum was the hardest to say. He'd ask him right away because he could hear him coming up the stairs.

When he arrived in their bedroom Piers asked Oliver the big question. 'Oliver, at your school do they know you're an orphan like me?'

'Yes.'

'Everybody knows?'

'Well, at first it was just my friends, but I think it was bound to get out. I just assume everyone knows now.'

'Doesn't it make you feel weird?'

'Nothing they can say makes me feel any weirder than I do already after these last few months. And anyway, most people aren't mean about it, or even nice about it. They're just kind of awkward and don't know what to say. So most people just sort of ignore it.' Oliver got into bed.

'You haven't cleaned your teeth and you haven't washed your face.'

'So?'

'You should. Every night. Dad said.'

'Can't say it now, can he?'

Piers was silenced by Oliver's stone-cold cruelty.

'I know he can't, but you shouldn't not get washed and not clean your teeth.'

'It was him went and died, so what? I can do as I like now.'

'You can't. He still counts as our dad.'

Oliver thumped his pillow, saying, 'Not any more he isn't. Those days are gone. There's no one to tell us what to do. No one. *Absolutely no one.*' It sounded to Piers as though Oliver wished he did have someone who would tell him what to do.

'There's Uncle Graham.'

'Huh!'

'He is trying.'

'Very trying. I agree.'

'Oliver! I think it's wonderful Myra thinking up this idea all because of your art proejct. Aren't you pleased? I would be.'

'That's because you're only ten.'

'You were ten once.'

'Not now I'm not. I'm nearly thirteen and I can see why.'

'Why what?'

'Piers! Shut up. Just shut up. I've gone to sleep. Right?'

'You haven't, you're still speaking.'

Oliver beat Piers with his pillow as hard as he could, Piers objected and before they knew it they were fighting. Uncle Graham raced upstairs and switched on their bedroom light.

'That will do, boys. Thank you very much.'

'It's Oliver, Uncle Graham. Not me. He started it.'

Oliver protested. 'He won't shut up talking. It's driving me mad.'

Piers shuddered as that familiar fear rose up from his stomach. Here it came roaring up his oesophagus and a great fountain of his bedtime hot chocolate poured out of his mouth all over the duvet before he had time to get to the bathroom. He froze. Froze solid. That beautiful image he'd had earlier of them being secure here at 12 Spring Gardens had vanished.

He heard Auntie Myra arrive in their bedroom but couldn't look at her. She'd see the mess he'd made all over her bed linen and that would be that. In his mind, he faced the children's home as bravely as he could. But he wasn't brave, not at all. He was shaking with fear. There would be punishment, above and beyond, he knew it.

Uncle Graham took hold of him under his armpits and heaved him out of bed, and dragged off the disgusting mess that had been his duvet cover. Auntie Myra stripped his pyjamas off and quickly spirited a clean pair out of his pyjama drawer. She held on to him and calmed him down while Uncle Graham found a clean duvet cover and put it on. In what seemed like seconds

Piers was back in bed. OK, the pillow case didn't match the duvet but who cared, certainly not Piers.

Auntie Myra suggested that maybe the time had come for separate bedrooms. 'We'll discuss it in the morning over breakfast. Not now. Would you like that, Piers, your own bedroom? You have a think about it. Right?'

But he wasn't thinking about bedrooms. He needed an immediate answer about children's homes and such. 'You're not going to send me to a children's home then?'

'No. You have my absolute promise on that. You're staying here. This is *your* home. Now, Piers Butler, bed and sleep and no more fighting.' She kissed his cheek, gave him a hug, then another kiss, and tucked him into bed, saying again, 'No more fighting. Right?'

Oliver apologised too because he knew more than anyone how terrified Piers was about children's homes. Delphine used to threaten him with it whenever she felt like it, being well aware how frightened Piers was about the whole idea. Thank heavens they weren't with her any more. If his dad had ever known what a scary woman Delphine could be he would never have left them with her. When his dad was there Delphine was charming, thoughtful and very obviously a caring person but when he wasn't there – which was an awful lot of the time, especially in the school holidays – she was a shocker. Oliver never let on about her because what alternative did his father have? As the older brother, he shielded Piers as much as he could, but not always successfully.

When Oliver knew Piers had at last fallen asleep he crept out of the bedroom and down the stairs. The sitting-room door was not quite closed so he tapped on it and then walked in. Both Myra and Graham were reading and they looked up surprised.

'Sorry. I need to tell you something. It's about Piers.'

Graham closed his book, patted the space next to himself on the sofa and said, 'Sit down, Oliver, and say whatever you want to say here right now, don't keep anything back. Auntie Myra and me, we're both tough and if we need to know, just *say* it. If it helps.'

Oliver paused, wondering if he should go ahead.

'Yes?' prompted Myra. She closed her book and waited for him to speak.

'He's frightened about children's homes because when Dad was in hospital, Delphine used to threaten to send him to one if he didn't do exactly what she wanted. He dropped a jigsaw box once and all the pieces fell out on the carpet and she was furious, said that was it, she'd take him to one first thing the next morning, "and then you'll see who looks after you the best. Me. Delphine. I do, and this is how you repay me. You won't like it there. You won't even have a jigsaw to drop. Nor top-of-the-shop computer games like you have now. Oh no! Nothing, because they can't afford it."'

He got no immediate response from either Myra nor Graham so he decided to go back upstairs. He slowly began to turn to go but Myra stopped him.

'We'd no idea she did things like that. Poor Piers. I'm shocked. Thank heavens you've told us. Did she threaten you with it too?'

'Once or twice, but Piers was a better target because he took it so badly. She preferred the stick for me. Dad didn't realise what she was really like but he had no choice, had he? People willing to take on two boys don't come along often, Especially in the school holidays. All day, every day. Dad was glad she lived so close to us. And she always put on her best side whenever Dad was there.'

Finally Graham spoke. 'Thank you for telling us, Oliver. I appreciate you taking the time and explaining it so well. Myra and I will find the right moment and talk to Piers about it all and help him to rid himself of his demons. It was very wrong of her. He's lucky to have such a caring older brother, it makes me very proud to be related to you. Would you like to sit down with us for a while in case there's anything else you need to tell us that would help with Piers?'

Oliver, glad for their company, stayed where he was, wishing so hard it almost broke his heart, wishing his real dad was there and that they'd never met Delphine. 'The other thing is ... I don't know if I should say ...'

Myra claimed that if what he wanted to say was the truth then he'd every right to say it, here and now.

'I once saw her going through Mum's jewellery and putting something in her pocket from out of the box. Dad kept it hidden in his bedroom and showed it to me once. I nearly told Dad but I daren't because he'd have had to find someone else to care for us. Don't tell her I told you, will you?'

Graham, faced by yet another unpleasantry to do with Delphine, sighed loudly. In front of Oliver he did not say a word, but waited until the boy had returned to bed after they'd reassured him he'd done the right thing by telling them.

Myra was furious. 'How dare she, with her holier than thou attitude to us all.' But before she could continue, Tyke made his presence felt. 'Stop chewing my shoe, Tyke, if you please. Go away. You're Graham's dog too, so go chew his shoes.'

With no more ado, that was exactly what Tyke decided to do. It seemed a very attractive activity to a five-month-old puppy. Myra began to giggle, Graham to protest, and the two of them rolled about laughing so much they became helpless with laughter. Myra got up to rescue Graham from his torturer, tripped in the struggle to reach Tyke and at the same time stop him deciding to chew her shoes again, and between the two of them she fell on top of Graham, which made them laugh louder still. Their completely uncontrollable laughter delighted Tyke who was enjoying the trouble he was causing by clamping his teeth on their shoes time and again, harder and harder.

Oliver, halfway up the stairs, came back down again when he

heard the fuss. But as he got back down the laughter stopped. He opened the door and for the first time, witnessed a real kiss between two adults related to him.

And what a kiss! This must have been what it was like when his dad still had his mum, he thought. He would never understand why grown-ups behaved the way they did – he didn't know whether to be mortified or amused. Best just to be glad they were happy, he thought. He quietly shut the door and tiptoed back upstairs to bed.

Chapter 19

Graham and Myra spent what was left of the evening drinking gin and tonic. Not three, but four glasses each. Just as before, Graham had to carry Myra upstairs. But this time she didn't need help undressing, but she let him all the same. Tenderly he stripped her of her clothes and when he searched under the pillow for her pyjamas he found the black lacy clinging nightdress she'd bought. She smiled and slipped it on. But before she could appreciate the effect she was having on Graham, she'd fallen fast asleep. So Graham sat on the edge of her bed to admire her. Certainly the nightie was a wonderful choice and she looked heart-stoppingly wonderful wearing it. This was a completely different woman from the one he'd known for the last how many years?

Tomorrow, he promised himself he'd spend his lunch hour in that same shop buying her another nightgown for her birthday next week. Not a book token, nor two cinema tickets, nor a box of chocolates, nor new cushions for the sofa in the sitting room like in past years, nor a new kettle like last year, it would be one she would feel beautiful in and one he wanted to see her wearing. She turned over, opened her eyes and reached to kiss his lips. 'Oh, Graham!'

He bent his head and kissed her back but she'd already fallen asleep again. Maybe a bit less of the gin and more of the tonic next time and then perhaps ten years of ignoring each other's needs might at last come to an end. The way they'd kissed, and laughed and kissed some more this evening made him feel like they were newlyweds again. She wanted him, and he certainly needed her with a passion he scarcely recognised.

He'd choose turquoise tomorrow, he thought, as Myra slid silkily across towards him and sleepily placed her hand in his. His hands smoothed her nightgown over her body, down over her hips, not quite as bony as of yore, but now much more tempting, down her thighs, then both thighs in unison, and felt her wriggle with pleasure. This was a much more sensuous Myra than he remembered from before but then 'before' was a long time ago. Graham enticed her to respond to his caresses by slowing down the pace, and at the same time closing the space between the two of them, lying closer, closer still, increasing the tremor of his hands, breathing deeply in the hollow of her neck so his hot breath mingled with her warmth and his heart beat fast and then faster still. 'Myra. Myra. Myra.'

'Not so loud, Graham! Hush. The boys! ...'

'Oh, God. Yes!'

They broke apart, amazed as they were by their urgent desire for each other. It simply wasn't them. Not them at all. It was as if they were two completely different people, not safe old Graham and Myra any more. But who? Who were they? In that moment, it no longer mattered to either of them. What mattered was the depth of their enjoyment, their deep sensuous pleasure in each other, their rediscovery.

Chapter 20

Driving home from work the following evening, more eager to get home than he'd been in years, Graham looked forward to the new rituals of family life. Dinner and shared stories of their day, maybe some help with homework. Oliver always had something he needed to look at on the internet. He paused – and wondered why Piers didn't seem to want to be on his computer. In fact, it occurred to Graham that ever since Piers had lived in their house – what was, it three months now? – he'd never seen him using his computer. Now they each had their own bedrooms, where was Piers' computer? He remembered how thrilled John had been with the speed at which Piers absorbed knowledge about computers even as a young child. Piers was obviously a natural, John had admitted and it seemed odd that he hadn't asked for his computer to be set up. Was it still in the boxes in the garage? He'd ask as soon as he got home.

Piers froze in response to Graham's question. Oliver spoke up without being asked. 'He's gone off computers for the time being, thank you, Graham. He'll get round to it soon, I expect.' Oliver looked at Graham very directly with an expression that brooked no argument and Graham, becoming more of a real dad than he had ever hoped, took the hint.

After Piers had gone to bed, Oliver asked if he could broach the subject of Piers' computer.

'Dad always sat with him when he used his computer. He said it was because he didn't want him wasting his talent on silly games, but I think it was because he was proud of how good

Piers was. I think he was wrong about games anyway, I think you can learn a lot from messing about with games.' Oliver shrugged. 'But now Dad's not here he can't bear even having a go on mine. It was one of his special things with Dad and now it makes him cry, and he's tired of crying but he can't stop it. It just happens and he wishes it didn't.'

'I see. Well, I won't push it – and I certainly don't want Piers to think I'm trying to take his dad's spot at his side, but I'll have to make sure he knows that when he's ready, it can be his job to bring me and Myra up to speed on computers and the internet. But there's no rush. Time is a great healer. If you get a hint he's feeling better about it, let me know.'

Myra, overhearing this conversation while stacking a neat pile of freshly washed towels ready to go upstairs, decided that Oliver was the most grown-up, sensitive, thoroughly lovely boy she had ever come across. Then laughed at herself, for how many boys had she ever really known before Piers and Oliver came to live with them? None.

What a change they'd made for her and for Graham. The two of them were rapidly becoming more relaxed with each other and she could tell the boys sensed it, too. In fact, as she placed the last of the towels on the neatly stacked pile, she knew she was definitely a different person to who she was the day they arrived. More understanding, more willing to adapt, more—. Myra listened. Was that Piers crying again? Should she go upstairs and hug him?

No, she wouldn't go in straight away. It was something she was learning – when to swoop in and when to give him space. This time she would let him get it out of his system a little and then casually amble upstairs with the towels and have a word. On the way she caught a glimpse of herself in the mirror by the front door. Her new hairstyle, courtesy of an afternoon in the salon that day, really suited her. It was easier to keep looking smart compared to the overly long old-fashioned bun style she'd had for years. In fact she looked like someone who could buy clothes at the next New to You Sale the school was holding in the new year. She might very well go to that this time. Myra paused for a moment longer to admire her new warm silk shirt with the toning cashmere waistcoat she'd bought that morning.

'Yes. You do look good in that outfit.' Graham had sneaked up behind her. He had been so amazed at her new haircut when he'd got home, that he'd barely had a chance to appreciate the new clothes that skimmed her figure.

Myra blushed at the thought of being caught admiring herself. She turned round to answer Graham just as the doorbell rang furiously. Myra carried on upstairs and left Graham to open the door. She glanced down from the landing and saw Betty from next door standing there on the step. She stood there apparently speechless with shock. Myra looked again and did a double-take. Dear God! In Betty's hand was a carving knife copiously covered with blood. Not hers, though, one supposed. This did not look like a little accident carving the roast. Surely it wasn't Roland's blood? She hadn't killed him . . . had she?

'I've done it. I knew I would one day and I have. At last. Kept wanting to and now I have. Graham, will you ring the police?' She calmly asked him again when he didn't react. 'I'm not afraid. Prison will be paradise after the years of hatred I've tolerated from Roland and his temper.' Betty gestured with her hands to indicate she didn't want to use them, covered in blood as they were. 'He's dead. He can't beat me any more. Those days are gone for ever. Sorry for the mess, I'll stay outside. Myra won't want her carpet ruining, she's very houseproud, I know.'

Graham still hadn't done what she'd asked of him. Ordinary people like Graham Butler didn't do dramatic things like ring-ing the police and reporting a murder; a lost boy or a stray dog, but not *murder*. It felt like a long time before Myra came back down the stairs though it was only a handful of seconds. Graham kept his eyes fixed on her face as she came to stand by his side. He waited for her to collapse at his feet because that was what Myra did when things got too much for her: passed out and left it all to him.

But Myra's first words were for Betty. 'I didn't know he was hitting you. Hold tight to yourself, Betty, keep a clear head, the police will want to know how it all came about. Believe me, I've every sympathy with you, Betty. Living with abuse day in day out. If only we'd realised. Keep steady.'

The three of them stood silently for a moment, but when Myra became aware that Piers and Oliver had joined them she swung into action. 'Boys! In the sitting room please, this minute. Graham, will you sit with them please and close the door. Right now. If you please. I'll stay with Betty.'

Graham looked again at Myra. How she had changed. At one time she would have fainted at the sight of much less blood than this, it was easing its way over the threshold as it dripped from Betty's hands, and very soon it would be touching the pride of Myra's heart, her lavender hall carpet. He mustn't let it happen, he'd have to take action, else ... but it was Myra who stepped forward.

'I'll ring the police for you, Betty.'

The blood still dripped and puddled. The grandfather clock carried on ticking. Graham whisked the boys into the living room. Through the door, Myra could hear Piers using his inhaler and Oliver endeavouring to be the caring elder brother murmuring helpful words she couldn't quite make out. She brought her focus back to the doorstep. Betty was endlessly talking. But now there was a tremor in her voice as though the realisation of what she'd done was inevitably dawning.

'I always knew this would be the end of him, me polishing him off. Such a charmer he was, in his twenties. My mother told me not to marry him. She said "his eyes look cruel even when he smiles, don't be too eager, let him be the ship that passes in the night".' Betty looked directly at Myra. 'I'll bring the train set round tomorrow. It's still wrapped up like when you saw it last. Our Col would be glad for it to go to a good home. At least now I shall be able to see Col whenever I want to … '

Myra didn't think it wise to point out that it was unlikely Betty would be at liberty to drop the train set round tomorrow or see Col easily – unless she was thinking about visiting hours on remand.

'He won't be upset about Roland,' Betty continued. 'Roland made his life a misery. Hell on earth.' She bowed her head, the gory carving knife fell from her hand and lay on the doorstep of number 12 Spring Gardens, pointing ominously at Graham who had emerged again.

'Here's a chair …' Graham beckoned Betty inside.

'No, don't put it down in the blood.' Myra swiftly whisked the chair leg away from danger and went to pick up the phone.

Graham pulled himself together, and as Betty inched her way into their hall he took care to assist her balance by gripping the one blood-free wrist nearest to him. He looked at the doorstep making sure that the blood-covered knife wasn't visible for their boys to see at close range – no doubt one would be listening at the door and the other peering out of the window with ghoulish fascination. He didn't want his boys to see it. Not a blood-stained murderous weapon. Heavens above, they'd never forget. Graham grew in stature, feeling more a father with a protective role to play than he ever had. He must protect them from this harrowing sight. The poor woman had chosen the largest domestic carving knife he'd ever seen. She'd certainly meant to finish Roland off.

Then the whole atmosphere changed. She showed them the bruising on her leg where he'd trampled on her right calf so deeply there was the imprint of the pattern from the soles of his boots left behind on her flesh, vivid purple and blue stains on her skin. The man must have been a monster, thought Graham. No wonder she'd turned on him.

Graham looked into her eyes and saw steely hatred in them, sheer unadulterated scarifying emotion. Though he knew it wasn't aimed at him, he felt the portion of it that must group all men in with her tormentor. He couldn't believe this had been going on in Spring Gardens. All that ghastly hatred and cruelty behind the lovely arched windows and the elegant primrose-coloured front door of number 10.

In the street everyone heard the distant police siren advancing. But it won't be coming into Spring Gardens, they all said to each other. We don't see the police from one year to the next. Then they jerked with surprise as the two cars roared up the road. There was nothing untoward in Spring Gardens. Never. All the same, the two cars stopped outside number 10. Every single neighbour went outside to see and were horrified to watch Betty being led away by the police. Now if it had been Roland, that would have been conceivable, but Betty? Lovely kindly Betty? Instead, the onlookers and assorted faces hidden behind twitching curtains were surprised that old Roland wasn't out protesting about the officers arresting his Betty. When a bulky body, well-wrapped, was taken away from the house they were bewildered. He must have had a heart attack. Poor old chap. She will miss him. They were devoted, weren't they?

Only Graham and Myra knew the actual truth. Surely, thought Graham, it won't be prison for Betty? She had been driven to the worst possible act of desperation to finally get rid of her torturer. But there was no one to stand up in her defence, for no one had ever witnessed his cruelty, there had only been Betty present. What an unholy mess to be in. Standing there watching and waiting, Graham was stunned into silence. He watched Myra calmly telling one of the policemen what had happened. She looked so poised. She turned round to look for him and they drew strength from that glance at each other. Were they now drawing nearer to being a real married couple in the proper sense? Two real people working together instead of two half people staying as far apart as possible? He felt ashamed that he was asking this question of himself. A grown man asking questions of himself, analysing himself like a teenager would. If he'd been different, would he and Myra have avoided those long years of not being man and wife in the real sense of the word? He knew deep down how much he needed to be a whole person, he remembered the long forgotten urges, the passion, the excitement. Ever since the other night desire had crackled between them like electricity. Even now. This instant. This precise moment. As Myra finished talking to the policeman and came back in, their eyes met and Graham knew his hunger would be present in his eyes. She would know, she would recognise his desire. Her cheeks flushed. She knew all right! For one brief second their eyes met again and they felt to be the only people in the house and then the moment was broken by Piers calling out.

'Uncle Graham, is Roland actually dead now, do you think?'

'Yes, I suppose he is, Piers.' Graham felt embarrassed and ashamed that all he'd been thinking of was making love to his wife at a time when there were neighbours in such dire straits. But Graham realised he and Myra were one step nearer to each other despite his anguish about Roland and it all happening so close to hand. 'But don't let it worry you, Piers, the police are here sorting it all out.'

Oliver heard a different timbre in Graham's voice when he'd replied to Piers, one he hadn't heard before and grinned to himself. He wasn't entirely sure what it was he could hear that was different in Graham's voice but Oliver knew it was a change for the better.

Piers, meanwhile, was thinking how lucky he was he didn't have a dad like Roland. He then realised he was thinking about his own dad and not crying. He practised thinking about him again and this time decided that maybe he was growing up. He was ten, remember, he told himself. As he tried to think about

253

his dad more and more he found it was the first time he could think of his face and smile. All these last weeks without Dad the days had dragged along and now in an instant he felt the warmth of happy memories bubbling up inside him alongside the sad thoughts. In his mind, he saw his dad sitting alongside him, both of them hunched over his computer. Yes, his wonderful state-of-the-art computer that he'd loved from the very first time he saw it, but had left untouched since coming to live here, even though Graham had quietly moved the box into his room the other day without saying anything. Maybe it was time to get it out and have a play with it. His dad would want him to, wouldn't he? He pictured his Uncle Graham helping him with the computer instead of his dad. How alike they were. Perhaps ... perhaps ... he could make do with his Uncle Graham. He was sure his dad wouldn't mind, seeing as they were brothers.

Graham and John. Oliver and Piers. Brothers were pretty amazing, he thought. Brothers were loyal and proud of each other's achievements. He dashed away a tear that had sneaked down his cheek, took a deep breath and decided he must allow his life to speed along and be splendid and interesting as it was before, and that Auntie Myra and Uncle Graham would be the next best thing to parents to have with him along the way. First thing: unpack my computer, he thought, no time to waste. He'd begin tonight to help shut out that terrible image of the bloodied knife. Piers gulped at the memory of it but then took hold on life again with enthusiasm. He decided that before he actually began getting familiar with his keyboard again he'd just have a word with Tyke. The two of them rolled about on the hall floor, went in the kitchen and found Tyke's ball quite by chance and played with that until they were both exhausted.

Thinking of his computer again, Piers headed upstairs. He quickly grew so involved with his computer that he didn't notice that Uncle Graham had been observing him for quite a few minutes, until his uncle coughed unintentionally and broke his concentration.

'Hello, Uncle Graham. Just thought I'd have a go. Would you like to look at it?' Piers glowed with pride.

Graham admired it with tremendous enthusiasm and after a moment, asked if he could have a go?

Piers was delighted. So for a whole hour the two of them wallowed together in this miracle of modern technology, although it took only moments for Graham to realise that his brother John had been right about Piers' talent with computers. He showed him games he'd designed, told him what coding was and how to use it and even told him how to be safe online.

'Aren't I meant to be the one telling you that?' Graham chuckled. 'Anyway, that's enough for now, Piers. It's late and time to relax ready for bed.'

Piers objected. 'But I am relaxing, my computer always makes me relax. A bit longer please. Please.' Piers' splendid bright blue eyes won the day.

Graham, who was in truth enjoying himself immensely, agreed he could have another ten minutes.

After Piers was finally in bed, Graham told Myra about his amazing talent. It was a relief to have something else to talk about rather than the blood and drama of earlier.

'He takes after John undoubtedly, you know, even at this age! It's amazing.'

'Both you and John were always computer-savvy. Graham, you're a genius with all the computers and systems at work, remember that too.' She said this so wholeheartedly that Graham was almost embarrassed. Never free with her praise to anyone, child or adult, Graham was surprised to find himself on the receiving end of her admiration. He looked her full in the face and found admiration in her eyes that matched his own. For one brilliantly scary moment they looked into each other's faces in a way they hadn't looked at each other for years.

Embarrassed, the two of them withdrew their gaze and then returned it, finding themelves greedy for more. Myra reached out to touch Graham's cheek with gentle fingers, caressing first his right cheek then his left cheek with a tenderness she'd never found before, not even in the heyday of their passion. In one shattering second they were clinging to each other, breaking apart only when Oliver came to speak to Myra about coming home late from school the next day because of an unexpected football match.

Oliver didn't choose to look directly at either Graham or Myra because of the flush of bright red on her cheeks and the hungry look on Graham's face. Blimey, Oliver thought, is it romance in the air? At their age! Then he remembered Graham's makeover the other night and the fact that neither of them were as old as he'd originally thought. He felt acutely embarrassed but at the same time a sense of optimism went through him from head to toe. At least perhaps it might make them more ... well, more relaxed perhaps, more normal. He left them to it, and once he was out of earshot, chuckled to himself. But a glimpse of the blue lights still visible between the gap in the curtains reminded him of the cruelty that had played out next door. He was mystified at the way adults could treat each other. He thought of the obvious frostiness between Graham and Myra when they'd first got here. But he had to admit though, Myra was much kinder and more open than she had been. Maybe she had changed. She showed real sympathy for that Betty, and as for Tyke ... he'd seen her holding him close, rubbing her face against his forehead or tickling his tummy when she thought no one was watching. Tyke had taken a shine to Myra, that much was clear, and dogs instinctively knew about things like that, so if Tyke loved Myra then Myra was all right for him and Piers to love. She still needed a few corners to be rubbed off, but – Oliver heard Graham laughing in a carefree way he hadn't laughed before – maybe it wouldn't be far off. Perhaps he and Piers should try to show more appreciation to them both, after all there was no law that said they *must* take two orphan boys on board, was there? It must have been hard for them. Yes, there had to be a plan for him and Piers to show how much they appreciated being taken care of. Since the debacle with the card and the collage, the boys had felt awkward about showing their gratitude. That time when he'd seen Iain, that boy from school who'd been taken into care and looked so wounded that he, Oliver Butler, hadn't been able to acknowledge him, he knew now he should have spoken to him. That boy needed friendship like a drowning man a lifebelt. Next time he saw him in town he definitely would speak to him and perhaps find out where he was living and invite him home, here for tea. Somehow for Oliver the ground rules felt to have changed. All right, his Uncle Graham was a funny old stick compared to his own dad but it was him who'd taken them into his house and was doing his best to make the rough deal they'd been dealt bearable. He'd go right away downstairs to find Myra, his very own Auntie Myra and ask her what she thought of the idea of him finding Iain and asking him over. She was even more of an odd sort than Graham, but she was his, and right now that seemed to be all that mattered. He had heard her leave Graham in the sitting room, and found her in the kitchen putting the finishing touches to one of her huge fabulous cakes – cherry and coconut this time.

When she answered, she hesitated for a moment while she placed the final cherry on the top, then agreed he could and another night they'd have a friend of Piers' home for tea.

'Do you think your friend would like that? A Friday tea then he could stay later with it not being school the next day.'

'I know he would, Auntie Myra, I know he would. I don't need to ask. And thank you. Very much indeed. He had to move schools but I've seen him in town once or twice so it shouldn't be too hard to find out where he lives. That's sorted then. Thank you.'

She was turning out to be quite nice was Auntie Myra. Better than he'd ever expected. Now, thought Oliver, what can we do to show our appreciation to Myra and Graham? He had the answer! That idea of making memory quilts and soft toys for Auntie Myra to sell at the Christmas Fairs, he'd not found the heart to do anything about it yet and very soon he'd be running out of time. So he'd get on with them because all the success of it would depend on his art work. He'd sketch them out today, right now! Show them to her tonight before he went to bed. Filled to the brim with enthusiasm, Oliver sketched out a bear, an elephant and even a giraffe. He even left room on their paws for Myra to embroider on names in case people wanted to make them even more special. Somehow they were among the best drawings he'd done. Perhaps he did his best work when he felt extra happy. That was it! He should only do his art when he was happy, not when he needed to cheer himself up, because being miserable for him was a stumbling block to doing his best work. Myra was thrilled when she saw them and so too was Uncle Graham when he came in to inspect his handiwork.

Oliver went to bed delighted with his efforts and thrilled to have found something to do as a thank-you to Myra and Graham. He got a great big hug from Myra, but Graham shook Oliver's hand, which made him feel grown-up, much more so than half a dozen of his Uncle Graham's oddly peculiar clumsy kisses. A handshake was much more acceptable for someone thirteen years old. In fact that night everyone in the Butler house went to bed full of promise and the prospect of making a start on their Christmas project.

The next evening, sitting round the table planning out the work that would be needed to get ready for the fair, Myra decided they would work in two-hour shifts so it would not be too onerous or disrupt homework, especially for Piers. If she wasn't careful he would be her favourite, but having witnessed the pain that favouritism had brought to Graham and to Oliver she had made up her mind that neither of the boys would be favourites, they would be equals always. Suddenly she felt like some wound had finally healed inside herself and found her new situation so rewarding she wondered how on earth she had functioned as a whole person all these years without this new comfortable feeling she had discovered deep within her. Maybe it had always been there but never emerged before. Perhaps that was why she kept surprising herself by unexpectedly saying motherly things at the right moments. Maybe she'd always been waiting in the wings, so to speak, to be a mother, or something like it, and hadn't realised it. Whatever, this coming together of the four of them to achieve this new state of affairs was perhaps how family life was meant to be. Myra contemplated that new phrase she'd found: *whole person*. She never had been a whole person, had she? No, she hadn't. For years she'd deliberately kept part of herself hidden away, denied Graham her body, denied herself pleasure, remained aloof, kept herself to herself so that she never had truly shared her life with him or anyone. Myra glanced across at him from the other side of the kitchen table and studied him closely, until he suddenly sensed her gaze, when she dropped hers and then looking at him closely again she knew he recognised something in her eyes he'd not seen for years. What a fool she'd been. She recalled the embarrassment of Viv telling her everyone in Spring Gardens knew they didn't sleep together. The whole street had known and she was so wrapped in herself it had never occurred to her they all knew until Viv told her. Myra flushed red, the very brightest red all over her face, Graham saw it, Oliver saw it, and even Piers, engrossed in the scroll he was drawing round the word Christmas, saw her colour up, but only Graham understood. The boys were too eager pressing on with their scheme to bother to analyse what was going on between the adults around them, and for that Myra was grateful. Viv was right, a husband and a wife showing affection did make the wheels of a marriage turn – be that a hug, sharing a bed or making love. All she'd done was achieve nothing with her disregard of an essential of marriage. John might have been more glamorous than Graham when she'd first met him, but she couldn't imagine a man more patient, more loyal than Graham in the love stakes. There was no one to beat him when it came to faithfulness. Nor tolerance, nor kindness, nor consideration. She looked across at him again and saw not just how caring he was, but how good-looking he was, saw how decidedly he deserved her devotion. Yes, definitely ... devotion.

'Time you boys threw in the towel and went to bed, you've worked so hard tonight. How about a slice of cherry and coconut cake with your hot chocolate? Yes? Thank you so much, boys, for all you've done. And you, Graham, for helping us. I don't know where we would have been without your superb organisation. We've assembled so much more than I'd anticipated. Five bears all ready cut out. I love the one out of your old school uniform, Piers. And we shall have fun making one out of those funny old 1970s shirts of yours we found, Graham. I shall start on the stitching tomorrow. I can't wait to do their faces – you've chosen such cheeky expressions for them in your sketches, Oliver. Brilliant! We'll get quicker at it with experience, too!'

Myra looked at each of her helpers in turn and gave all three of them warm encouraging smiles. Graham caught Myra's eye briefly and winked at her. He'd never properly winked at her before. Ever. Married fifteen years and never winked? Surely not. Well, not a genuine wink, maybe an awkward attempt, which like his smiles, used to be oddly twisted. Surprising what two young boys could do to you even when they weren't aware of it. Graham looked at Piers as he carefully tidied things away. If he'd had a son of his own he would have moved like that. Too late to be thinking that. He did have a son in a way, well, two sons in fact, the very nearest he possibly could to two of his own. Graham dwelt on the idea of being a parent. The sensation sat comfortably on his shoulders. Strange how life worked out. Somehow tonight his whole life felt sorted, no more half living, he'd done with all that looking back full of regret, forlornly, uselessly, wishing ... he sensed he stood on the brink of a new life. He glanced across to Myra and actually saw the changes in her that he felt within himself. She wasn't visibly shrinking into herself any more, cold as ice and shuddering at the thought of human contact. She was sitting there full of delight about the success of their evening's efforts, and he, Graham Butler, was smiling properly, he could see his reflection in a mirror on the kitchen wall so he knew for certain he was. He felt Tyke snuffling along under the table looking for bare toes to nibble and he knew whose toes he found, for Myra was soon wriggling and laughing. At one time she would have shrieked as if under attack if a dog even approached, but not now. Now she half grumbled but half laughed at the same time. What a change! Tyke was making it Piers' turn to wriggle and laugh, then Oliver, then Graham himself. Soon all four of them were laughing. Graham remembered how much as a boy he and John had wanted a puppy. Recollected the unbearable pain he felt when he realised he and John would never get one. But he had now. A puppy and two boys to raise. And two such different boys, for each of them had equal but different merits, different gifts, different quirks. And so different in looks, too. Graham admired Oliver's curls, envied Piers' gentian blue eyes and loved them both. Then his eyes lighted on Myra and genuine love for her flooded his entire body. Was there any man anywhere in the world with better prospects than Graham Butler? In fact, was there any woman who deserved loving more than Myra Butler? He thought of all the changes she'd made within her to accommodate the two boys. After all the pain that there'd been between the two of them, life now looked brighter than ever before.

261

48. 00

58. 50
18. 00
40. 00
3. 00
---
109. 50